"A smart, resilient [...] are all too real and much to [...] d from a modern ER into dre [...] waking and everything in Between make for a sparkling debut novel. Most enjoyable."
— Carol Berg, national bestselling author of *The Daemon Prism*

"A rich wonder of a fantasy, full of life, death, dreams and nightmares becoming real, and dragons. I was swept away."
— Robin D. Owens, award-winning author of *Heart Fortune*

Hit and run like hell . . .

Vivian tried to break away, but her head was pulled inexorably downward by hands that should not be this strong. The chain bit into the flesh at the back of her neck, forcing her so close to the old woman's face that hot breath touched her lips like an evil kiss.

"So you're the special one. Don't look like much."

"Let me go."

A twist of the chain, and then another, cutting across her windpipe, restricting her breath. Vivian clawed at the tormenting hands. Fear and confusion and rage flooded through her. Black spots danced before her eyes.

And then a surge of power burned through her synapses, and without even thinking, with the last of her breath, she gasped in the voice of command, "Release me."

The pressure on the chain eased and the hand fell away as the old woman's eyes widened with shock. She snarled with hate and spat a blast of spittle into Vivian's face. It clung, slimy and malign, blurring her vision, running over her cheeks.

Vivian swiped at her face and eyes with her sleeve. When she was able to see again, there was no broken old body lying on the pavement. Only the van, sideways in the street, and the freezing rain.

Ace Books by Kerry Schafer

BETWEEN
WAKEWORLD

WAKEWORLD

~ A Book of the Between ~

Kerry Schafer

ACE BOOKS, NEW YORK

THE BERKLEY PUBLISHING GROUP
Published by the Penguin Group
Penguin Group (USA) LLC
375 Hudson Street, New York, New York 10014

USA • Canada • UK • Ireland • Australia • New Zealand • India • South Africa • China

penguin.com

A Penguin Random House Company

WAKEWORLD

An Ace Book / published by arrangement with the author

Ace Books are published by The Berkley Publishing Group.
ACE and the "A" design are trademarks of Penguin Group (USA) LLC.

For information, address: The Berkley Publishing Group,
a division of Penguin Group (USA) LLC,
375 Hudson Street, New York, New York 10014.

ISBN: 978-0-425-26124-8

PUBLISHING HISTORY
Ace mass-market edition / February 2014

PRINTED IN THE UNITED STATES OF AMERICA

10 9 8 7 6 5 4 3 2 1

Cover art by Larry Rostant.
Cover design by Judith Lagerman.
Interior text design by Tiffany Estreicher.

For David, who holds my heart

ACKNOWLEDGMENTS

First and foremost, great love goes to my family, who share my time and attention with the stories in my head without complaint. I am especially fortunate in my Viking, who reads early drafts and dares to give honest opinions. Your willingness to engage in brainstorming, butt-kicking, motivational speeches, and hugs, even when I bite the hand that feeds me, is priceless.

Much love also goes to my agent, Deidre Knight, who frequently steps outside the demands of her job to also serve as counselor, advisor, shoulder to cry on, and friend.

I'm ever grateful to my talented editor, Danielle, who always sees how to make my books stronger, and to Brad in PR, for being so responsive to my requests and so pleasant and lovely to work with.

I also want to thank all of the medical providers who cared for and about me during this sometimes difficult year. Dr. Moline, Dr. Cooper, all of the nurses and scheduling people, and the wonderful tech who nurtured me after my biopsy—bless you. Without your kindness, responsiveness, and skill, my encounter with breast cancer would have been so much more traumatic, and I think I would never have made my deadlines. So I also owe this book to you.

As for my friends—you are many and wonderful, and I can't begin to thank you all. Julie and Leigh—you have been there through the good and the bad, and I doubt the book would have been born without you. Huge thanks to Jenn and Susan, not only for your friendship but also for quick reads at crucial moments and great feedback. Alex, our sprints and accountability program helped so much in getting my edits done. Thanks to my sisters at the *Debutante Ball* for all of the support and friendship as we went through this debut year together. And the rest of you—both online and off—even though your name isn't on this page, please know that it is in my heart.

Last, but far from least—my heartfelt thanks to everybody who reads, buys, borrows, loans, or loves books. The whole point of writing stories is to have them read, and without you, publishing this book would be a meaningless endeavor.

One

It was chilly in the old cabin. Vivian tucked her feet up underneath her to escape a draft and wrapped the faded old quilt closer around her shoulders. It smelled, incongruously, of cinnamon. The old gray cat in her lap purred on, undisturbed, but the penguin across the table fixed her with an inscrutable gaze and made no sound at all.

The cat's name was Schrödinger, but other than that there was nothing more mysterious about her than any other cat. The penguin, on the other hand, did not belong to any recognizable species. He stood a little larger than an Adélie, smaller than a King. His beak was a little too yellow, his breast too perfectly white, except for a crimson splash over his heart. He'd been standing in the same spot for hours, staring in silence, and showed no signs of wandering off to do other things.

And the penguin, never flitting, still is sitting, still is sitting . . .

Precisely the reason why she had named him Poe.

One dim overhead light illuminated piles of books and documents propped drunkenly against each other on the table in front of her—each one important, each one selected with care from the shelves in her grandfather's secret room and carried out to the relative normalcy of his kitchen.

Dream theory, string theory, alternate realities. Psychosis. Mythology. Anything that looked like it would shed some light on the nature of the Dreamworld and the Between. Some volumes were printed and richly bound in leather with gold embossing; others were nothing more than handwritten notes, loosely tied together with string.

Vivian had taken a leave of absence from work to give her time to study. On the dotted line that asked for a reason, she'd written *executrix of a complicated estate*, which was true enough. Nobody needed to know that being the executrix also meant inheriting the role of Dreamshifter, a task she was woefully unprepared to take on. Her grandfather had taught her absolutely nothing before her initiation in the Cave of Dreams. All sorts of good and valid reason for that, but it didn't change the fact that she knew next to nothing and was responsible, alone, for monitoring all of the portals between dreaming and waking and that place between, where realities and dreams shifted together. She was the last, he'd said, the only living Dreamshifter, which meant there was nobody on the face of the planet that she could ask for help or advice.

And so she and Zee had taken refuge here in her grandfather's old cabin, which offered not only safety and concealment but also a treasure trove of information. The first thing she'd waded through was the Code—based on oral tradition and handed down from one Dreamshifter to the next. At some point it had been transcribed in a cramped and difficult hand. Others had crossed things out and added things in, so many voices from the past offering up their point of view on what needed to be done. Instructions for keeping the balance, when to close the doors and when they could be opened. Guidelines for the teaching of the heir. Protecting oneself from danger. A listing of creatures known to roam the Between.

There was a lifetime of information to absorb, and she had so little time. Besides the dream doors to mind, there was the matter of the missing dreamspheres and the Key to the Forever. Not to mention the dragon loose in the forests surrounding Krebston. Vivian kept the police scanner on at all times, monitoring the calls as they came in: something seen flying above the river at night, a UFO with wings. A fire in the Colville National Forest, which witnesses claimed was started by some giant animal breathing flames.

No deaths yet, but it was only a matter of time.

Right now, though, the scanner was quiet and Vivian's head was stuffed full of lucid dreaming theory, alternate reality continuums, astral projection, and practical theory for locating and walking through doors. Her eyes gritted and stung, blurring the words until she blinked them back into focus. Maybe she should go lie down, close her eyes for just a few minutes.

To sleep, perchance to dream. She feared her dreams—what she might become, or what might materialize. The last time she closed her eyes it had been to a vivid dream where the otherworld self of her ex-lover had beaten her nearly unconscious. She had shifted into a dragon and consumed him. She could still taste blood, could feel the separation of flesh and bone, hear the horrible shrieking sound he had made just before he died. And because of who and what she was, she wasn't entirely sure that what she dreamed wouldn't become a reality in the waking world.

Sleep was out of the question. She got up and started a fresh pot of coffee, put eyedrops in her burning eyes, and returned to the table, wearily shuffling through the books and papers, overwhelmed by the staggering volume of print and her own fatigue. Poe hopped down from the chair, knocking over a bamboo cylinder that she had propped against the table. As she bent to pick it up, she noticed that something about it seemed wrong, but it took her a moment to realize that although the cylinder itself looked weathered and scratched, the wax sealing the end was fresh. With the aid of a paring knife fetched from a kitchen drawer, she incised the wax around the top, taking care not to cut into anything that might lie beneath.

The scent of dust and mildew made her sneeze and sneeze again as the wax seal came free. Gingerly, she tipped the cylinder upside down, cupping her palm beneath, and withdrew a scroll so ancient she feared it would disintegrate in her hands.

Wide awake now, all thoughts of other problems pushed out of her mind by the excitement of discovery, she cleared the table, stacking books and documents in uneven piles on the floor, and set the scroll down where she could examine it. The paper was brown and brittle, crumbling at the edges. Stains blotched its surface. Unrolling it would surely cause damage, but the desire to open it outweighed all of her scruples.

Anchoring one end with a book, she began to unroll the scroll, cringing as the paper cracked and flaked in her hands. Using books, she weighted it at regular intervals to minimize the damage. It was handwritten, and not by a single person. At the very top, a heading in a script that looked like it had been written by a medieval monk read, *Chronicle of thee Shyfters of thee Dreame.*

Underneath the heading was written a name, *Taliesin.* Beside it, the legend, *lost in battle at Camlann.*

Vivian touched her finger to the name in wonder. Taliesin, a fascinating mythological character in Celtic and Arthurian legend. At least she'd always thought him mythological, but everything she had once believed was turning out not to be true. She'd encountered him in *Le Morte d'Arthur,* in the *Mabinogion,* had loved him enough to track down *The Book of Taliesin.*

> *I have been a tear in the air,*
> *I have been the dullest of stars.*
> *I have been a word among letters . . .*

Beneath his name several others were written in the same hand, each with the manner of death. Typical medieval things—*a fevere, ded in his sleepe, by sworde in battle.* After that the writing changed, and with it the ink. And then changed again. And again. Names. Thousands of them. Some of them in languages she couldn't read—Chinese,

Cyrillic, Russian, even what looked suspiciously like Sanskrit.

When the scroll had unfurled as far as the end of the table, the entries had begun to include dates alongside the cause of death. She went back and rerolled it at the top, forcing herself to work slowly and methodically to preserve the fragile paper as much as possible. By the time she reached the bottom of the list her hands were shaking, her heart fluttering at the base of her throat.

The final entries were written in a spiky black script that Vivian knew well as belonging to her grandfather, George Maylor.

Xiaohu, poisoned, 1656
Amrit Nehru, combustion by dragon poison, 1689
Mary Miller, hanged as a witch, 1692
John the Cooper, dead of a wasting disease, 1775
Evan Evans, a dragon took him, 1778
Niklas Kappel, slain by a giant bear, June 1887
Edward Jennings, murdered, 1925
Weston Jennings, missing, 1925
George Maylor, murdered, October 2011

And beneath it, on the last line at the bottom of this long list of people, all long dead, *Vivian Maylor.* No date or cause of death, but her fate seemed to be lurking in the empty space, only lacking the means and the date.

Vivian shivered, this time not from the cold. She retrieved the quilt and pulled it tightly around her anyway, taking some comfort from the warmth and the softness of the old fabric.

"Viv, it's three A.M." Zee stood in the shadows on the far side of the room, dark hair tangled on bare shoulders, faded jeans riding low on his narrow hips.

"I couldn't sleep."

He crossed the room toward her, light-footed as a cat, and tired as she was she smiled at the combination of softness and lethality that was Zee. The hair, those clear agate eyes, bespoke the artist, while the hard muscle of his arms and chest, and above all the still-healing scars that marred his face, brought to mind the warrior.

"You can't go on like this." Zee moved behind her, hands warm on the tightness of her shoulders, and she relaxed back against the solid strength of him, letting his hands knead away some of the tension and fear.

"It's the dream thing, isn't it?" he asked her. "Sit, this will be more effective."

Vivian sank into a chair as he directed. Dreams lay at the heart of her, and although she feared her own, she craved them with an intensity that frightened her. Something whispered that she must dream, or she would die.

"Did you dream?" she murmured. "Tell me."

His strong fingers hesitated, then moved to her neck, working the clenched knots at the base of her skull. "Pizza," he said.

She snorted, disbelieving. Her dreams, forever and always, had been big dreams—dragons and shadows and the twisting mazes of the Between.

"The rest of us mortals," he said, moving his hands back onto her shoulders so his thumbs could isolate the muscle just below her shoulder blades, "often dream about silly things. Like pizza. Now, did you want to hear my dream or not?"

"I'm sorry. Tell."

"We ordered pizza. About three days later it showed up in the U.S. Mail van. The driver tried to fit it into the mailbox but it wouldn't bend, and then Poe flew out to get it, only he ate it on the way back."

"You made that up." But she was laughing, caught out of herself and leaning back into him, her head comfortable against his chest. His hands slowed; she heard the catch in his breath and felt her own heart start to race. Head tilted back, she caught the expression on his face, the question in his eyes.

The kiss hung there between them, ready for the taking.

She pulled away, leaning forward on her elbows and rolling her shoulders experimentally. "That feels better."

"What did you find?" His voice was a little too casual and she knew she had hurt him, again, and hated herself for it. There was nothing to be said, so she leaned aside so he could see the scroll, argument and conclusion in a list of names and dates of death.

A long moment of silence. When she dared to look at him again, his jaw was clenched, all the softness of sleep wiped away.

"You want to know what I really dreamed?" he said. "I dreamed that a dragon came after you and I killed it. None of those people on that list had me standing guard. Do you understand?"

She did. This was the face of the warrior, scarred and lethal. He would die to protect her, and maybe she was underestimating him. Maybe he loved her enough to encompass all that she was—including sorceress and dragon. Her body and soul yearned for him, to slip into his embrace and be—safe.

There was no safety, though, not now. Not being what she was.

As if to emphasize these thoughts, the scanner let out a burst of static and then the voices came on. A woman's voice, first. Dispatch:

"Control two eighty-seven, do you read?"

"This is two eighty-seven."

"I've got a report of fireballs at Finger Beach. Two injured. Need ambulance, fire, and all patrol units."

Zee asked the question with his eyes. Vivian nodded. No need for a word between them. It was time do something about the dragon.

Two

H ey, sleepyhead, we're here."
Vivian thought she felt a hand stroke her hair and rest warm on her shoulder, but by the time she got her eyes open Zee was checking his weapons—slamming a cartridge into the .38 he'd found at her grandfather's cabin, loosening the sword in its sheath.

It was a good four-hour drive from the cabin to the town of Krebston, and she'd lost the fight against sleep within about the first thirty minutes, drifting on the margins of dream without ever going under. Or so she'd thought. Now she wasn't sure whether she'd dreamed the hand stroking her hair or if it had been real.

Yawning, she stretched and surveyed the situation. They'd both been worried that Finger Beach would be crawling with uniforms, but the parking lot was empty except for one black-and-white, a county car, empty. Yellow crime-scene tape marked off the path leading down to the river.

"I wish you'd stay in the car," Vivian said, knowing Zee's response.

"Yeah. Something in there about beggars and horses and genies." He grinned, lopsided and sweet, and then just as rapidly sobered. "Besides, that's what I was wishing about you."

"Not likely."

He opened his door and she followed suit. "But Zee, there's probably a warrant out for you. And there's a cop around here somewhere."

She filled her lungs with the clean cold air. It smelled of snow. A vee of geese flew across a morning-tinted sky, their haunting calls tugging at Vivian's heart as they always had, with a longing for flight. Beyond the beach, still under cover of darkness, flowed the Pend Oreille, a steady background susurration. Even though the Finger Stone was screened from her sight by trees, she could clearly feel its power, could have found her way to that massive red thrust of rock blindfolded.

Letting her mind reach out above and away beyond the stone, she found the dragon. Her thoughts met his and at once the world took on an extra dimension, crystal edged and bright. In that moment her consciousness split into two: one body shivering in a cold wind, clinging to the open door of the van with rapidly numbing fingers, while the other flew above the clouds in a world bright with the first rays of the rising sun.

In the distance she could hear Zee calling her name, his voice sharp-edged with worry, while the dragon spoke directly into her mind.

Hail, Dreamshifter. Will you fly with me?

Almost as if they were her own, she could feel the beat of his wings, the free flow of cold air over scales, the star-bright pleasure of flight.

"Vivian?" Zee's hand was on her shoulder, drawing her back into a body restless with the call of the sky. Her heart felt too tight, her thoughts too hard-edged and sharp to fit back into the soft human brain.

As she came back to herself, she knew she should tell Zee about the dragon hidden in the mist, but a reluctant loyalty silenced her tongue. Zee was a slayer of dragons, and all at once she didn't want this one killed.

As it turned out, there was no need to tell him anything. His body stiffened, his chin swung over and up, and he snuffed the air like a hunting animal. His eyes followed the invisible flight path that she could sense but not see. Without a word he strode off toward the beach, ducking under the crime-scene tape.

Vivian dashed after him, stumbling a little in the dark, her senses still divided between earth and sky. "Zee, wait—the cops are down there."

"Please go back and stay in the car," he said. The first rays of sunlight cleared the tree line and glinted on the naked sword in his hand.

"Zee," she protested, trailing along behind him. "You can't kill a dragon with a sword."

He didn't answer. His eyes were on the sky over the river, where a dark blot emerged from out of the mist.

"Just because you slay them in your dreams it doesn't mean you can do it here. Not in Wakeworld," Vivian called after him.

He stopped and turned. His face looked fierce and wild, no trace of the softness that had always been there for her.

"Zee! We have to do this together. Listen to me!"

His eyes focused on her face, gradually warming into recognition. "I swore to keep you safe. And you're asking me to give you the chance to become blood spatter."

"He's not going to eat me. He's young. He just wants to play."

"So does a tiger. A dragon isn't a house pet, Vivian. One mouthful, and that's the end of you."

"I want to call him back into the Between," she said. "Please. Let me try."

The doubt in Zee's face nearly broke her. Feeling suddenly very weary, she said, trying again, "Let's go. Together, Zee."

"One chance."

"What?"

"One chance to talk this monster through a door. And if it makes one wrong move, or so much as looks at you funny, I kill it."

In the sky, the dragon continued to call to her. At play in this moment, perhaps, but she knew he was built to be a fighting machine, armored and dangerous. As was Zee. She didn't want either of them dead.

If she put the Voice on Zee, she could stop him in his tracks. Protect him from himself and, more importantly, from all that she was capable of. But the thought of interfering with his free will sickened her. If she ever once did that, any trust they held between them would be shattered forever and there would be no going back.

"Fair," she said, holding out her hand to seal the deal.

Zee took her hand but didn't shake it, his clear agate eyes searching hers for what she worked so hard to keep hidden. Her breath caught in her throat; her knees went weak. "You're wrong, you know. About us."

She was still searching for the right words to respond to that when he released her. "Your hands are cold. You should wear gloves. Let's go."

Vivian needed time to get her breath under control and to stuff her heart back where it belonged, but Zee had already turned and was striding away from her. She followed. The path was heavily shaded by cedars and the dim light hadn't yet penetrated the thick boughs. Tiny needles of freezing mist pricked the exposed skin of her face and hands. Her muscles tightened and clenched against the cold.

As she emerged from the trees she could see the river flowing placid and smooth across an expanse of sand, silvery under a sky now lightening to gray. Both the geese and the dragon had turned and vanished into the mist rising off the river.

Nothing else moved as far as she could see.

To the north, the Finger Stone thrust up out of the sand, red and raw. Power zinged through the nerves of her body as she approached it. She could feel an awareness of doors, so many doors in all the worlds. Some stood open, some were closed; all of them called to her. At the same time the inner dragon stirred and she felt the beginnings of change: the tightening of skin, the itching at her shoulder blades.

No. Gathering the strength of her will, she forced the dragon fire back into the by-now-familiar heat at her core.

The boundary was so thin here between Wakeworld and

the Between that she could almost see the winding of the labyrinthine paths that traversed it between one Dreamworld and another. It pulled at her, the moon to the tide, and she thought maybe when the dragon came she would walk with him for a little way, at least.

An unexpected voice swung her around in dismay.

"Dr. Maylor. This is a crime scene. What on earth are you doing?"

"Deputy Flynne. You look better than the last time I saw you."

"Answer my question. What are you doing down here?"

"Pretty much the same as you, I'm guessing." She chose her words carefully, not wanting to set him off. Last time she'd seen him he was raving about an attack by penguins, and now he was back in uniform with a fully stocked belt of tools, including an automatic pistol and a Taser.

"I'm not a nutbag," he said defensively, as if catching the tone of her voice. "I've had a whole psych battery and been declared fit for duty. Some sort of medical thing, they think."

"And what do you think?"

"What else would I think?"

"It was a strange thing, Brett. You were so cold and there was no reason for it. I couldn't warm you at all. And you were talking about—"

"Penguins." His eyes widened and his gun was in his hand, level, aimed at something over her shoulder and behind her. She looked and took a step to the side, blocking the shot with her body.

His hands were shaking. "It's a freaking devil of a—" He swallowed.

"Penguin. Yes, I know. He's with me. His name is Poe." She walked backward as she spoke, ever so carefully, stealing quick glances to maintain her trajectory until she reached the penguin and scooped him up in her arms. "Are you sure you're fit for duty, Deputy? You seem a little edgy."

"I dreamed them," he said. "Giant penguins with sharpened beaks."

"The penguins are coming." He'd repeated the phrase

over and over before succumbing to hypothermia and being too cold to speak.

"Through there—a place by the Finger. Thousands of them. All of them taller than me, with human eyes. Behind them—I couldn't see it, but you know how dreams are—a giant ice field strewn with the dead, all with empty sockets—"

"Deputy!" She spoke firmly, bringing him back. "It was a dream. A nightmare. But you're not dreaming now. This is a real, flesh-and-blood penguin." Technically this was a lie—Poe might be flesh and blood, but he had walked straight out of a dream.

Poe wiggled and twisted and she bent and let him slide to the ground, still keeping her body between him and Deputy Flynne. She was going to have to tell part of the truth. The dragon was headed back this way, and she wasn't going to let this man be killed because he'd been sucked into something by accident.

"Going to sound crazy, Brett. You know the thing that killed the teenagers, that was shooting firebolts around last night? It's a dragon. It came through the same thin place where you saw penguins."

"And they call me the crazy one."

"You need to clear the beach, Deputy."

"And leave you here, I suppose."

"Yes."

This earned her nothing but a look. "It's my job to protect this town. Which includes you."

"Actually, protecting her is *my* job," Zee said.

Flynne's weapon was drawn in a heartbeat, but Zee was faster.

"Ezekiel Arbogast, drop your weapon."

"I don't think I can do that, Officer. With all due respect."

"You are under arrest."

"For what?" Zee was watching the sky and not the gun trained on his heart. "It's coming," he said to Vivian.

"I know—how can you tell?"

"Vibration, a change in the wind. I don't know how. But I know."

"Excuse me," Flynne said, "can we get away from discussing the weather and back to the arrest?"

"Right," Zee said, still watching the sky. "Charges?"

Brett hesitated. "Well, suspected murder. Of Vivian Maylor."

"Who is standing right here, alive and well. For the moment." A definite bitterness in Zee's tone let Vivian know he still wanted her off the beach and away safe somewhere.

"That's for the judge to decide." Brett reached for his radio.

"I don't think you want to do that," Vivian said. She edged closer to the stone. The dragon would be in sight any minute. She needed to call him to her and away from the others. "You want to explain to dispatch that you've found Ezekiel Arbogast, along with a penguin and a dragon?" She gestured with her chin, and he turned to follow her gaze.

Above the river, small yet, but growing rapidly larger, appeared a creature that couldn't be a bird—four legs; a long, naked tail—winging its way toward them.

"One chance," Zee said, in a voice she'd never heard him use before. He paced across the sand to the place where two weeks before a giant white bear had lain dead.

Vivian turned to Flynne, allowing a note of pleading to creep into her voice. "Deputy. Brett. This is more dangerous than you can imagine. Please move off the beach."

He shook his head, stubborn, adjusting his grip on his pistol.

The dragon was close now, occupying all of her senses, and she had little thought to spare for anybody else.

Come. Dance with me. The sky is ours for the taking.

Vivian's body responded to the call. Her blood ran hot with the memory of flight and power. She fought it down. She was not a dragon, she was Vivian. Still, the voice she used to return the call was full of an untapped power that exhilarated and frightened her all at once.

Not this time, little brother. Come here to me.

She settled herself with her back supported against the

stone, letting its power flow through her, and opened the door into the Between.

The dragon flew in low over the river, sunlight striking glints of rainbow color off his scales. He flew a loop, a spiral, shot bright jets of flame from his nostrils.

Vivian called again, dragonmind to dragonmind, *Come, little brother. Come here to me.*

Wind gusted around her, raising a flurry of sand that scoured her face and hands. There was a thunder of giant wings. For a moment the sun was blotted out and then he landed, so much more lightly than expected, so much more beautiful. Mellisande had been old, her scales dull with age. This beast shone diamond bright. He dipped his head in respect and spoke into her mind.

Greetings, Dreamshifter. Why will you not fly with me?

You must go home, little brother. It is not safe here for you.

I do not choose to go back.

This world is not yours—you do not belong here.

Even so. I have chosen.

Please. I will walk with you a little. The Between is not what it was, now that the Sorceress is dead. There are wide skies on the other side.

He snorted a small puff of bright flame. *I will not go.*

There is death for you here.

I don't fear death. But there was a question, a wavering. Vivian took a step toward him.

He stretched his wings and clapped them over his back, raising a wind that pushed Vivian back and to her knees.

A single shot rang out. The bullet struck fire from the scales on the dragon's side and ricocheted away into the sand.

He opened his jaws wide and unleashed a cry of pain and rage, spreading his wings and shooting off a full jet of flame.

"No!" Vivian shouted, her voice lost in the thunder of wings as the dragon lifted off from the sand. "Please," she cried, stretching her arms toward the sky.

Another shot, this time from where Zee stood, across the beach.

A spike of agony through her eye. Wings drooping, heart quivering. Blackness pouring in.

And then she was fully back in her own body and the pain was gone. A shout of warning. Something heavy struck the earth with enough force to throw her off her feet. She lay still and futile in the sand, hands pressed against her eyes, the cold and damp insinuating itself through the fabric of her jeans and into her skin.

She pushed herself up onto her knees. Less than two arm lengths away a dark ungainly form lay twisted and motionless, wings splayed wide. The dragon's right eye was a shattered cavern. Black blood steamed in the cold air.

Zee stood over his kill with the gun still in his hand, his scarred face alight with victory.

Vivian watched him, wordless, fighting to draw breath. Silent tears ran down her cheeks.

He saw her trouble and the light went out of his eyes. Kneeling in the sand beside her, he reached out a hand to touch her face. She flinched away, and he let it fall back. "Vivian. It needed killing. You must see that." A fresh burn on his cheek, etched there by a splash of dragon blood, emphasized his words.

Not his fault, she told herself. Brett had fired the first shot and made it necessary. The dragon had killed before and would have killed again. She knew that, but it did nothing to ease the pain at her heart.

"He didn't know better, Zee. He was so young . . ." Young and beautiful and alive beyond imagining.

"Don't cry, Viv. It was just a dragon."

She laughed, short and bitter, as his words went home. "Blood of my blood," she said.

Realization dawned in his eyes, too late. "No, you are not one of them, not really—"

"But I am. And you were made to hunt them. What are we to do about that?"

A low whistle broke the moment. "It really was a dragon,"

Brett said in a voice filled with awe. "Thought you guys were kidding."

Sirens wailed in the distance, drawing closer.

"You should go," Brett said. He spoke into his radio. "Number three seventy-two on scene. All clear."

Stiffly, Vivian levered herself to her feet. Inside her boots her toes had gone numb, and she stomped her feet to get the blood moving.

"You may have a slight problem explaining that away," Zee said, eyeing the dead dragon.

Brett shrugged. "I found the creature already dead. I never saw a thing. Not that I'd mind taking credit for killing the murdering son of a bitch."

"Are you sure?"

He shrugged. "I can't tell them the truth. It's the next best. Go."

Vivian ran up the trail after Zee and they drove unhindered away from the beach, passing two police cruisers and a border patrol pickup on their way to a scene they couldn't possibly have imagined.

Vivian felt a yawning abyss between herself and Zee. He didn't know, couldn't know, how much the dragon encroached already on the integrity of her self. The heat in her blood, the flashes of time where every sensory detail became extraordinary and three-dimensional, the desire to unfold powerful wings and take to the sky. Very small she felt, walled in by unbreakable glass, untouchable and afraid. More than anything she could imagine, she wanted to slide over beside him, feel his arm around her, relax into his strength. Instead, she wrapped her arms around herself and hunched into them, breathing past the pain of unshed tears.

"Cabin?" he asked.

"Too far. And my apartment's trashed. We'll have to risk the bookstore."

He nodded, turning onto Main Street.

Vivian caught a blur of movement darting from the sidewalk to the street.

"Shit." Zee spun the steering wheel and stomped on the

brake. Vivian jolted forward against her seat belt as the van slid sideways and came to a stop, but not before it hit something with a dull thud that reverberated in the pit of her stomach.

An instant of shock, while body and mind caught up with what had just happened, and then she was out of the van, staring down in horror and dismay at the limp body crumpled beneath the tires.

Three

"D ear God," Zee said. His face in the glare of the head-
lights looked dead white. "She just stepped out in front
of the van."

An old woman lay on the asphalt, legs splayed, arms
flung wide, palms up and open. Gray hair, unkempt and in
need of a wash, straggled around a wrinkled face smudged
with dirt. Her eyes were closed; her mouth drooped open
over broken snags of teeth.

Vivian's hand went to the pendant that hung at her breast,
a penguin caught in a dream web. It was her talisman and
served to help her mark the boundaries between one world
and the next. In Wakeworld it was always there, warm and
comforting. In Dreamworld, it vanished. Now it was all too
solid and real. This was no nightmare.

She knelt on the wet pavement, long practice pulling her
mind back into a cool assessment of the crisis. "We need to
call 911."

"Haven't got a phone," Zee said. "Have you?"

"Lost it, Between. You'll have to go to the store and call."

He hesitated.

"Go. We need an ambulance. Also, we need to not
have Poe."

The penguin had followed her out of the van and stood

on the other side of the victim. His feathers were ruffled and puffed up, and he hissed once, the way he did when he felt threatened.

"Come on, you," Zee said, picking up the penguin. "I'll be right back."

"No," Vivian said, assessing her patient. Airway clear, chest rising and falling with a regular breath. Pulse steady. No visible bruising or lacerations.

"No, what?" Zee asked, lingering.

"Don't come back. I was driving, not you. Understand?"

The old woman's eyes fluttered open. They were the color of molasses, wide with fear. Pupils equal, neither dilated nor constricted. Her lips quivered. "Don't hurt me."

"Easy now. Nobody's going to hurt you. What's your name?" Vivian's hands began, all on their own, to feel for broken bones or bleeding. She glanced up at Zee. "I'll take care of her. You're no good to me in jail."

"It's not just her I'm worried about."

"I'll be fine. You've already killed the dragon." Her tone was harsher than she'd meant, the words hanging between them like living things, winged and dangerous. Too late she tried for softness. "Please."

She'd hurt him. She saw his eyes shutter, even as he nodded and turned to run down the street toward the store, Poe clasped awkwardly in one arm.

A feeble whimper drew her attention back to the injured old woman. "Where does it hurt?"

The question earned her only a shake of the head and an attempt to scrabble backward and away. "You're trying to kill me."

"I'm a doctor. I'm trying to help you."

"The man drove his land ship right over me. Intent to kill. He hates me."

"He doesn't hate you. He doesn't even know you. Does your head hurt? Is it hard to breathe?"

Spittle ran down the old woman's chin, slick and shiny. Dirt was embedded in her pores. Foul breath heated Vivian's cheek, hotter than it ought to have been. She wondered if the old woman had been sick with a fever. Maybe delirium had driven her out into the street in front of the van.

"Where did he go, the killer man?"

"He's gone to find help."

"You're sure he's gone?"

"I'm sure. Nobody's going to hurt you."

The old woman's eyes went cold, no confusion in them now.

Fast as a striking snake, her gnarled old hand grabbed at the pendant. Vivian tried to break away, but her head was pulled inexorably downward by hands that should not be this strong. The chain bit into the flesh at the back of her neck, forcing her so close to the old woman's face that hot breath touched her lips like an evil kiss.

"So you're the special one. Don't look like much."

"Let me go."

A twist of the chain, and then another, cutting across her windpipe, restricting her breath. Vivian clawed at the tormenting hands. Fear and confusion and rage flooded through her. Black spots danced before her eyes.

And then a surge of power burned through her synapses, and without even thinking, with the last of her breath, she gasped in the voice of command, "Release me."

The pressure on the chain eased and the hand fell away as the old woman's eyes widened with shock. She snarled with hate and spat a blast of spittle into Vivian's face. It clung, slimy and malign, blurring her vision, running over her cheeks.

Vivian swiped at her face and eyes with her sleeve. When she was able to see again, there was no broken old body lying on the pavement. Only the van, sideways in the street, and the freezing rain. She felt, more than saw, a closing door in the middle of nowhere, and then she was kneeling in the street alone.

In the distance a siren sounded.

Perfect. What the hell was she supposed to tell the attendants when they showed up?

What happened here, Doc?

Well, Jim, we ran over this frail old lady who attacked me and disappeared into another dimension.

Yep. That was going to fly.

She wished she were still asleep in the van with Zee warm and steady beside her. That there had been no dragon killing today, no old woman who was not what she seemed. That all of this was some horrible dream from which she could wake up. But there would be no waking up from this, not now, not ever. There was no going back to this morning, no do-overs.

Her hand reached for the pendant at her breast.

It was gone, the chain broken. Frantic, she crawled around the site on hands and knees, groping blindly in the shadows, searching. But she knew in her soul that the old woman had taken it, and that whatever it was wanted for was surely nothing good.

Four

Morgan Weathersby slapped at his neck, silencing the whine of a mosquito just a few seconds too late. His hand came away smeared with blood, and a dozen other spots on his body itched already. Damned bloodsuckers. More of them than there ought to be this late in the fall, but it would be cold enough tonight to knock them down a peg. He tossed another chunk of wood on the campfire. A knot of pitch flared and popped, sending sparks up into the dark night, illuminating the faces across from him.

Time had carved its mark on the man he knew as Carpenter. Unlike Morgan, who looked the same now as he had twenty years ago, the old man had aged visibly since they'd last met. His hair remained thick but was nearly white. The line of his jaw was both leaner and softer, and he moved with a slight hesitation, as though not entirely certain the ground would be there when his feet came down. Not surprising, that. It had been damn near twenty years since their last trip.

Carpenter had brought his youngest son that time. The trip was a family ritual by then—a rite of passage, and even though this third son of his had been less than enthusiastic about hunting in general and scornful about this expedition in particular, Morgan had never been one to turn down the solid reality of bills in his wallet.

It was understandable, bringing your sons out to take a beast as a ceremony to mark the transition from boy to man. He admired it. But this trip was different, and he had protested until Carpenter won him over with extra cash. Women had their own rites to mark entrance into adulthood, and they damn well shouldn't have anything to do with guns and killing.

This was no place for a girl, especially a girl with night-dark hair and eyes of a brown so deep you could barely see the pupils, a girl self-contained and light-footed and too goddamned capable for her thirteen years. She'd kept up easily on the hike yesterday, had carried her own pack, never made a single sound of complaint.

Morgan scowled at her, sitting motionless on an upended chunk of a log, gazing into the fire as though she saw secrets there. Grace had been like that, always looking into the depths of things and keeping what she learned locked behind an impassive face and unreadable eyes.

Grace was not safe to think about.

"We start at first dawn," he said, needing to get the girl out of his sight. "You might want to turn in."

Carpenter sniffed the air. "Temperature's dropping—frost by morning."

"Good hunting weather," Jenn said. Her voice was deep for a girl, slow rolling, like a shallow river over stones. She turned to her grandfather. "Which rifle will I carry?"

"The Winchester."

"I like the AK."

"The tradition is the Winchester, Jenn. That's what your dad used."

"You just want to use the AK yourself." She smiled at him, a slow smile that made her eyes even darker.

"Your dad got his bear with the Winchester."

"Lucky shot," Morgan grunted. "Boy couldn't aim and was shaking like a junkie."

Carpenter's white teeth gleamed in the firelight. "The

girl's a crack shot, Morgan. Takes after her grandpa, not her old man. Wait and see."

Morgan snorted. "In my experience, the apple don't fall far from the tree." It was an insult to Carpenter, but he couldn't abide the way Jenn occupied her own skin, eyes measuring him up with an expression that bordered on disdain.

Not often he thought about his appearance, but those eyes made him remember that it had been a few years since he'd cut his hair, that his beard was untrimmed and bushy, that the flannel shirt he wore was overdue for a wash. Not that he cared what she thought about anything, her or any human creature.

A sound startled all three of them into stillness, a sharp retort, almost like a gunshot.

Only one thing made that sound in the forest: a tree, breaking under stress, branches cracking and rustling as gravity pulled it down to the earth. But trees didn't fall randomly on quiet nights. They broke in high winds. Or when something big enough pushed them over.

Morgan picked up his shotgun, chambered a shell. Carpenter was a few seconds behind him, the girl even quicker.

It took a pretty big critter to break a tree. A grizzly might do it, if the trunk was rotten or not too big around. And there were strange creatures out here in this forest, not registered in any *Hunting the Northwest* guidebook.

Twenty beats of his heart, and then a sudden onrush of wind that brought down leaves and set the trees to keening. A shadow blotted out the stars overhead, a sinuous, long-necked shape. And then, as suddenly as it began, the wind was gone, the sky was clear, the normal forest sounds returned.

"What the hell was that?" Carpenter's useless gun was still trained on the empty sky; might just as well try shooting at the stars.

"Freak burst of wind, I reckon," Morgan lied. "One of those dust devils. You get some strange weather up here."

With all of the rules he'd broken over the years, a few things had managed to sneak past him from Dreamworld into Wakeworld. But he was damned sure he would have noticed a dragon. And if there was a dragon here, then something had gone very wrong with the worlds, and this part of the forest was a particularly dangerous place to be.

At least the creature had flown over, had kept on going. Still, a dragon could cover a lot of territory with speed; it might be back. He sat back down by the fire, covering his unease with a casual tone. "Cold tonight. Hope it don't turn to snow or some such. Get the girl to bed, Carpenter. She'll be good for nothing in the morning."

Jenn smiled, that smile that hid what she was really feeling. "Come on, Grandfather. Old men need their sleep." Carpenter grunted, allowing her to grab his hand and tow him toward the tent.

"Get some sleep yourself, Morgan," he said. "Good dreams."

Good dreams. Now there were words to choke on. Morgan would be a happy man if he never needed to dream again; there was no peace for him there. And there would be no sleep for him this night. All through the long hours of the dark, at the mercy of memories that refused to stay contained no matter how many years came between, he listened for the thunder of dragon wings with the loaded shotgun across his lap.

Just before dawn, when the sky began to be visible above the trees, he banked the fire. After lowering his pack from where he'd hung it away from bears, he slapped bacon into the cast-iron pan and put the kettle on for coffee. The girl emerged from the tent first, looking young and vulnerable with her hair tangled and the Dreamworld still fading from her eyes.

"Smells good," she said, breathing deep, and he couldn't help approving the fact that she seemed to be referring as much to the scent of frost and evergreen as to the bacon.

She vanished into the trees, off to relieve herself. Despite his fatigue, Morgan remained on high alert. He didn't like the girl out of sight. His eyes kept scanning the sky, ears straining for any sound out of place. The quiet of the night had done nothing to allay his unease, had intensified it if anything.

Jenn returned unscathed and sat down by the fire. "I dreamed about a dragon," she offered. "Blacker than night."

"Dragons aren't black," he said automatically, then nearly bit his tongue out for acknowledging that there might be such creatures in the world.

She responded as though it were a rational conversation. "That's what made the dream so weird. All of the movie and book dragons are green, with maybe purple and red mixed in, or brown. The ones in Pern were bronze and green and gold. Anyway, this black dragon just looked at me, and I thought maybe I shouldn't look back—all of the books say not to look a dragon in the eye, of course—but I did. And it was like it was talking to me in my head. Which isn't really so weird, I guess; everything talks in dreams."

His belly tightened at her words and he looked up at the sky, almost certain a dark shadow had fallen over the world. Nothing different about the darkness, though. The sky continued to lighten in the east. A last lingering planet shone bright just above the tree line.

"What did it say?"

She frowned. "I can't remember. What if it was important?"

"I doubt it. I've got no use for dreams, girl. That's what comes of marshmallows at bedtime. Wake your grandfather— we need to be moving."

The three of them ate almost in silence. When they were done, they stowed away food and cooking gear and hoisted the pack up again on a rope between two trees. They checked their guns, packed up ammunition. Morgan extinguished the fire and led them out. Timing was everything, and he guided his little party along at a calculated pace.

He had to get them to precisely the right spot and through into the Dreamworld during that short window of time just past dawn when it was light enough to walk without tripping over their own feet, but still dark enough that they wouldn't notice a door in the middle of the wilderness.

People tended not to see what was right in front of their eyes if it didn't fit with what they knew of the world. And the location where he opened the doorway was strategic. A red rock bluff butted directly up against it on the right, a cluster of bushes on the left. If you didn't happen to look at the air too closely around you, it was easy to pass right through and into the Dreamworld without pause. But he always took precautions, just to be sure.

When he'd first started guiding hunting parties here, he had experienced guilt, easily silenced beneath the weight of his rage. He hated both the Dreamworld and his ability to access it. This dream was a so-called gift from the Guardian, given to him at his initiation in the Cave of Dreams. He wanted no truck with it, but on the other hand, living in Wakeworld required hard cold cash and the Dream was at least good for that. Hunters would pay good money for a shot at something slightly unusual, and this dream was lousy with creatures. Bears and wolves predominated, but stranger beasts had been sighted.

He'd seen one or two of the creatures the Indians named Shunka Warakin, one of which had been shot and ended up in a museum well before his birth, which meant he wasn't the only one who had played around in this Dreamworld.

Hunters he guided out here all signed an agreement not to tell where they'd been, or who brought them. Sure, they were likely to talk anyway, but he didn't worry about that overmuch. If the authorities came looking for the place, or the wolves or bears that were taken from here, all just a little "off" from regularly occurring species, they would never find the door. The rare beast that had managed to escape into the forest stayed pretty well hidden.

At the same time, folks were willing to pay extra for the opportunity. He had permitted rumors of Sasquatch sightings to judiciously leak into the community. Bigfoot hunters paid even better than the average sportsman. Truth was, he'd had a few glimpses of the big beasts in the dream landscape, including one too-close encounter that left him wary, but although he saw them often enough, they always slipped out of sight and left him well alone.

Of dragons there had never been a sign. The creatures

had powers of their own, and doors were never a barrier to them, but they tended to keep to the Between and he'd never seen one in Wakeworld or Dreamworld before.

He was in the middle of wondering what had drawn a dragon to the forest, when they stumbled onto the kill. It was just light enough to see what they'd almost stepped in. A few feet to left or right, and they would never have noticed. Not that there was much left to see—fur, a few bones, bloodstains on the grass. A black circle surrounded it all, the grass turned to ash. There were footprints too, four craters in the blackened earth, each as big as the girl.

"Holy mother of God," Carpenter said, surveying the damage.

Jenn walked up to the edge of the black ash, sniffed the air. "Smells a bit like sulfur."

"You've outdone yourself, Morgan—this is a huge and rare beast. How do we track it?" The other man's voice held a note of awe.

"We don't. What the hell do you suppose that thing is? You really want to have your granddaughter anywhere near it?"

"Maybe it's aliens," Carpenter said. "Spaceship could make a circle like that, landing. Makes more sense than anything else."

"Whatever it is, it could come back," the girl said.

Morgan couldn't help liking the kid. She was matter-of-fact, stayed calm. He felt a sudden need to get her the hell out of here and back to safety. "We should go back," he heard himself saying. "I'll refund your money."

"Buck up, man. Never took you for a coward." Carpenter strode forward and Morgan ground his teeth together to keep himself from saying anything he'd regret. Get in, let the kid get an animal, get out. Sooner the better.

"Right about here, I think." Carpenter came to a stop close to the bluff where Morgan always called a halt.

"Yep. Good memory." He pulled the blindfolds out of his pack. "Put these on, if you would."

Jenn rolled her eyes. "Are you for real?"

"You go in blindfolded or not at all. That's the rule."

"Oh, fine." She tied the strip of fabric over her eyes and Morgan adjusted it, then checked Carpenter's.

"All set? Great. Form a train. Here we go."

With everybody touching and their eyes covered, it was an easy thing to open both doors and lead them into the Between and then immediately into the Dreamworld. To disguise what he had done, he led them forward about twenty paces, asked them to duck down low and mind their heads for another ten, and then gave permission to remove the blindfolds.

"Great territory here," he said, gesturing at the subtly changed terrain that lay ahead. "I've never once brought somebody in that didn't find some sort of trophy. Dangerous and strange things, too, so keep your wits about you."

The horizon was light now, clear and beginning to be blue. In the plains the sun would be rising but not here, where mountains thrust their bulk between land and sky. The landscape was only dimly visible, leached of color like a black-and-white movie. All as it should be, and yet Morgan's gut churned with an alarm he didn't understand. Something was off-kilter and wrong.

The dream felt dark.

Despite what his eyes showed him—the normal progression of dawn—he kept expecting to see nothing but black. Every time he blinked he found himself surprised to see light. Here, through the doorway and into dream, all of the extra senses he tried to keep closed down were wide open.

Instability in Dreamworld was dangerous beyond words, but he would need something tangible to call off the trip. Carpenter had paid a couple of grand for this expedition. And the girl was primed—had probably been pumped up for this one hunting expedition since she could talk. Neither of them was going to go back because he had a bad feeling.

Which meant all he could do now was follow, stick tight, stay alert, keep them from straying into some other dream where there were creatures more dangerous than bear and wolves, or into the Between where anything could happen. Nothing he could do, though, if something decided to come through an open door. At least it would be light soon. Most dream creatures didn't care for the light.

They walked single file, the girl in the lead. She was good, he had to admit. Carpenter had taught her well. Taking her time, scanning the trees, watching for signs, listening, sniffing the air. The old man was on higher alert than he had been with his sons, though, a little more protective. A little less at ease. Maybe he sensed something too, seasoned old hunter that he was.

Jenn led them down into a ravine where the darkness congregated thick and undisturbed, even though the sky was now very nearly blue. A good choice if you were looking for game. Not so great considering the invisible threat. Above, on the higher ground, birds had been rousing, beginning a chorus of tweets and chirps. Breeze in the trees. Racket from a couple of frogs that hadn't yet dug down into the mud for the winter.

Down here in the ravine it was too quiet. No birds, no frogs. Not even the wind in the trees. Just a dead calm.

Morgan's unease grew, although in his mind he was still trying to argue it away with logic. It was normal for it to be darker in the ravine. Quieter, too, he reminded himself, because of the dark. Plus, they were shut out from the sounds above.

He stepped on a dry twig and his heart skipped at the sound of its snapping.

At first there was only a whiff of an unpleasant scent, rapidly growing into a solid sensory assault, part skunk, part carrion, that set him to coughing. He recognized it, knew what it was, and his heart hammered a warning. He was aware of the others, watched them cover mouth and nose with their sleeves. An unearthly screeching howl rose up dead ahead, in the direction they'd been going. An answering howl came from the other direction, echoing, bouncing off the rocks, a sound that made his blood congeal, his knees go weak.

Boq, Sasquatch, Bigfoot. So many names, so many jokes. But there was nothing remotely funny about the creatures. The Indians had long known them for their supernatural powers and kept a deep and respectful distance. You couldn't shoot them, it was said. Guns exploded, bullets went wide. They could shift time, work tricks with water and fire.

Puzzle pieces clicked into place, remembered images flashing one upon the other. *A wounded Sasquatch. The flash of a blade. Blood.*

"Up, back to high ground, now!" he shouted, following his own advice without looking around for the others. It was a blind scramble over rocks and loose dirt, sliding, grasping onto branches and roots, and dragging himself up one-handed, still clutching the rifle with the other.

At the top, he paused to look back.

Hell and damnation. They hadn't followed. He could barely make them out down in the shadows, braced back-to-back with rifles ready. Down the ravine on either side, branches swayed. A loud banging sound, as of sticks against tree trunks, and then that howling again that turned his bowels to water.

He tried to shout but found he had no voice. He ordered his body to go back down, told himself that he must not abandon his party. Throughout his long life he'd faced down all manner of creatures without fear. Now he stood silently cursing himself, shivering like a rabbit under the paw of a coyote, and watched the hunting party, his hunting party, that he had abandoned and run away from.

Two dark shadows were visible now, emerging from the trees. The offensive stink was almost unbearable, wafting up to him in waves that set him retching.

The beasts were well within range, out of the trees now and visible. They were roughly man-shaped but covered in brown fur, bent forward a little at the hips, with long apelike arms and human hands. As they moved, they banged on tree trunks with sticks, keeping up a constant howling.

Carpenter's rifle leaped and then exploded in a burst of fire. The man went down with a scream and one of the beasts leaned over him, blocking him from sight. The girl, still self-possessed and externally calm, took aim in turn. Her finger pulled the trigger. The rifle clicked. Nothing happened. She tried again. Another click.

Still the creature advanced toward her.

At last she screamed and broke into a run. One of the man-creatures shambled in pursuit, graceless and awkward, but fast.

Dropping to one knee, trying to steady his shaking hands, Morgan drew a bead on the Sasquatch and fired. It kept running. He fired again. Saw in disbelief a spray of dirt and rock as the shot struck way wide of his target.

But even as he fired again it picked up speed, long legs covering the ground in a shambling stride, caught Jenn around the waist and swung her up over its shoulder. She struggled and fought, beating with her fists on the beast's back. Her eyes found Morgan and she began to scream, still not in a panicked fear but half plea, half command. "Help me! Morgan—"

Both of the creatures turned then to look up at him. He felt the full force of their burning eyes, a pressure on his brain, a searching.

Revenge.

The girl's cries twisted in his heart, but Morgan stood transfixed, his hands loose and nerveless on his gun, his feet grown into the dirt and incapable of movement.

And then they turned away. Carpenter's limp body now dangled over the shoulder of the first creature as it vanished into the trees. The second lumbered into the forest after his mate, dragging the girl. She had stopped screaming. The last glimpse Morgan had of her, she had stretched her arms out toward him, hands reaching as though all of the space between them did not exist, as though she were a child seeking safety. A bitter and desperate hope still animated her face. And then went out. She was not one to go easily into death, however, and she shouted one last word back before she was lost to him in the trees.

"Coward!"

It echoed, bouncing off cliffs and trees and the memories stowed deep beyond his conscious thought.

Coward.
Coward.
Coward.

As the last echo died away he shook himself, released from the spell. It wasn't the first time that word had been hurled at him by a girl, and goddamn it if this time he'd let it stick.

Five

Zee sprawled in one of the armchairs at the back of A to Zee Books, head tilted back, eyes closed. His face looked softer in sleep, the artist again, and not the hardened warrior who took wild joy in slaying dragons. A book lay open in his lap—Joseph Campbell's *Hero with a Thousand Faces*. His right hand lay on the arm of the chair, relaxed and easy, but his fingertips grazed the hilt of the sword, unsheathed and resting against his thigh.

Vivian had run in through the back entrance, using the fire escape to reach Zee's upstairs apartment, but it made sense he would be watching for her here. Part of her wanted him awake—she needed to tell him about the lost pendant, to make plans to search for it. On the other hand, she didn't want to talk about what happened on the beach or any of the hurt that lay between them.

She picked up the book, set the bookmark, and laid it on the coffee table beside an unfinished chess game. He was dreaming, his eyes rolling behind his eyelids, a touch of a smile on his lips. Vivian found herself envying him. Always, dreams had been serious business for her, even before she knew there was such a thing as a Dreamshifter, or a possibility of being lost in a Dreamworld. What must it be like to dream with casual abandon, to have dreams of pizza delivery and flying penguins? This looked like a pleasant dream, and a deep yearning filled her. She feared her own dreams, but maybe it was possible to dip into his.

Poe, standing on the far side of the coffee table, stared at her out of obsidian eyes that radiated disapproval, as if he knew what she was thinking.

"I'm not going to hurt anything," she whispered. Matching the rhythm of her breath to Zee's, she laid her hand on his forehead and closed her eyes.

The dream was there, just beneath his skin; she could feel its ebb and flow tugging at her, and she let go of her control and let it pull her in.

Immediately she wished she hadn't.

He was naked, and he was not alone. He stood with his back against a shelf of old books with leather covers etched with gold-embossed titles. A woman stood on tiptoe, the entire length of her naked body pressed up against his. He was kissing her, eyes closed, as though his lips on her skin were the single most important fact of the universe. His hands were tangled in the fall of her hair, tipping her head back so he could run a line of kisses down the length of her throat.

Vivian felt a twist of jealousy in her gut, a visceral yearning. She wanted him, wanted all of him. What she had denied herself in real life was eminently possible in dream. If she could enter the dream, surely she could also shift it. Put herself in the place of the other woman so that she could experience what she had forbidden herself in the waking world.

Something familiar about the auburn curls stopped her, the line of the back, the swell of the hip, images glimpsed over and over in a mirror. And then she realized: It was her own dream hands caressing the smoothness of skin over muscle, her own breasts and belly straining against him, always wanting more.

Her body heated at the thought that Zee was dreaming of her. She could almost feel his skin against hers and it would be easy now, so easy, to slide into the place of her dreaming self. A breath, a moment of focus, but just as she pushed toward the Dreamworld, an itching of her shoulder blades jolted her back into waking. As she watched in dismay, the Vivian in the dream sprouted wings, her naked white body transforming into a monstrous shape with scales and teeth and the weight of an armored tail.

"Vivian," Zee cried, his voice loss and despair. At the instant the cry left his lips the dream shifted again and he was dressed in leather and chain mail, the drawn sword in his hand, and his eyes were those of the dragon slayer, not the lover.

Her body trembling with a potent draught of adrenaline, desire, and grief, Vivian slid out of the dream. Zee still slept, restless, and she retreated to a chair on the other side of the coffee table, grabbing the first book in reach along the way. She watched him through a screen of her hair as he stirred and his eyes opened and fixed on her. "How long have you been here?"

"Only a few minutes."

"You should have wakened me."

"You needed the sleep."

"How is she?"

"What is she, you mean."

He shook his head and rubbed the sleep from his eyes with both hands. "Explain."

"She's not really a fragile old woman and she wasn't injured."

"Vivian—"

"She stole my pendant and went into the Between."

"But—"

"No buts. I don't know what she is, but I'm betting it isn't human." Her voice trembled on the edge of tears, her hand automatically groping for the missing pendant. Its absence was palpable, a negative space that felt more solid and real than the book in her lap.

All softness vanished, Zee leaned forward and touched his index finger to the broken skin at her throat. "I should have stayed." There was a huskiness in his voice. The clear agate eyes searching hers brought the heat to her face, set her heart to beating at a ridiculous rate.

"I—put the Voice on her, Zee. I wasn't ever going to use it again."

His big hand cupped her chin and raised it so she was forced to look into those dangerous eyes. "Just maybe— since she was trying to kill you—it was a permissible thing." And then his face broke into an unexpected grin. "What on earth did you tell the ambulance?"

"And the cops. The fact that we were driving Grand-father's hippie van didn't help any. If they didn't know me, I'd probably be locked up about now." She dropped her face in her hands, grateful for the ability to hide and regain a measure of composure.

"Hopeless search party has been activated?"

"I told them that she ran out in the street and I hit the brakes but couldn't stop in time. And that she appeared to be unconscious, woke up, refused to stay still, and ran off. I said I thought she'd gone down the alley across the street."

"The mud's frozen and there's no snow, so no big surprise if they don't find footprints," he said. "That will keep them busy for a while."

"Honestly, I doubt they'll look too hard. More important things afoot. Nobody cares about an old homeless woman."

"Are you sure you're okay? Nothing broken."

She nodded. "Fine. Except—I've never been without the pendant, since I was seven. How do I even know if I'm awake?"

"Welcome to my world. That's the thing—most of us are always guessing."

"I don't like it." Her voice sounded small to her own ears, childlike. Which, she realized, was how she felt. About five years old, powerless and afraid. And if Zee said one gentle word to her now she was going to dissolve into a quivering mess of hysteria. The warmth of the hand cupping her chin was bad enough.

He withdrew his hand. "You're not dreaming."

"How do you know?"

"Because *I'm* not dreaming."

"And you know this because?"

"You are sitting over there with all of your clothes on and I am not kissing you."

And with that she was a long way from childhood, her body burning with memory of his dream. She should tell him what she had done, but that would open the door to a conversation that she wasn't ready for.

"What now?" he asked. "What is the creature after?"

"I don't know."

"We need to find the Key, and those missing dream-spheres."

"And my pendant. So—back into the Between?"

"I was thinking about paying a visit to your old friend Jared."

Just the mention of the name invoked the sensation of his unwelcome hands on her body. She wrapped her arms around her belly, containing a transitory sense of flying into pieces. A toxic mess of emotions bubbled dangerously near the surface—fear and rage, loss and shame, and other things she couldn't put words to. Zee would notice, she knew he would notice. And he would ask, and she would fly into a million pieces.

"Do you think he knows what his dream self was up to when he—did what he did?" Her voice sounded far away and foreign to her own ears, as though somebody else were speaking.

"Only one way to find out. By the way, your book is upside down," Zee said, as though she wasn't disintegrating before his eyes, as though a nuclear-strength emotional charge wasn't lying between them. "*The Inbreeding of America: A Photographic Journey.* No wonder you're having night-mares."

Intense gratitude welled up in her that he had chosen to sidestep the land mine. She dared not meet his eyes, not yet, but her heart settled back into a regular beat, her body felt like it would hold together after all. One deep breath, another, and she heard her own voice saying, "All right, then. Let's go pay a visit to Jared."

Six

Jared fumbled off the alarm and buried his head under the pillow. The faint light seeping in around the window shades was enough to send a laser beam of agony into his brain. His tongue felt three sizes too big and tasted foul; his stomach gurgled and churned.

Hungover.

On a Monday morning.

He could count on the fingers of one hand the number of times he had allowed himself to get drunk, and three of those five occasions were named Friday, Saturday, and Sunday of the week just past. For the moment he couldn't remember why he'd been drinking, or put together any sort of logical thought.

Aspirin. Water.

The two words lined up beside each other in a way that made some sense, and he crawled out of bed in search of the cure, groaning with every movement. His body felt like it had been trampled by hundreds of pairs of feet. The bathroom, usually pristine, was a disaster. A wet towel lay in the middle of the tile floor on top of a jumble of cast-off clothes; the toilet was foul with vomit.

Mouth-breathing to quell a new surge of nausea, he flushed and turned on the fan to dissipate the stench. A spritz

of deodorizer made it worse, the sweetness of flowers blend-
ing with bitter putrefaction.

He found aspirin in the medicine cabinet. Ran water into
a tumbler. Swallowed. Swallowed again and again to keep
it down.

His eyes managed to focus long enough to read the clock.
Half past nine. He was going to be late. He was never late.
Which meant calling in with some sort of an excuse—stuck
in traffic, something. His cell phone was in the pocket of
the pants crumpled on the floor. His head pounded with a
whole new intensity as he bent to retrieve it. There was another
object in the pocket.

Small, square box. Velvet.

Memories swarmed in without restraint, firing every
neuron in his brain at once. Vivian had rejected him, turned
down a diamond worth ten thousand dollars. After which
he had dreamed strange dreams of acts far beyond the
reaches of the law, so real they lingered on his skin weeks
later. Insanity might start this way. A confusion between the
dream and the reality, the two shifting places so that the real
became the dream and the other way around. Maybe he had
done it after all: had forced himself on the woman he loved,
beaten her, been complicit in feeding living humans to
dragons.

That thought dragged him back from the rabbit hole.
Whatever sort of mumbo jumbo philosophers and physicists
might bandy about, there was no way that dragons were real.

Feeling marginally better, he showered and dressed casually in slacks and a sport jacket, skipping the badly needed
shave. If TV ads meant anything, the unshaven look was a
thing; he'd pretend to have done it on purpose. And when
he arrived at the office he would claim illness, make a point
of how dutiful it was for him to show up while obviously
ravaged by some vicious flu.

Head still throbbing but slightly subdued by the aspirin,
he put on his shoes and walked out into the hall, where he
froze, taking in the unexpected.

Vivian stood in the middle of his living space. Everything

about her was unchanged: the auburn hair curling over her shoulders, the jeans and T-shirt he could never break her of wearing, the serious, listening look on her face that had drawn him to her the first time they met.

Only her eyes were different, glowing amber as if lit with an inner flame, and she was not alone. A tall man leaned against the door frame, watching, waiting. Jared had seen that face before, waking and dreaming. He felt the walls of his own house pressing in, his breath suddenly loud in his throat. He swallowed, hard, finding his voice with difficulty.

"So I was right. You do have a lover."

Neither one of his guests responded to the barb. They didn't flush or fidget or look at each other. They just waited. Uneasiness grew; his stomach churned and the pounding in his head intensified. This was not a social call.

Breaking a silence that seemed to span a lifetime, he shifted his gaze to Vivian. "You might have knocked."

"But I still had a key. This just seemed easier." She crossed the room to stand facing him, no more than an arm's length away. Once he would have reached out and touched her; now there might as well have been a million miles between them.

Her eyes were all wrong. They had been gray, a little uncertain, changeable like smoke or mist. Now they were hawk eyes, golden and fierce. He knew full well that it was impossible to read somebody's mind, and yet he felt that she could see deeply into him, past all the carefully cultivated layers of civility to the inner self that he kept under lock and key. Unable to sustain her gaze he looked down, only to see that the eyes were not the only change. An intricate tattoo marked the skin at the base of her throat and onto her shoulder.

Almost like lace. Or scales. He shivered as he slid into a memory that raised the fine hairs on the back of his neck, tightened his belly, turned his heart into a trip hammer.

Vivian, chained to a stone. She was dressed in a flowing white gown, her hair loose on her shoulders. A dragon stood facing her, its teeth stained red with the blood of other humans recently consumed. And then the unthinkable: Vivian shifted, changed . . .

"Jared. Look at me."

Vivian's voice. Vivian here, in his house, and not in some dream where she had turned into a dragon. He obeyed the command. She was very pale, and he saw now that her hands were shaking. Those eyes were a torment, but the words that followed were worse.

"Do you remember what you did to me? Do you know?"

He shook his head in denial, looking away from the disconcerting eyes only to catch the stare of the man who now stood only a pace away. Jared had reason to know that those hands, though they might look easy and relaxed, were capable of swift and lethal violence. He swallowed hard as his stomach rose in rebellion.

"What do you want?" he said, shifting away from both of them. "I need to go to work."

"You're not going to work today," Vivian said. "We need some help."

Her words loosened his tongue, heating his blood to anger. "Why should I help you with anything?" But even as he said the words, he felt the guilt run through him like a poison. In that dream, where the dragon had been about to consume her, he had been complicit. And there was the other thing that he had done. Still, the jealousy boiled. "If you wanted something from me, you should have come without your boy toy."

"His name is Zee."

"We've met. I have no idea what you think I can do for you."

"We're interested in your dreams," Zee said. "Maybe you remember something about a Key."

"I don't—I don't know what you're talking about." He tried to push past Vivian, but Zee blocked his path.

"You need to leave my house."

"I think you do know something about the Key, Jared. All you need to do is tell me where it is."

"I'm calling the cops." Jared pulled out his cell phone, but Zee knocked it from his hand, casually, like a cat batting at a piece of string, and sent it sailing across the room.

"It doesn't really look like a key. More like a cylinder, made out of black stone." Vivian was no longer shaking. The golden eyes burned, for all the world as though there were flames behind them. The pattern on her neck had darkened and spread down her arms and onto the backs of her hands.

Panic built inside him. They were here to kill him. In the dream they were both killers, and now they had come to exact revenge for the crimes he had committed. In a dream.

Vivian put her hand on his arm, her face puckering as though there were something slimy on his sleeve. "Let's go."

"Go where?" The panic was alive now, beating at him, and he tried to twist away from her but Zee was right there, blocking him.

A door appeared where no door should be, right in the middle of the sitting room. It was green, with a brass knob. For one thing, he would never have such a plebeian-looking thing in his house. For another, it hung in the middle of the air, not connected to anything.

But Vivian opened it with her free hand, and through it he saw not the couch and the other side of his sitting room, but a thick forest with old-growth trees.

"You're going to show us what your dream self did with the Key," Zee said.

Jared wanted to say that he didn't know what they were talking about but didn't trust himself to speak, let alone to formulate a believable lie. Because everything they said was true. The minute that strange door opened, the dream memories seemed more real than this scenario playing out in his living room.

And if those dream memories were true, if what he'd written off as nightmare was real, then he was in the sort of trouble from which there would be no coming back.

Seven

Zee wasn't sure what he'd been expecting to find on the other side of the door, but it wasn't this. The part with the trees was all right, even vaguely familiar. What was unexpected was the sudden weight of memory that didn't belong to him.

He knew full well that he'd never stood in a forest that looked anything like this one, populated by fairy-tale trees older than any tree had a right to be. Vines wrapped around their trunks; sheets of gray-green moss hung down over their branches. The undergrowth was thick and impenetrable, save for one path wending its way between the massive trunks. He caught himself expecting the sudden appearance of Ents.

Jared twisted his arm free of Vivian's grip and began puking up his guts into some bushes. Zee watched without sympathy, entertaining the image of his sword at the man's throat. One swift cut and whatever the asshole had done to hurt Vivian was avenged. Except that dead Jared was of absolutely no use to anybody, and it probably wasn't fair to punish a man for what he'd done in his dreams, asshole or not.

"What is it?" Vivian asked, her hand on his arm, gray

eyes wide with concern, and Zee realized that he had forgotten to hide his own distress.

"It feels like I've been here before; done things here before. But that isn't possible."

"The Warlord," she said, matter-of-fact. "Your alter ego, as the Chancellor is Jared's. He could have been here—I don't think we're far from Surmise."

That made sense, and simply understanding the problem eased Zee's discomfort. The Warlord was dead, so there should be no weird encounter of self with self, and his memories could be valuable.

"Which way do we go?" he asked. Surmise was off to the left, if memory served, but there was no path leading in that direction.

Vivian shook her head. "I don't know. Paths shift all the time in the Between—every time somebody dreams a new dream, or an old dream dies."

"Make it stop," Jared said. "Please." He looked like he was about to faint, his eyes taking on the dazed look of shock. "Something's messing with my brain."

"There is one Dreamworld we all know," Vivian went on, not even looking at him. Her voice was very quiet, and Zee guessed where this was going with a jolt of apprehension.

When she turned to Jared, he held up both hands as though to ward off an evil. "I have no idea what you're talking about. I've never been in any Dreamworld . . ."

"You're lying. But it doesn't matter. Think of a garden, Jared, one where there is a fountain, and a stone bench."

He shook his head. "No—"

"If it helps, you can think about a penguin skewered on a sword. Maybe that will make you feel big and powerful and you won't be so scared. Zee?" She grasped Jared's limp hand in one of hers and held out the other.

"Got it," Zee said. He'd expected her hand to be cold, but it burned with heat like fever. The pattern of scales had spread up her neck and touched her jaw. The golden eyes burned.

A sense of loss came over him for the gray-eyed girl who

had slipped into his store a few weeks ago, pursued only by the wind, but there was no time, not now.

"Close your eyes," she said, and it was a quiet command.

Zee waited for Jared to comply. Dreamworld or Wakeworld, he was an unreliable bastard who required watching.

An elbow in his ribs from Vivian reminded him to follow suit.

"Think about that garden, the fountain, whatever brings the place to mind."

Zee closed his eyes, let himself slide into a memory of a place he had never been.

Darkness, with a red and bloated moon overhead. The garden had a light of its own, though, enough to see the blood on the stone bench, the bruise blossoming on Vivian's cheek, the penguin lying dead in the grass. And in his own heart a mixture of rage and grief and shame that nearly sent him to his knees with the weight of actions both done and undone.

"Keep your eyes closed. Hold the focus." A tug on his hand followed the words and he followed, walking blind, holding the image with both mind and soul. He felt the shift as they stepped through the door. Heard the splash of water on water from the fountain, smelled the roses.

Vivian let out a little gasp and her hand tightened convulsively. Zee's eyes sprang open, all senses on alert.

For a moment everything was a muddled swirl of reality and dream that stole his breath. He knew he stood holding Vivian's hand. Jared stood on the other side of her, and at their feet was a penguin, alive and well and making a hissing sound like a small steam engine.

In the garden, equally solid and real, lay a dead penguin and a man that looked like Jared, except that he had long hair and was dressed like a prince in a fairy tale. All strange and surreal, but it was the warrior in chain mail who threatened to derail Zee's sanity. The man's face, scarred by so many knife cuts it barely looked human, was inhabited by a pair of agate eyes that had looked back at Zee out of the mirror for thirty-five years.

Zee rubbed his eyes. The Warlord was dead. Had taken a knife meant for Vivian's heart in his own. Even as he entertained this thought, the Warlord began to fade, growing wraithlike and insubstantial so that the fountain showed through him. Then he was gone. The dead penguin dissolved an instant later, but Gareth the Chancellor remained, all too solid, all too real.

Jared was puking again. This time Zee really didn't blame him. At least with his own dead alter ego out of the way he was able to pull himself together enough to fight if necessary.

The Chancellor looked them all over with a condescending stare. "Well, this is interesting."

"I hoped to find you here," Vivian said. "I had no idea whether it would work—whether Jared's vision of this place would summon you."

"That's his name? Jared? What is wrong with him?"

"Seeing you, I suspect. Being hit with memories of all of the things you have done."

"Why don't I have memories of the things he has done?"

"You do. Think of your dreams, Gareth."

The man's face altered.

Vivian seemed taller. The pattern of scales on her skin had deepened and darkened. Zee could feel waves of heat wafting off her. His nostrils caught a hint of hot, clean stone. Dragon. His heart beat the word with rage and hate. But this was Vivian, who hadn't asked to be Dragon, or even Dreamshifter. He couldn't stand by and watch what would follow if she changed; time after time he had seen it in dream, and always it tore the heart out of him.

She took a step toward the Chancellor.

He took a step back, his eyes wide.

"You killed my penguin, right here. You tried to rape me . . ."

"No," Jared moaned, off to the side. "No, no. I didn't. I wouldn't. What is happening? I don't understand . . ."

"You." Vivian's head turned in Jared's direction, all predator now, even her body posture changing as the scales spread. Only an instant and it would be too late. "You dared—"

Zee stepped between her and the prey, put both hands on her shoulders, forced himself to look deep into eyes now soulless and hungry. "Vivian. Stay with me. Please."

If she shifted, he would be dead, unless he killed her first. Three full breaths, and then recognition came into her eyes; the scales began to fade.

"Are you back?"

She nodded, laced her fingers with his, and gave Jared a look of pure contempt before turning back to the Chancellor. "Gareth," she said, as if there had been no interruption, no threat of a dragon emerging from her body, "you helped me, in the end. You said you thought I was right that your counterpart was a better man. Do you remember?"

The Chancellor nodded, wary, keeping his distance.

"I'm offering you another opportunity. We're looking for something you can help us find."

"I can't imagine what that would be." Color had begun to return to his cheeks; he breathed more easily. His fingers toyed with something in his pocket.

"Of course you do," Vivian said, her fingers tightening around Zee's. "Where did you hide them?"

Zee put his free right hand to the sword hilt, ready for either one of the assholes to make a wrong move.

The Chancellor had his hand out of his pocket now, something hidden in the palm. *Dreamsphere.* Zee leaped into a full-scale tackle, his weight bearing the other man to the ground, preventing him from looking into the thing he held in his hand. As they hit the ground he jarred Gareth's elbow against a stone. The fingers opened and a small crystal sphere rolled onto the grass.

Releasing Gareth, he secured the dreamsphere before it could do any harm, careful not to look at it. The Chancellor was no longer a threat—the blow to his elbow had crippled his right arm, which hung limp at an awkward angle. Through jaws clenched with pain Gareth said, "You can kill me, but I won't tell you where to look."

"What about if you tell her?" Zee gestured toward Vivian. "She's got plenty of reason to hurt you without even thinking about what you've got hidden away."

"I'm guessing this dreamsphere will take us to the general location," Vivian said, taking the thing from Zee's hand. "I suggest we start there." She crossed the clearing and knelt beside Gareth. "Oh bother, you've gone and broken his arm."

"It was an accident—" Zee couldn't believe he was apologizing for hurting somebody who had done the things Gareth had done. Or that she was even worrying about the bastard's health and well-being.

"We'll have to splint it. We can't drag him off into some Dreamworld with it flopping around like that. Here, hold the dreamsphere. Do not look at it. Understood?"

"If I do, I get sucked away into some dream somewhere?"

"Right. And I'm not sure how to find you."

Zee tucked the thing into his pocket. He didn't like the way it vibrated, as though it picked up some sort of signal he couldn't hear. And he definitely didn't like the idea of being pulled away into a world from which he might never return.

He watched as Vivian scoured the forest floor for what she needed, and came back with two straight sticks.

"What are you planning on doing?" Beads of sweat stood out on Gareth's brow. "I don't trust you . . ."

"She's a doctor." Jared spoke for the first time since they'd landed here. His face was pale, and his left hand was holding his own right arm as though it hurt him. "Let her fix it." He sat down in the grass and let his head fall into both hands.

Still on high alert, Zee watched them all, watched the sky, the forest, the earth. Listened. Reached out with his senses. Something was out there. No sound, no movement, no flash of light or color. He caught a whiff of hot stone on the breeze and glanced at Vivian.

She was engaged in wrapping strips of fabric around the sticks to splint the arm of her enemy. No hint of the dragon there.

"We need to hurry," he said, sniffing the air again, feeling an unease that could not be defined.

"Dragon," Vivian said. "I feel it too. Jared, come over here. Zee, grab Poe."

"Can you talk to it?"

She shook her head. Her eyes were wide and uncertain. "I—it's blocking me. Join up. Let's get out of here."

Jared didn't argue, probably scared spitless by all this talk of dragons. They all laid hands on Vivian, who was holding the dreamsphere. At the last minute the Chancellor tried to pull away. "I don't want to do this. And if you make me, I won't tell you where to look."

"Maybe we can help you change your mind," Zee growled. He was out of patience, had wanted nothing more than to give this man a good beating since the moment he'd laid eyes on him. Maybe now he had an excuse.

"It's all right." Jared's voice shook a little, but his face was resolute. "I know where the things are hidden. I'll show you."

Eight

They stood in the open doorway of a one-room cottage. Stone walls, straw roof, an earthen floor. Not at all the sort of place Vivian would expect the Chancellor to spend his time, but maybe that was the point. One glassless window let in light, but also wind and dust. A herd of about twenty goats grazed nearby, and something that looked more or less like a chicken squawked inside the cottage, running out between their legs to join the flock scratching and pecking in the hard dirt outside.

There was nothing inside the cottage other than a narrow platform bed with a worn blanket, a wooden table, and a single chair. Clean. Barren. Nowhere here to hide anything. No disturbance of the packed-earth floor.

Vivian's senses were all on high alert. She had clearly felt the presence of a dragon but had been unable to read anything at all—whether it was male or female, its age or size, or its intentions. All she had been able to pick up was a clear sense of power.

Zee too was on edge, like a stalking cat, deceptively relaxed but ready to pounce. This did nothing to set her at ease, and she just wanted to find the Key and get out of this place.

"Where do we look? Not a lot of hiding places."

"Under the bed, maybe," Zee said.

"Try the garden." All eyes swung toward Jared.

"Traitor!" Gareth spat. "Whose side are you on?"

"The side that gets me out of this place and back home." Jared crossed the small room and sat down on the chair.

"Aren't you going to show us where to look?" Vivian asked, trying to contain her irritation at his erratic mix of cowardice and courage.

He shook his head. "Dig up the potato plant, fourth row in, fourth plant over. Watch out for the chicken things."

Gareth took a step toward the bed, but Zee stopped him. "You are coming with us."

"You don't seem concerned about him—"

"He didn't do this. You did."

The Chancellor drew himself up to his tallest height, exuding all of the imperial authority he'd flung about in Surmise. "And if I refuse?"

"Please do." Zee's face was impassive; his agate eyes showed no emotion. But there was a quiet note of warning in his voice. "This is not Surmise, Gareth. You are no longer the Chancellor and I am not the Warlord, bound by your command or Jehenna's. I won't attack you, since you're injured, but if you press me . . ."

The warning was clear. Gareth's green eyes sparked outrage, but he said, "Oh, very well then."

Vivian led the way, out the door and around back, where a neat garden was bounded by a white picket fence. She had little experience with gardens, but she recognized cabbages and tomatoes. She didn't have a clue what potato plants looked like and hesitated right inside the gate.

"There." Zee pointed to the far end of the garden.

A chicken scratched in the dirt on the narrow path in front of her, blocking her way. Its neck was too long, and it was yellow like a canary. Vivian didn't think she'd ever seen a yellow chicken, but then her experience was pretty much limited to what she bought in the grocery store, mercifully feather free. Dreamworld. It figured.

Jared's warning saved her. Instead of shooing it with her

foot as she might have done, she flapped her arms and kept her distance. The chicken squawked and came at her in a flurry of wings and extended claws. Poe stepped between her and the attacker, his own neck extended, hissing.

And then Zee was there. A silver flash and the chicken's head hit the earth, while the body continued to run around in meaningless circles.

Vivian managed to get her breath back, taking in Zee with the sword in his hand, the body of the chicken now careening through the garden, and the head lying at her feet. The eye staring up at her focused in. The pupil contracted, the position shifted. The beak snapped open and closed, revealing a double row of sharp teeth.

She couldn't take her eyes off the horrid thing or bring herself to walk past it. "It's not dead," she said.

Zee came up to stand beside her. "You're the Dream-shifter."

Right. There had been something in the books about changing the contents of a dream. Vivian concentrated. She pictured the chicken head as belonging to a real, ordinary chicken. Just a beak. A normal eye. White feathers. No teeth. And the thing on the ground in front of her changed to match what was in her mind. She performed the same thing for the body still running around, giving it white feathers, and then laying it down on the earth, still.

She shivered. The thing was now dead, needed to be dead, but she was the one who had stopped its heart with her thoughts. This was a power she wasn't sure she wanted to possess. *Only in dreams,* she reminded herself. Which was small comfort, but she would take whatever she could get.

"Can you do the rest of them?"

It seemed possible. Vivian turned her mind on the rest of the flock, focusing on plain white feathers, normal-sized necks, beaks with no teeth. Exhilaration flooded through her. Power. Dreams weren't so scary after all—not if she could shift the contents into something harmless. She picked out one chicken and made it a rooster—gave it the long tail, turned its feathers red and green and gold, and then for fun added a blue topknot.

She grinned at Zee, but he wasn't looking at her. His eyes were scanning the horizon, still searching for something she couldn't see. But she felt supercharged and no longer afraid. If some new nightmare thing came along, she could shift it. They could do this. Get the Key and the spheres and fix the mess that began long before her birth.

"Which are the potato plants?" she asked.

"City girl," Zee said. "You've never seen a potato?"

"Well, potatoes, yes."

He pointed. "Those plants."

She followed the path through the middle of the garden to the plants he'd pointed out. Gareth followed, sullen and silent, with Zee behind him, ever watchful. Vivian glanced back at the cottage to see Jared framed in the open window, watching.

The moment of euphoria she'd felt after shifting the chickens faded. She wanted only to secure the Key and the dream-spheres and get the hell back home. Potato plants, thank all the gods, were not all conjoined and woven together like the other vegetables in the garden. Each stood alone in a little mound of earth, so it was easy enough to count four rows back and four plants over.

"Should have brought a shovel," she said.

Zee grinned and lifted an eyebrow. She smacked the back of one hand to her forehead. "Right. One shovel coming up."

Not so strange, really. Lucid dreaming, only here the things were real. She pictured in her mind the implement she wanted—a spade, with the sharp rounded end and a smooth wooden handle, splinter free. It appeared in her hands, solid and real. She dug awkwardly into the dirt at the base of the plant she wanted.

"Here," Zee said. "Let me."

She stepped back and watched as he grabbed the base of the plant with one hand and thrust the spade into the earth at the edge of the mound with the other. In one smooth movement he brought a clump of earth and roots up into the light, including five or six fist-sized potatoes. "Shame to waste them," he said, but he tossed them aside and kept digging. Two more strokes and the spade clanged against something solid.

Vivian sank down onto her knees, plunging her hands into the bottom of the hole. Her fingers found a rectangular shape, hard and smooth. She scrabbled at it, trying to get a grip. At last she pried it loose from the dirt and lifted it into the light. A box, plain, wooden, without ornamentation. There was no catch or lock, and it opened easily, revealing a cylinder carved from black stone. The Key. Her Key.

A shadow crossed the sun.

Poe hissed.

The rush of power struck her like a blow. Before she could shout a warning Zee was already in motion, turning to meet the five men who flowed over the fence. There was a subtle wrongness about the way they moved, as though they were not limited by flesh and bone. Their skin was gray, the sockets of their eyes empty, save for a glowing spark of red. Each wielded two blades, black as death, ten shadow blades against Zee's one.

Gareth, standing closest to the fence, fell before he could run or scream, blood spurting from a gash at the base of his throat. Vivian felt weighted, as though somebody had filled her feet and brain with iron. She must do something but couldn't think what that might be.

The men were almost on her and she was going to die, standing here stupidly with the Key in her hands.

Zee stepped between her and the attackers, sliding into a smooth and deadly rhythm. Vivian watched him parry the blows, the ring of sword on sword an assault to her own senses, still unable to think what to do.

Something was here, powerful enough to turn her brain to mush. Nothing moved, other than the fighting men. Jared was still visible in the window, watching, too far away for her to be able to read his expression, but she knew there would be no help from him.

A lurch in the rhythm of the swords, a cry, the thud of something heavy hitting the earth. Her heart convulsed in an agony of fear, but it was one of the attackers who had fallen. The death dance resumed, Zee still on his feet. He fought brilliantly, but there were too many.

She had to help him, had to fight this heaviness that immobilized her.

Shift them, change them. If she could eliminate even one of them, it would help Zee. A moment later one of the men held only sticks in his hands, futile against Zee's sword. There was time for fear to cross his face, and then he was dead. Two down. She turned her mind to the next, hope springing up in her breast. They could do this, she and Zee. She would disarm them, he would kill them. The third man fell after his weapons just vanished, leaving his hands empty. And then the fourth, without her having done a thing. Zee and his last opponent stood a distance apart, studying each other, holding off before making the final move.

Dead bodies lay sprawled in the dirt, limbs tangled in vegetation. Blood spattered Zee's face and clothing, and it wasn't all the blood of his enemies. An ugly laceration ran from shoulder to elbow of his right arm. He'd shifted the sword to his left hand. His breath came too hard and he moved slowly, as though gravity had increased its pull on him.

The gray man didn't even look tired. He spun his swords up into the air and caught them. White teeth flashed. Vivian shifted his swords to sticks, but they shifted back before Zee could make a move.

The man whirled, the two blades dancing. Zee blocked and parried one, but the second got past him and traced a line of crimson down his side.

"Surrender!"

Zee managed another blow. It drew blood. His opponent staggered and one of his swords dropped to the earth.

Vivian's heart leaped in hope as she again focused on a shift, this time making the remaining blade disappear altogether.

And then, so unfair, more warriors swarmed over the fence, an army of loose-jointed figures with fresh blades.

"Surrender!" the swordsman facing Zee shouted again, brand-new blades shining in his hands, as the wave of reinforcements swept up behind him.

"Vivian, go!" Zee shouted, bracing himself for a hopeless defense. One last swing, and the onslaught bore him to the ground.

There had to be a way to fix this. Vivian grabbed the first image that came to mind and started the shift. The men began to sprout white feathers, to shrink. Their noses grew sharp and beaklike, their necks elongated.

The transformation was almost complete when an override struck her brain with an agony that nearly blinded her. Her legs felt like rubber; nausea surged in her belly. But Zee was going to be killed and she tried again. This time the pain dropped her to her knees, whimpering.

"Pitiful," a woman's voice said. "And stupid. Now give me the box."

Vivian couldn't move. Breathing was an agony that threatened to blow her head apart. Even the blood traveling through her veins created too much sensation. She willed herself to run, to do something to save the Key, but movement was beyond her.

She felt the box taken from her hand.

No more clanging of swords, no thudding of fists or grunts of effort. Nothing but her own too-loud breath.

When the voice spoke again, she tried to get her eyes open, but the light stabbed like daggers and the first attempt turned her stomach inside out.

"Get her out of my sight," the voice said, dripping with disgust.

"It would be easiest to kill her." A male voice now, accented and unfamiliar.

"Leave her alive. She may yet be of use. The rest of you—bind the warrior before he wakes."

Hard hands grasped Vivian's arms and dragged her to her feet, sending brand-new daggers of agony stabbing into her brain. The Voice of command was too far away for her to reach; her muscles didn't belong to her. Bracing herself against the pain, she managed to stiffen her knees, force her eyes open, but then the hands lifted her and flung her through an open doorway.

The pain was beyond enduring and all the world went dark.

Nine

The sun had already dropped behind the mountain, laying heavy shadows beneath the trees. Soon it would be full dark. Morgan was racked by indecision. If he kept going, he risked losing the trail, blundering through the forest with nothing more than a blind hope that he'd somehow stumble across his quarry. But every time he thought about stopping he saw Jenn's hands stretched out to him, the hope fading out of her eyes.

His fault—because he had been too slow to act today, and because of what he'd allowed to happen a year ago.

He'd been short on funds, and against his better judgment brought a young hothead hunter out looking for bear. After a long day of hunting and coming up empty they'd stumbled across a dying Sasquatch. What had happened to bring the creature down, Morgan couldn't tell. Maybe it was wounded; maybe it was just sick, or old. It lay on a creek bank with its legs and feet trailing in the water, stinking to high heaven. When it saw them it struggled, briefly, trying to get to its feet but falling back and staring up at them with damn near human eyes.

And the imbecile hothead killed it. Not a mercy shot to end its suffering, or even a quick knife kill. No, the idiot began carving away at the neck with his hunting knife, carried away by the idea of lugging the head home as a trophy. Morgan had time to hear a near-human scream emerge from the creature's throat, to see the eyes cloud with pain and fear before he'd put his own shotgun to one of those eyes and pulled the trigger.

He'd been uneasy ever since then about the man-beasts, and now the innocent were paying the price.

Trying to keep his emotions locked up tight so that his mind would be clear, he'd pushed himself all day long, moving as fast as he could without risk of losing the trail, not stopping to rest. He ate power bars from his backpack to keep up his energy. Drank water from the canteen. Welcomed the pain of overworked muscles and the creeping fatigue as a small punishment for an unforgivable failure.

At the edge of a small meadow he paused as his nostrils caught a hint of skunk gone bad. There were several large depressions in the grass and another smaller flattened area that could have been made by Jenn's body. He saw no signs of blood. Maybe the creatures were more humane than the humans and his worst fears would not be realized.

Fingers tightening around the shotgun, he searched through the gloomy shadows for the trail. At first, his eyes passed right over the thing half buried in moss beside a decaying cedar. Just another bit of log, or an earth-covered rock. He had begun to follow the trampled grass out of the cleared space before his brain registered what he had seen.

Sick with remorse and dread, Morgan retraced his steps and knelt beside the body half buried in the leaves. He brushed away the debris to reveal Carpenter's face, eyes open and staring blankly at the darkening sky. The old man's face and hands were the color of a ripe plum. Dried blood clotted around a jagged piece of shrapnel embedded in his forehead, gift of the exploding gun. Blood matted his once-white hair.

The cause of death could have been brain injury and loss of blood from the head wound. If he had actually died hanging over the beast's shoulder as his swollen face implied, then they hadn't deliberately murdered him, had only dropped him off when they found him dead and even had the decency to cover him.

Which meant Jenn could still be alive.

Morgan's weariness lifted in a burst of hope and renewed energy. Maybe he could still find her before dark. He didn't want her to spend the long night hours as a prisoner, startling at noises in the dark, terrified of what her captors might do. He shut his mind against all of the possible harm that could come to her, willing his nerves steady and his mind clear. He could not afford to make any more mistakes.

Carpenter deserved a decent burial and his granddaughter would need that sort of closure, so Morgan took care to register the landmarks that would enable him to find the place again. He hadn't gone far before a sound that had been just at the edge of his hearing became audible.

Running water.

Somewhere nearby there was a stream, and his quarry was headed toward it.

Morgan abandoned the trail and picked up his pace. Too dark now to catch the signs, but if he lost the trail he could backtrack to the clearing and try again by daylight. If they were heading for the water, it would be easy to find footprints in the soft earth at the margin of the stream.

As the sound of the water increased so did the stink, the air seeming to thicken with it. It spurred him to greater speed. He was on the trail; he had a chance to rescue the girl and at least partially pay for what he had done. This time he wouldn't freeze if the hairy man-monkeys looked at him wrong. If they threw his shots off target, he'd tackle them with his bare hands. And if they killed him, what was death to him? A small thing, his life. He would be more than willing to trade it for the girl's safety.

It was a noisy little creek, maybe ten feet across, cut deep into the earth. A pool about twenty paces downstream was edged by shallow muddy banks, lousy with footprints that would have given a Squatch hunter wet dreams, but Morgan didn't even look at them.

Jenn lay half in, half out of the pool. A ray of light shafted through the trees and illuminated her face. She was moving, thank God, and her dark eyes were open. During the endless seconds it took for him to reach her they seemed to follow him, judging. One of her boots was caught under a branch that had lodged against two submerged rocks, anchoring her body in the stream with torso and head floating in the pool. Her long hair rippled with the moving water. Her arms were spread, palms open, much as they had been hours earlier when they had been stretched out to him, beseeching.

Coward.

Morgan waded out to her, icy water seeping into his boots, numbing his legs. Seen up close, the eyes were not looking at him, were not looking at anything. No breath animated the chest. The movement of her arms was an effect of the flowing water.

His own breath kept hanging up on a snarl of something that felt like barbed wire. He knelt beside her, heedless of the icy water and the sharp rocks tearing into his knees. Tilting her head back, he sealed his mouth over hers and blew air into her lungs. Her skin was cold and clammy and he knew even as he breathed breath after breath into her that it was far too late.

This was his fault. His. He had brought her to this place, had failed to protect her. Had been too slow—too slow—to find her.

Coward.

Grace's face flashed before his mind's eye, her face spattered in blood. It was not something he could bear to think about. Not now, not ever, and he shoved it away as he always did.

Jenn's body was heavy with water, his arms rubbery and weak. It would have been easier to put her over his shoulder, but he wouldn't do that to her, not after what she had been through. Instead he pressed her head onto his shoulder, the long wet hair tangling around his arm, and tried to warm her against his heart. He caught himself rocking her as though she were a frightened child and forced himself back to sanity.

His feet sloshed inside his boots as he splashed onto dry

land. His arms ached with the weight of his burden. Pain was only the beginning of the penance that he would pay, and he embraced every signal of discomfort that his nerves sent him. One slow step at a time he retraced his path. It was now dark in earnest under the trees, and he stumbled over rocks and fallen branches, moving more by instinct than by landmark.

But it wasn't far and his sense of direction was well honed. At last he collapsed onto his knees in the clearing and laid the girl on a bed of moss beside her grandfather. As he knelt over their bodies, still struggling to breathe past the tangle in his throat, a memory long suppressed fought its way past all of the guards and wards he had built against it.

Blood, everywhere blood. The sick sweet smell of it, thick and clotted on his own face, slick on his hands. The walls—whitewashed once by his own reluctant labor—now patterned with an indelible splatter of crimson. The bodies, so many of them, like empty containers discarded on the floor, emptied of their souls. Underlying the smell of blood the bitter tinct of gunsmoke. Only one living face, besides his own, dark eyes staring accusing into his.

His body shook with a sick palsy that wouldn't permit him to take refuge in physical flight. The one scene played in his memory, over and over again, an old-time movie reel broken and spinning, tick, tick, tick. The room, the blood, the dead, Gracie's face, alternating with flashes of light and dark.

Guilt was an unbearable torment.

He could put the barrel of the shotgun in his mouth and end it now, but that was a death too easy for the sins he had committed.

His hand went to the leather thong around his neck. In Wakeworld a pendant hung from it, a raven in a dream web, carved from strange black stone. He was a Dreamshifter. He had the power to re-dream this nightmare, to cast himself as a hero able to rescue both the girl and the old man. Or he could dream a dream in which the Sasquatch had never appeared. He could dream himself and the girl into ravens, flying high above the forest and looking down at a miniature Sasquatch far below.

One small problem.

In all the years of his life, Morgan had never used this power, not once, and had no idea how to do what needed to be done. Right now he would gladly have given up his life to know how to change this story, but that didn't help a damned thing. The knowledge that would have helped him was buried with all of the rest of the memories from his childhood.

He'd spent more than eighty years avoiding anything that reminded him of his childhood, his family, or the Dreamshifter lore. It was too late to do anything to save Carpenter or Jenn, but as penance for his sins the least he could do was face up to his demons.

Ten

"You've killed him."

Aidan felt the rage building. Her awkward human form, vulnerable and inadequate to contain so much power, threatened to disintegrate.

"It was kill or be killed. He fought well." The captain of her shadowmen, either very brave or foolhardy, dared to stand before her and say the words.

She smiled, letting all of her teeth show. "Do you think I care if you lose some of your worthless men? There were more than enough of them to take him down without a death wound."

"We lost seven, to his one." He too was wounded. A gash in the thigh, one in his side. The blood scent filled Aidan's mouth with saliva, pushed her toward the shift. The captain was a creature of the Dreamworld, far from human, but he could still bleed and be killed.

Step back, if you value your life.

Like humans, the shadowmen never heard her when she spoke into their minds, but still she considered it fair warning. And while the captain may not have heard the words, her face and toothy smile must have told him something. He stepped back one pace, and then another. Not far enough, if she let herself shift. Still within easy reach of jaws and teeth. It was to his credit that he was able to contain the fear, keeping face and body under harsh control.

Aidan surveyed what had once been a neat little garden, now broken and trampled. Seven bodies lay in a row, no red spark in the empty sockets, limbs folded, given the respect of a death well won. One man lay crumpled next to the fence, green eyes wide and staring, his throat cut from ear to ear.

He would serve as dinner, once she was done here. The body was still warm. Not so good as a fresh kill, but it would do. It would also serve as a reminder to the remaining shadow-men of the tenuous balance of their service without inciting a rebellion by disrespecting one of their own.

One other body lay untended, the earth around him stained crimson with his blood and the blood of others. His right hand remained clamped in a death grip around the hilt of his sword.

This was the death that should not have happened. The man had fought well, well enough that it was possible that he might be the Warrior, but the years lay heavy on that old hope. So long had Aidan been seeking that she hardly remembered the reason she had begun.

"A Warrior is born in every age," her mother had said. "Find him. Make him your ally. He will help to put the old wrong right. Only remember this: Once you find him, never, ever let him know that you are descended from the dragons."

Ages had come and gone, one after the other, and the Warrior had never come. Aidan had seen men who were brave, men who could fight. A few of them had been put to the test, but not one of them had survived.

Of late she had begun to wonder if the Warrior was of any importance. She was used to a lone existence—the drag-ons of the Between were too uncouth and degenerate to be company for her. Humans were too soft, and so easily turned into prey. Trust and companionship had ended with her mother's death, at least a thousand years gone.

But the Key in her hand sang to her now, bringing back all of the dusty old stories from her mother's tales and mak-ing them shine like a ruby fresh from the river of gold.

Funny how that image rested in her mind, solid and bright, as though she had seen the river with her own eyes and not only through childhood tales.

From the dream matter I made him, the first of the Warriors, fit to be a companion for me. But it was not safe for him in the Land—the King would have been jealous and one man, no matter how mighty, cannot fight against all the dragons at once. And so I sent him away into a Dreamworld.

When you find the Warrior, do not let him slip away. From the River he comes, as surely as do you, and there he is able to return.

The number of the years Aidan had been seeking this Key had been lost so long ago that she could not begin to count them. She had watched her mother, human, even though she could move between the Dreamworlds, fade and die. Had bided her time, watching the Sorceress Jehenna spin the web that was Surmise. Had been standing by, watching and ready for the moment Jehenna unlocked the Forever, but that attempt had failed and the Key lost once again.

Now she had to wonder. What if this man lying dead before her was the one, at last? What if his help was needed and she must wait another age before another warrior would come to help her meet her long desire? Fury flowed through her veins and she felt herself begin to shift. She would kill the ones who had done this, one by one. And when she had slaked her thirst for blood she would take the Key and find her way to the Gates, Warrior or no.

A shout from one of the men barely reached her.

"He lives."

She was nearly too far gone to care, but her vision, already transforming the world into a thing of sharply defined lines and colors, saw the man's chest rise and fall. She pulled herself back from dragon to fully human, clenching the Key in her hand.

"Barely," she said. The man's face was bruised and swollen. A deep gash ran down his side, and another, still bleeding, ran the length of his sword arm. But he was breathing. Strong enough to kill seven of her best men and live. If he could survive this, there was a chance he could survive the other.

"Let him be put to the test."

The captain looked at her, as though he wished to speak but did not dare.

"What?" she demanded. "Say it."

"He is already very weak. It is a harsh death you decree."

"If he is the one I seek, it will heal him. If not, he will die anyway. See that it is done."

"And the other?"

She barely even glanced at the hovel. The face that had watched through the open window had moved out of sight, but she knew the man was still in there. A coward. She detested cowards. Not worth the sword thrust it would take to kill him and of no use to her, now that she had the Key. "Throw him into the Between and leave him to wander."

Eleven

Coming back to consciousness was a difficult thing.

Vivian's heart pounded against her ribs as though her chest had grown too small to contain it. Breathing felt awkward and wrong. After several futile attempts she managed to get a full breath into her lungs. It hurt, but as she practiced the discipline of *breathe in, breathe out*, the pain eased and her body remembered the way of things and took over. Her hand sought the pendant and then she remembered, with a burst of panic, that it was gone. Stolen.

Fighting the inertia that pinned her, Vivian managed to roll over to her side, and from there up onto her knees.

She was just inside the front door of A to Zee Books. The store was dark and shadowy, the glow from the streetlamps outside illuminating the hanging sculptures that twisted and spun on invisible threads, the only moving things in the empty store.

Memory was tenuous, but she knew that she'd been hurt in some way; there had been terrible pain. The discipline of her training took over and she ran her hands over her head, checking for bumps and bruises and signs of injury, but her skull felt smooth and undamaged. No headache or nausea. Her vision was clear, no blurring, no distortion. No injuries other than a few minor bumps and bruises and the stiffness of long unused muscles. Nothing to worry about.

Except that she couldn't remember what happened. There had been a dream door. She had walked through it with Poe and Zee and Jared. Flickering images came and went, bits of memory tied together with dream sequences.

Zee dreaming in the chair. That was real. The book lay on the coffee table where she had left it. She picked it up, solid and heavy in her hands, the dust jacket smooth and cool to her touch.

Jared, unshaven, his shirt untucked and his shoes unshined. They'd gone to his house. That was right. Looking for the Key. That's where the dream door was, so what the hell was she doing here? Where were Zee and Poe, and for that matter, Jared?

And then memory turned into a battering ram and hit her all at once. Zee attacked, wounded, overcome by too many warriors. Her own failed attempts to save him. The woman's voice and the debilitating pain.

"Zee!" she shouted. "Poe!" She ran up the stairs to the apartment above, driven by fear.

His bedroom and kitchen were untouched and empty. No sign of Zee anywhere, but she found Poe in the bathroom, standing in the empty tub. He looked up at her hopefully and she flung herself down on the cold tile floor and hugged his feathery body, pent-up tears pouring down her face. He was bony and stiff and not at all cuddly, despite the softness of feathers, and he wriggled out of her grasp with an expression that rivaled embarrassed teenager.

"Where is Zee?" she asked him.

He stared back out of obsidian eyes, ever silent, then waddled over to nudge the faucet with his beak.

Vivian scrubbed at her tears with the back of her arm. "Fine," she said. "As you wish." She ran the tub, watching Poe carefully for signs of injury as he immersed himself in the water, but he seemed unhurt and little by little she stopped worrying about him. Leaving him to his soak, she walked to the end of the hallway, hesitating in front of a closed door.

It was an ordinary wooden door, unlocked, and she opened it to reveal a large room with a hardwood floor. Natural light flooded in through windows in the three external walls. Whatever wall space wasn't taken up with windows was hung with paintings strange and wonderful. Recognizable mythological creatures featured in many of them. A manticore snarled at a knight wielding a familiar sword. A phoenix plummeted from the sky in flames. There was a centaur and a cyclops. But most of the paintings followed two main themes.

The first was a faceless man with a sword, engaged in the art of dragon slaying: small dragons and huge, dragons old and young and in between, in good health and bad, wounded and full of vigor. All that remained the same was the knight who fought them.

The second theme was Vivian herself. Her face, her eyes, repeated over and over again on at least a score of canvases. In some of them she was her old self, in that time so far away now when she was not a Dreamshifter or a dragon woman, but only Vivian. In others, she was part woman, part reptile, her eyes golden, her flesh covered in scales.

How had Zee painted all of these pictures and not seen what she was? Her breath a tangled knot in her chest, Vivian selected two paintings and moved them to stand side by side against the wall. In one, her face, still gray-eyed, her hair blowing as though in an invisible wind. And beside it, a sinewy dragon in purple and gold, the warrior clinging to its neck and thrusting a triumphal sword into one of its golden eyes.

To this grouping she added one more picture, this one of a creature part dragon, part human, with golden eyes and a reptilian face covered in iridescent scales.

Vivian stared at these paintings long and hard to imprint the message on her heart. Zee loved her. Zee was a dragon slayer. And the dragon inside her, wanting to come out, was ever present and growing stronger. This sort of conflict could destroy a man, his love set against his hate.

Sobs tore at her throat and she swallowed them back, her entire body shaking with the effort it took to contain the pain. She fled the room, checked in on Poe, went to the kitchen and ran a glass of cold water. Her hands shook so badly that water sloshed over the edges of the glass and she could barely get it to her mouth, but she managed to drink several long swallows.

The water steadied her, and the last bits of memory slid into place. *Jared, watching through the window of the cottage. The dead warriors. Zee falling beneath the onslaught. The box taken from her hands.*

There was a chance that Zee was still alive and held as a prisoner somewhere. She couldn't assume that he was dead, not as long as there was the tiniest hope. She had gotten him into this mess, and she must find her way back to him. The best place to start would be where she had left him. Surely she could find it again. Three doors—into the Between, into the fountain at Surmise, and on into the Chancellor's dream.

The Chancellor was dead, but surely that wouldn't matter. It hadn't been his dream to start with; he'd used the dream-sphere. Which meant it was a stable dream that could be entered by any Dreamshifter.

Wrapped in a blanket, Vivian descended the stairs to the store and curled into one of the chairs to breathe and clear her mind. When she was calm, she created a door to the Between. It was so easy. Just a thought and an intention, and a green door materialized right in the middle of a shelf of books. She crossed to it, put her hand to the knob.

It wouldn't open.

She twisted the knob harder.

There was no give.

"Open!" she commanded. And still the door remained locked. She rattled the knob, panic welling up inside her. Stepping back, she hit the stubborn thing with her shoulder at a run, rebounding with a pain that took her breath away and promised a colorful bruise.

She knew she could not afford the panic; too much depended on her. So she counted to ten. Walked into the bathroom and splashed cold water onto her face. Sat down in one of the chairs, closed her eyes, and breathed. Only yesterday she was able to create doors and walk through them. Now, for some reason, she was barred.

Why? She hadn't had the pendant last night when she'd created the door at Jared's house, so that wasn't it. Maybe it had to do with the fact that she'd created a door to the same place at Jared's. It was closed, but maybe if it was still there she couldn't create another.

Closing her eyes she focused on a different area of the Between, and when she felt the door emerge she approached it with a heart full of hope. But again it was locked and would not allow her entrance.

Sinking back into the chair she confronted the possibility that she was locked into Wakeworld. Maybe the unknown source of power had broken her, rendered her incapable of opening doors.

This was not acceptable. She had to get to Zee, had to find that Key before somebody else put it to use. She was still not entirely clear what evil thing was going to come about if somebody did get the freaking thing. Jehenna had been after everlasting life. So what. Let somebody have that for all she cared. What would it hurt?

Well, maybe a lot of things, if that somebody had a lot of power. Enough power, say, to lock a Dreamshifter out of the Between. Enough power to hammer a brain into mush.

Her thoughts circled round and round like an amped-up hamster on a wheel. The series of events played themselves over and over. There must be a solution to this problem; she must be smart enough to figure it out. There was nobody to go to, nobody to ask.

Poe waddled across the floor and bellied up onto the coffee table, where he took up his watchful penguin stance, fixing her with a disconcerting stare.

"What? I suppose you know."

She sighed and slumped down, stretching her legs out in front of her and letting her tired head rest against the back of the chair, her gaze drifting over the array of strange and wonderful hanging sculptures Zee had created. There was a flight of dragons, a waterfall made of silvery beads, a fleet of sailing ships.

And an intricate creation of tiny winged books, flying through a maze of stars.

Her eyes snagged on that one sculpture; the frenetic hamster came to a stop.

A fragment of poetry filled the calm space in her thoughts.

I have been a tear in the air,
I have been the dullest of stars.
I have been a word among letters,
I have been a book in the origin.

Poetry written by the enigmatic bard Taliesin, lost in battle at Camlann. Not dead, but missing.

There had been another name on the scroll reported as missing. Maybe, just maybe, Vivian wasn't the only living Dreamshifter after all.

Sitting here was stupid and futile, and nothing would be accomplished by wishful thinking. If she was locked into Wakeworld, maybe it was time to do a little digging into what happened to the man named Weston Jennings.

Twelve

Zee opened his eyes to stars.

They were not stars he had ever seen before: too bright, too close, too obviously balls of burning gas rather than the familiar pinpoints of cold white light. The constellations were also complex and strange—no friendly Big Dipper, no Orion striding across the horizon.

It didn't help that the light blurred in and out of focus, and it took a minute for him to realize that his vision was at fault, likely connected to the pounding of his head. He lay flat on his back with his hands folded across his bare chest. A line of fire ran the length of his right bicep, another along his left side. Every breath felt like a stiletto between his ribs. Thirst constricted his throat and papered his tongue.

A cool breeze flowed over him and he shivered. Whatever it was he was lying on was cold. Stone, if he judged by the hardness of it, probably a dungeon floor with not so much as a heap of straw beneath his naked shoulders.

Only if it was a dungeon, then why the stars? A hallucination maybe, a product of a severe concussion. He thought about moving his hands to feel what was beneath him, about sitting up to look around, but the act of even wiggling his fingers took an exorbitant amount of energy.

He'd lost a lot of blood, he guessed, and his body felt dry, dry, dry. He would need to find water soon.

Where was Vivian? She could doctor him up and they could get on with things.

Vivian. At the thought of her his heart beat faster, loss twisting in his gut. The last memory he had was of shouting at her to run, just before one of those gray bastards clobbered him over the head with the flat of a sword. Cowards, all. He had to find her. Would find her.

Just as soon as he could move. Tentatively he tested his muscles. It took a few trials before the brain signals got through to their targets, and the movements he could manage were sluggish and weak. His injured right arm moved at his command, but the pain made his breath hiss between his teeth. The left was stiff, but not seriously damaged, and his legs seemed okay.

Something rested on his chest, cold and narrow, long enough to run the length of his naked belly. He ran questing fingertips along its length. A sword. His sword. He wrapped his hand around the familiar hilt and instantly felt stronger.

Slow and careful, he eased himself up to sitting, taking the sword in his left hand since the right hung nearly useless. As he came upright his vision went dark and blood roared like ocean waves in his head. Little by little his vision cleared and he was able to take in his surroundings.

The giant stars lit the night as brightly as a full moon. He sat on a flat granite slab, one of seven set in a circle. On each lay the unmoving figure of a man. Each was naked to the waist, clothed only in white cotton breeches. Their feet were bare. Their hands were crossed over an unsheathed sword. No movement. No breath or other indication of life. All were scarred; some bore unhealed wounds. And their faces, one and all, were grotesquely twisted with agony.

Zee felt the prickle of fear on his skin.

His own wounds didn't seem to be life threatening. His right arm was caked with dried blood from a deep laceration that he knew needed cleaning and stitches. It was still oozing a little, but most of the bleeding had stopped so if it didn't get infected it would probably heal all right. Another jagged cut scored his ribs. This one was shallower but had also bled profusely. There was enough bruising to explain why it hurt so much to breathe, and the blood loss would account for his weakness. As for the blinding headache, he'd had enough concussions in his younger, fighting years to recognize that particular pain.

He was still alive and planned to stay that way, which meant putting distance between himself and the dead warriors with all possible speed. It would have been nice to know where he was in space and time, but a circle of rough standing stones blocked a wider view. They reminded him of the Finger Stone, all with that same sense of foreboding power, only these had been set in place by a conscious intelligence.

Zee didn't want to be here when the author and creator of this place showed up. This was either a Dreamworld or the Between—had to be, judging by the stars—so the body housing the devious serial-killer mind that had dreamed up a place like this could be literally anything. He was not strong enough to fight right now, which meant fleeing as far and as fast as his body would tolerate.

When he tried to stand, it seemed at first that he wouldn't be going anywhere at all. The earth under his feet wobbled and swayed and threatened to swing up to meet him, but he braced himself on the stone slab until he got his balance.

Gripping the sword in his left hand, he managed to get his feet moving and made his way out of the circle of the tombs, past the monoliths, and out into a wider space on top of a hill.

Nothing moved. There was no sound other than the harshness of his own breath. The stars shed just enough light for him to see a new pair of standing stones that towered over him, each carved into the shape of a dragon. A wide road sloped away down the left side of the hill. It was paved by outsized cobblestones, each as big as a small car. Walls barricaded it on either side, higher than his head.

He didn't like it, he'd be trapped if anything came after

him, but unless he wanted to walk back through the circle of tombs it was the only option. The thought of going back made his skin crawl, so he staggered off down the road, about as in control of his body as if he'd been thoroughly drunk.

Dim shapes arose out of the shadows ahead, huge, menacing, and he stopped his erratic footsteps to be still and pay attention. Another set of dragons. Only stone, but still his hand tightened on the sword hilt, ready for battle in case the things turned out not to be stone after all. Dragons had magic he didn't understand, and it wouldn't have surprised him at all if they came to life and followed behind him. Weak and injured as he was, his blood heated at the thought of dragons, but he knew there was no hope that he could win such a fight and he kept walking.

The road curved, and then curved again, spiraling ever tighter, marked at intervals by the stone dragons. At last an archway loomed out of the darkness, twice Zee's height and wide enough for the largest of dragons to pass through with ease. Through the arch a soft glow illuminated a spacious pavement, revealing vibrant jewel tones. At the center of the expanse was a bench, made from the same jewel-colored stones.

Zee's muscles quivered with weakness. He was parched with thirst; the pain of his wounds had grown intense. It would be good to sit and rest. As he passed beneath the arch, a bell toned one deep-throated peal. He paused, looking about him in wonder and alarm. There was no bell to be seen. He could not identify the source of the light, soft and gentle to his eyes, but it provided full illumination. The stones beneath his feet were truly cut from gems—slabs of ruby and jade and other stones he didn't know, with lines of beaten gold to seal them together.

He became conscious of his feet, muddy and bloodstained. If there had been water, he would have stopped to wash them, despite weakness and pain. As he neared the bench he noticed a bucket and rope, and realized that within the circle of the bench there was a well.

One more step, and he could smell the water. Not as one

smells a river or a lake, nor yet the salt tang of the sea; this carried the scent of rain falling on green grass, of an iced glass at the end of a long, hot day.

Thirst grew into obsession. He laid the sword down on the stone bench, grateful to be free of its weight, and dropped the wooden bucket into the well. For what seemed to him an eternity he watched the rope uncoil, marking the bucket's progress downward. At last the rope stopped moving and he heard a small splash. A moment to let the bucket fill, and then he began pulling it up, hand over hand. The motion opened the wound in his right arm and it began to bleed again. It didn't matter. Nothing mattered but that he slake his thirst.

Somewhere in the back of his mind his own voice clamored objections, but still he drew up the rope, hand over hand, until he held the dripping bucket. The liquid that filled it made water as he knew it a pale shadow of the real thing. Never had he desired anything with this level of intensity. Even his love for Vivian seemed a small thing in comparison.

And that made him hesitate.

He needed water and soon, or he would die. But this craving was beyond any thirst he had ever experienced. It had a compulsion about it; the bucket was halfway to his lips already and he hadn't made the choice to drink.

An image of the six men lying dead on the stone slabs flashed across his mind. They had not died in battle, or of wounds unhealed, or of loss of blood. The blackening of their skin, the agony etched into their faces even in death—that spoke of poison.

His hands began to shake with the realization of what he held.

If he was going to die, it wouldn't be because he had given in to an enchantment. He would set the bucket down and walk away.

And yet it remained in his hands, and the drive to bury his face in the icy water was almost overpowering.

A sweet voice behind him said, "Why do you tarry? It is permitted for you to drink."

She came around to face him, a woman with eyes like the mist when the sun shines through. He saw no evil in her lovely face, no lines of cruelty or secrecy, and his heart leaped with hope at her words.

Between the demands of his pain and the energy required to resist the water, it was difficult to speak. "I fear it is enchanted," he managed to say.

The maiden laughed, a liquid trill that reminded him of birdsong. "Of course it is enchanted. It will heal you. After you drink, you may bathe your wounds and it will ease your pain. Let me help you."

Light and graceful as a leaf on the wind she approached him. A slim white hand dipped a cup into the bucket and held it up to his lips. "Drink."

A drop spilled over the rim of the cup and rolled down his chin. He was vividly conscious of its path along his jaw; it was icy cold and held an unexpected weight. When it dripped from his skin, he followed its course with his eyes, watching it fall, jewel bright, and strike the stone pavement. It bounced and came to rest on top of a disc, perfectly round, mirror smooth. It was black, yet it refracted the light into a rainbow brightness. In it he saw his own face, and that of the woman.

"Drink," she said again.

His breath caught in his throat and he became deeply aware that he had set aside his sword and stood weakened and weaponless, at her mercy.

With an effort of will, he turned his head away from the tempting cup. "No. Thank you for the offer."

"There will be no help for you if you do not drink. No shelter. No water. No remedy for your hurts."

"And if I do drink, I will die."

"Perhaps," she murmured, "perhaps not. There are things worse than death."

"I do not choose this death."

"If you drink and live, I promise rest, shelter, and healing."

His whole body shook with weakness. The water continued to summon him. But what he had seen mirrored in the reflecting disc, and something about the disc itself, held him back. The maiden turned her face up to his, and as the light shifted something on her cheek shone diamond bright.

It was perfectly round, reflecting rainbows of light. Just like the large disc on the pavement.

Zee put out his hand and caught the shining thing on his fingertip.

A tiny dragon scale.

It all came together in an upswell of hate—the stone dragons, the precious stones, the shining black disc at his feet.

Summoning all of his strength he swung the bucket at her head, letting the momentum carry his body forward and then down onto the pavement, rolling away from her and the tide of water that hissed as it touched the stone.

He bumped up against the bench and was able to grasp the sword in his left hand. It felt too heavy to lift and there was no room to swing, but he would at least die fighting.

As the water struck the woman she seemed to melt, like wax in an oven. And then she began to grow and shift, as though giant sculptor hands were at work on a piece of malleable clay. An elongated body, four legs, an armored tail, a long serpentine neck. Deepest black she was, an absence of color so intense that all light seemed to be sucked into her and absorbed, creating a pool of shadow all around her nearly as dark as she.

Zee's hate was enough to get him onto his feet, even though the world spun around him. He locked his knees, gripped the sword, and prayed that he could kill the beast, even if it cost him his life.

But the dragon spread her wings and beat them over her back three times, creating a thunder and a mighty wind that knocked him off his fragile footing. He lay on the pavement of precious stones and watched as she took flight, until she was lost to him in the darkness and the fiery light of the stars.

Thirteen

The Krebston Library was a square, one-story brick building occupying the street corner across from the county jail. It wasn't much to speak of in terms of either size or inventory, but Vivian had discovered that the librarian was a fervent lover of books, and possessed an almost magical ability to procure requested reading material.

She paused in the doorway, breathing in the distinctive smell of books, old carpet, and people, a comfortable musty funk that some people might find unpleasant. To her, it was comforting, a reminder of the local library that had provided her with a safe refuge during her chaotic childhood. In books she had found world after world where she could walk freely and without risk. During the year she'd been in Krebston, she had frequented the library about as often as the grocery store.

The librarian waved her over. "Hey there! I haven't seen you in a couple of weeks. That new fantasy you were asking about came in, only I think somebody already signed it out. Want me to check if it's back?"

"That's okay, Deb—I'm actually after town history today. Can you point me in the right direction?"

"Depends on what you're looking for."

"Well—do we have any old newspapers on file? On microfiche or whatever?"

Deb snorted. "We're not totally backwater. No microfiche, but we're getting some scanned in and online. How old were you looking for?"

"Old. Early nineteen hundreds and on."

"Um—Krebston's not even that old, let alone newspapers."

"I was afraid of that—"

"Hold on, hold on. We have access to Spokane's stuff. They had a rag that might have included Krebston news."

Vivian didn't argue. The population had been smaller back then. Something that would be captioned as a massacre might well have made news in Spokane. For all she knew, the Jennings family might well have lived and died in Spokane. Or anywhere in the country, for that matter.

Deb led her to a back corner desk with a sign that said *Reference Librarian. Please feel free to ask for assistance.* "Here, you can use the computer at my desk. Quieter, without all those kids talking and messing around. I miss libraries when they were for books, but don't tell anybody I said so."

"And if somebody asks for help?"

"Nobody ever does. Just wave me over if you need me." She pulled up a screen. "There you go. Old Spokane newspapers here. May I ask what you're researching?"

"Family history." The lie came easy, along with the rationalization that it wasn't really a lie. It just wasn't her family she was looking at.

"Okay. Newspapers might not be your best source for that, unless they were gunslingers or politicians. Here—try these. GenWeb will give you names and dates of death, with weird and fascinating causes. And then of course there's genealogy.com—standby for genealogy nuts. Ooops, gotta go, there's a line up at the checkout desk. Let me know if you need me."

The line consisted of a young mother with a baby in arms and a toddler twining himself in circles around her legs, but

Vivian was glad to see Deb go. She didn't need anybody looking over her shoulder and asking questions.

GenWeb seemed like a logical choice, and she started there. It brought up a rough map of the state, by county. She tried Seattle first, looking at death records between 1900 and 1926. No Jennings. Nothing in Spokane County, or Stevens. Without much hope she clicked on Pend Oreille County and selected *F–J* from the alphabetical list.

Holding her breath, she scanned down and found:

> *Jennings, Edward C. Death Date 6/7/1925, Age Unknown. Birth place, Unknown. Cause of Death, gunshot.*

The sweat on her body felt like it had turned to individual ice pellets. This name had also been written on the scroll. *Edward Jennings, murdered in 1925.* And now here that name was again in official death records accessed through a word processor. In the library. Reality was strange. She shivered, and moved on.

> *Jennings, Ellie M. Death Date 6/7/1925, Age 21. Birth place, Fort Spokane. Cause of Death, gunshot.*
> *Jennings, William J. Death Date 6/7/1925, Age 17. Birth place, Krebston. Cause of Death, gunshot.*
> *Jennings, Jack S. Death Date 6/7/1925, Age 19. Birth place, Krebston. Cause of Death, gunshot.*

The next name was Kenton, Mary, who apparently died in her sleep, and Vivian was grateful.

Something very ugly had gone down on June 7, 1925, which also happened to be the year that one Weston Jennings, Dreamshifter, went missing. Four family members shot to death on one day. One gone missing.

Not sure she wanted to know any more, Vivian clicked over to genealogy.com and looked up Edward Jennings. He had been married to Evelyn, née Harper, in January 1903.

She died of a fall on ice on December 18, 1918. Before her death she provided Edward with five children—the three who had been shot to death on the same day he died, plus a son, Weston M., born in 1909, and a daughter, Grace D., who was born three years later. Edward, his eldest daughter, and his two elder sons were found shot to death in their home. Two members of the family, Weston and Grace, had escaped the shooting.

Vivian went to the newspapers, searching for the date of June 7, 1925. Sure enough, the *Spokane Times* sported a garish headline—*Four Dead in Krebston Massacre!!*—along with a grainy black-and-white photograph of a tangle of bodies that she wished she could unsee.

All blame pointed at sixteen-year-old Weston. Grace was on the scene, bloodstained and mute, while Weston was nowhere to be found. The girl revealed no information about the events.

Vivian went back into GenWeb. Grace Jennings died in 1977 and was buried with her family in the Old Krebston Cemetery. As for Weston, there was no date of death. It was as if he had vanished off the face of the earth.

Leaning back in the chair she rubbed the muscles in her shoulders. A rogue Dreamshifter who was accused of the mass murder of his own family. Maybe he was dead. But Dreamshifters lived well beyond the usual life span and he could easily be running around creating havoc in Dreamworld or the Between. If there was another Dreamshifter still alive somewhere on the planet, maybe he had information. Maybe he could get her back into Dreamworld; maybe he knew about the Key.

Maybe, just maybe, he had access to dreamspheres. If there was even a hope of that, she had to try to find him. Even if he was a deranged killer, which seemed likely.

She needed more information, and she thought she might just know where to find it.

Fourteen

Zee refused to die. Not here in this place that reeked of dragons.

Using the sword as a support, he tried to lever himself up onto his feet, but his right arm wouldn't work and his knees refused to stiffen. On the first attempt he fell flat onto his bruised ribs. Pain lanced through him, stole his breath, sent his consciousness scurrying off into dusty corners of his mind.

He held on, resisting the lure of the inviting darkness, until the pain eased and he was able to breathe. Then he tried again, planting the tip of the sword between two of the paving stones, grabbing on to the hilt with his left hand. He managed to drag himself up onto his knees but could get no farther.

Recognizing at length that his efforts were not only futile but draining the little energy he had left, he began to crawl. One slow inch at a time, shoving the sword ahead of him to free both hands, he dragged himself toward the arch through which he had entered. His arm began to bleed again, turning the hand slippery with blood so that it slid when he braced it against the stone to pull himself forward. His head spun; his heart lurched and pattered in an irregular rhythm.

Death loomed. He felt its presence, but he wasn't ready.

Not yet. Too many things left undone. He'd sworn to help Vivian and now here he was, dying before he'd done a thing to aid or protect her.

But even these thoughts faded away as the pain and the weakness and the necessity to move just one more inch became overwhelming. He didn't notice when he reached the arch, but he heard the bell toll, followed by a cracking, rending sound.

And then everything changed.

He lay facedown in soft green grass, instead of on the road he was expecting. Light filtered in through his closed eyelids and he felt the impossibility of sunlight warm on his back. When he lifted his head, he saw that he lay on a well-tended lawn in full daylight. To his right, a gravel road disappeared into a thick grove of trees. Tall grasses grew up along the far side of the road, blocking the horizon. To his left stood a battered fifth-wheel trailer, much like the one he had grown up in, with the difference of a carefully tended lawn and a garden of bright flowers.

A man sat in the shade of a gnarled and ancient tree. His head was bald and shone as if it had been waxed and polished. A thick white beard covered his chest, and he wore a robe sewn out of some sort of rough brown cloth, tied around an ample belly with a bit of old rope. Beside him, ready to hand, sat a rough wooden table bearing a jug full of water and two plastic tumblers.

"Well met, Warrior," the old man said. "Would you drink?"

"Please," Zee croaked, in a voice that seemed to belong to somebody else.

The man got up with some difficulty. The flimsy lawn chair in which he sat was a tight fit for his bulk and wanted to come with him. But once he had managed to dislodge it he filled one of the tumblers with water and put it in Zee's hand.

It looked like plain, ordinary water. No enchantment that Zee could detect, and the old man stepped back and waited, not trying to coerce him. Drink or die. He drained the glass, the cool liquid soothing his parched throat, but it was not enough. Before he could ask, the old man retrieved the pitcher and refilled his glass to the brim.

While he drank, Zee looked around. Nobody was to be seen except his benefactor. A wooden dream door hung in the middle of a hedge, maybe the one he'd come through, maybe another one. It was closed, which was good, although he knew well enough it could open at any time.

"Where is this?" he asked, his voice belonging to him once again.

"No place and every place. Do you not recognize the Between?"

The urgency that had driven Zee this far resurfaced. "I need to get back to Wakeworld." He tried to sit up, but the old man pressed him back and he wasn't strong enough to argue.

"Do not fear. You are safe for the moment—she will come for you, by and by, but not yet. Rest now. Let me dress your wounds."

Too weak to explain or to fight, Zee let his head fall back into the softness of grass. His weariness was an inescapable force and his eyes drifted shut. Somewhere a bee buzzed, and a gentle breeze touched his face. His hand groped for the sword and closed around the familiar hilt. Only then did he allow himself to sleep.

When he woke, the old man still sat in his lawn chair under the tree. The sun hung in the same place in the sky; the shadows had not shifted. But the stabbing pain in his head had receded; the raging thirst was gone. A neat bandage wrapped his upper right arm. The gash in his side had been cleaned. When Zee pushed himself up to sitting, the world spun for only a moment and then righted itself.

Wordlessly, his benefactor brought him another tall glass of water, and he drank.

"How long have I been asleep?" His hand went to his jaw, half expecting to find a Rip Van Winkle beard, and he was grateful to discover only rough stubble.

"Time has no meaning here; it comes and goes according to its own whims. Do you hunger?"

Zee realized that he was, in fact, nearly as hungry as he was confused. "I could eat. And I have a lot of questions, if you are willing to answer."

"The willingness is perhaps not the issue. Ask only questions for which I have the answers, and we will do well." The old man opened a picnic basket that now sat on the table beside him. "Ham sandwich?"

The sandwich in question was made from a small round loaf of bread, stuffed with a thick slab of ham and some sort of waxy yellow cheese that was definitely not cheddar. Maybe it was just because of his hunger, but the flavors seemed bigger, the textures more real, than any sandwich Zee had ever eaten. One bite led to another, and he had consumed the whole thing before he wiped the crumbs from his face with his sleeve and asked, "Who are you?"

"My name matters not."

"How long have you been here?"

The old man smiled, beatifically, and said, gently, "As I have said, time here has no meaning. Ask a thing that I can answer."

"All right. What are you doing here?" Zee gestured at the trailer and the empty space all around.

"I'm a hermit. Where else would I be?"

The Holy Hermit of the Fifth Wheel, Zee thought, with a mixture of amusement and frustration.

"Well, why then?" he asked. "Why are you here?"

"Waiting for you, naturally."

"Of course. And you are waiting for me, because . . ."

"You would have died were there no soul here to succor your hurts and offer you food and drink. My purpose is to commune with the ineffable and to serve the Warrior should he appear."

"Why does everybody keep calling me that? Warlord, Warrior—"

"You drank from the well and live to tell the tale."

"But I didn't drink. She tried to make me and I refused." The smile faded. "You refused the test?"

"Was I wrong? The others—there are six men in there,

dead. It looked like they were poisoned and I thought it was the water." Even speaking of the enchanted liquid set him thirsting for it again.

"It didn't tempt you?"

"It tempted me plenty. I didn't want to die."

The old man stroked his beard. "You are very brave, then, Warrior or not. But I fear our time together may be shorter than I had anticipated. She will not be pleased."

"She who? And you still didn't answer about the Warrior bit."

"Very well, I shall tell you. But I warn you that my answer will be in the form of a tale. This requires stronger drink than water. One moment."

The old man heaved his bulk up out of the chair once more and disappeared into the trailer, returning a few moments later with large stoneware mugs, spilling over with foam.

Zee accepted the drink pressed into his hand but hesitated. He had lost blood and wasn't sure how alcohol would affect him as a consequence. Also, no place in the Between was truly safe and he was already incapacitated. His eyes went to the dream door, still closed, and scanned the horizon for any sign of danger.

"Drink, drink," the hermit said. "It's good brown ale. Replenishes the blood. You are safe enough here for the moment." He guzzled down a long draught, belched happily, and wiped his face with his sleeve.

Zee took an experimental swallow. The ale was smooth and full and rich, nothing like beer, or even the brew pub ales he'd tasted over the years. It soothed his throat, eased his distress, but left his mind surprisingly untouched.

The hermit took another long swallow and leaned back in his chair. "So then. The Tale of the Warrior and the Dragon, as it was told unto me by my father and his father before him.

"Long ago, in the far-off days before recorded history, a Dragon King ruled the Forever. He was the first of all dragons, and the most beautiful. It is said that in the full light of day his scales shone so bright that even the dragons could not look upon him with eyes unshielded.

"How he came to be, nobody knows. Some say he crawled from the river, fully formed. Others that the giants made him—shaped him of beaten gold and then breathed life into him. Only the giants could say, and they keep their lore unto themselves.

"One day, by fate or happenstance or genetic mutation, depending upon your theory of the world and how it works, a special child was born. It was a girl child, and her mother named her Allel. She never cried, they say, but watched the world through big gray eyes, taking in all things and understanding far beyond her years.

"One night, when Allel was maybe six months old, her mother checked the crib at midnight and found it empty. She shrieked her fear and dismay aloud, and her husband ran to rally the villagers and they hunted for the child, one and all, through the long hours of the night.

"In the morning, the baby was found in her cradle, fast asleep.

"The villagers were angry. 'Foolishness of an overly fond mother,' they said. 'The child was never missing. Don't bother us again.'

"And so the next night, father and mother watched by the cradle and saw the child vanish before their eyes. All night long they waited, and as dawn struck and the sky turned blue, Allel appeared out of nowhere, lying in her cradle fast asleep.

"Nobody would believe, so the next night a small group of elders were invited in. This time they watched carefully at the time of dusk and sleep, and saw the child vanish before their eyes, and later reappear.

" 'She is a witch,' they said, afraid. 'She must be destroyed now, before she gains power.'

"The mother wept and pleaded. 'Not now, give me one last day. She is no harm to anyone.'

"Not being evil or having hearts of stone, the men agreed to leave a watch to make sure she didn't flee with the child.

All day long the mother rocked Allel in the rocking chair, her long hair screening her face from view. But she did not weep. And when she glanced up at her husband, he read the look in her eyes and nodded.

"Bit by bit throughout the day, when their unwelcome guest was looking in another direction—eating his meal of bread and cheese, stepping outside to make water, blinking back sleep—she scrambled together a few small things into one place. A water skin. A bundle of bread and cheese and three boiled eggs. A blanket and a change of clothes for the baby.

"As the sun moved toward the edge of the sky and began to drop, her husband took up his spear and confronted the watchman sitting on the threshold of his door. 'We leave now,' he said. 'My wife, my child, and I. We shall never trouble the village again, if you let us go. But if you do not . . .'

"The watchman hesitated, looking at the family, and then shook his head. 'She cannot be allowed to live.' He opened his mouth again, to call for help, and fell before he could make a sound with the spear through his throat.

"The three fled before anybody else could come looking. Many long days they journeyed, and hardships they encountered, before they reached the tunnel through the mountain that led to the land of the dragons. Long, dark, and treacherous it was, and they emerged famished and weak on the other side.

"In those days the dragons were yet wise and noble creatures. They kept their distance from the three travelers, not allowing themselves to be seen, but made sure that game was sent in their direction, and that they stumbled upon pools of true water now and again, for although the dragons were able to drink from the golden river, this water would kill a human.

"Even so, father and mother ate little, depriving themselves in order to feed the child. They traveled by day. At night, as always, the child would vanish and they would wait for her return.

"At length a dragon was selected to speak with them—because he was smaller than the others, and white of scale and wing, it was deemed that he might appear less of a threat. But the father shook his spear and the mother hid the child behind her back to protect her.

"Allel pulled away from her mother's hands, stepped forward, and said, 'The White One was talking to us, Papa, and you must be polite and put away the sword.'

" 'Dear one, it was gibberish only. Take your mother and run away.'

"But Allel, utterly fearless, walked between her father and the huge creature of wings and scales and fiery breath and said, 'I am Allel, and I have seen you in a dream.'

"The poor parents did not understand a word of this conversation and were terrified that some evil would befall the child, but they need not have feared. The dragon led them to a place where there was water, and wood to make a shelter, and let it be known that they were welcome to live here so long as they wished.

"Allel ran wild in the forest by day, and ran through the Dreamworlds at night. From that day forward the white dragon was her constant companion both waking and dreaming. He kept her safe in the Dreamworlds, showed her how to move between one world and another, and all the secrets of the Between.

"All of the time in Dreamworld saw to it that she aged slowly. Her parents grew old and faded away. One after another they died, and by this time Allel was a good half century in years of time, but looked no more than eighteen summers, with a cloud of night-black hair and eyes the color of fog when the sun shines through.

"The dragon saw that she was sad and alone once her parents were gone. He tried to make it up to her, but she said, 'I am lonely without my kind; there are none of them left except in the dream, and those are only for a night.'

" 'I shall teach you how to make a dream of your own,' he said, and took her to the pits where the raw dream matter lies.

" 'Take up a handful,' he said, and she did so. 'Now let your mind go quiet, and you shall see the desire of your heart.'

"In her hands the matter twisted and writhed, and she looked at her dragon, afraid. 'Do not fear,' he said, 'or we shall have a nightmare to deal with.' She listened to him, and from the matter a lovely thing was formed, the shape of a young man. Broad shoulders had he, and hair as golden as hers was dark, a smile as bright and blinding as sunlight on water. He was only tiny, not life-sized, but alive and real and warm in her hands.

" 'Do you wish for him to live?'

"For the first time in her life Allel felt tears upon her cheeks. Yes, she wanted for this perfect thing to live. She could not understand what it was that she felt, only that once in existence she didn't want for the man to die.

"And so the dragon created a bubble around the little man, and blew with his fiery breath, and the bubble floated away and vanished. Allel cried out to see the man float away, but the white dragon showed her how to find that Dreamworld, so that she might visit whenever she wished.

"But it was against the dragon lore to teach such things to a human, and a summons came that both the white dragon and the girl should present themselves to the Dragon King. When he saw Allel, clothed only in the fall of her own hair and gazing at him with sheer delight in her silver eyes, he was enchanted.

"All of the dragons were assembled, but Allel was not frightened by the glittering throng. She stood quietly before them, self-possessed, and only inclined her head, ever so little, to show respect but not fear.

"And the King was moved by her beauty and the clearness of her eyes and the quickness of her mind. Within him stirred a new emotion—a hot and writhing thing. He had no name for it but could not bear to lay his eyes on the white dragon as he stood there beside the maiden.

" 'The law has been broken and there must be consequence,' he said.

"The white dragon moved to stand between the maiden and the King. 'You shall not harm her. The fault was mine.'

"'Precisely,' said the King. 'And yet we cannot allow her to return now into the world, to share what she has learned. She will stay here, not as a punishment but as a precaution. You shall bear all the penalty of what you have done, and that penalty is death.'

"A silence followed such has never been known before or after that time. The sound was sucked from the trees, the river, and even the sky. Breath and birdsong, breeze, flowing water, the scurrying feet of a mouse, even the inaudible flicker of a dragonfly wing went silent. And through the minds of the dragons, thoughts traveled from one to the next. Some thoughts were loyal to the King—whatever he did must be right. Others disagreed that the life of a human should be held sacred over the life of a dragon.

"And then the King set upon the white dragon and killed him.

"Through the ranks of the dragons ran a murmur of dissent. 'This is wrong. We will not be ruled in this way. We are a free people.'

"Others, accustomed to following the King's thoughts and deeds, cried out against the rebellion. A war broke out then, dragon against dragon. Allel stood unscathed in a swirl of battling dragons on sky and land, for all were agreed on the one point that she should not be harmed.

"But in that moment a great and lasting hatred was born within her heart—for the King, and for all those dragons who served him.

"At last the King came to his senses. 'Enough!' he cried. 'We must not fight among ourselves. Those who do not wish to honor an allegiance to me may go; the others may stay. Make your choice and make it well, for there will be no turning back.'

"Fully half of the dragons took to the air and flew away. Allel stood beside the body of the white dragon and watched them go. *There shall be reparation for this,* she thought, but she kept her thoughts unto herself, buried deeply within her heart.

"And so when the Dragon King shifted his form by magic to appear to her as a golden-haired young man, she smiled at him and allowed him to believe that little by little he won her love. At night, though, she vanished into the Dream-worlds still—visiting the man that she had made and telling him the tale of all her wrongs. Although Allel's hatred fell only upon the dragons of the Forever, and especially upon the King, her tales took on a life of their own in the breast of the man she had created.

" 'They are all alike,' he said. 'Marauding, cruel, and evil.' His hate grew until, in time, he began to hunt them, as did his sons, and the sons of his sons. The dragons were strong and many of the dragon hunters died, so that the seed of Allel's first Warrior was very nearly extinguished.

"But not quite—for it is said that in every generation, still, one Warrior will be born.

"As for the dragons outcast from Forever, they kept largely to the mazes of the Between. It was not that they could not enter the Dreamworlds, as much as that they did not care for the strangeness and unreality. They loved to fly, to hunt, to eat. Although they retained the ability to speak to one another, mind to mind, they lost the ability to speak aloud. Much of the magic and the lore was forgotten, for dragons are long lived but do not live forever, and what was passed from generation to generation grew less and less.

"Allel bided her time, and one starlit night she allowed the Dragon King to make love to her beside the golden river. Her body began to swell with child. In all that time she kept her thoughts to herself. For the Dragon King she would only smile, allowing him access to her physical self but keeping the rest of her—the part that he desired to know and possess—a secret unto herself. He grew increasingly jeal-ous, confining her to a single room so that she would not wander away. And with this also she complied, only with the exception that at night she vanished utterly away, and try as he would he could not hold her.

"At last, within the silken prison cell he had made for her, she gave birth to a child—a daughter, with her own dark hair lighted by gold, and silver eyes. And the King was moved by awe and wonder and great love for the tiny creature. Still, Allel waited and watched. She allowed him to grow more and more attached, and then one night she took her daughter with her into the Dreamworld and did not bring her back.

"The Dragon King waited, believing that she would return as she always had. But days went by, and then weeks, and months. Strange things began to happen. Dark shadows found their way into his kingdom, at first by night and then by day. They took the form of monstrous bears and wolves with jaws of iron. There were creatures that were a travesty of dragons—things of bloated bellies and bulging eyes with dragon wings and scales. They crept through the land, banding together to attack full-grown dragons, or attacking the young when unattended.

"The dragons all waited for the King to grow wrathful and lead a war against the invasion, but instead he wandered for hours by the golden river, often in his human form, pining for the woman and for his child. At length he did grow angry and led invasions out into the Dreamworlds, seeking what he had lost and wreaking destruction along the way.

"Word came at last to the Queen of the Giants, in those days the wisest and most just of all living beings, and she saw that if this war continued it could lead to the destruction of all the worlds. So it was that the giants went to work to craft doors of adamantine to block the entrance to the Forever. One by one, each of the lesser doors by which Allel had traveled into the Dreamworlds were sought out and sealed. The only connection left between the worlds was a single cave that bordered on the pits of raw dream matter, so that it might flow into the Dreamworlds and back again as needed.

"A dragon was chosen to serve as guardian in the Cave of Dreams, ensuring that nobody passed in or out of the Forever. And then the doors were made and put in place, and the giants shut them, that the dragons within would remain within, and the dragons without would remain without. And a key was made and a spell was cast upon it, that only she who could restore the balance would be able to open the Gates."

"And the dreamspheres?" Zee asked.

"Nobody knows why the Cave of Dreams exists, any more than they can tell how the Dreamworld or the Wakeworld came into being in the first place. Made by the gods, it is said, but where are these gods now? They are not talking. Every dream has its dreamsphere, and except for those given to the Dreamshifters as a gesture of goodwill, all rest in the cave. Thus it has always been."

Zee set aside his tankard in frustration. "You have told me fairy tales. How does any of this answer my question?"

The sound of a heavy motor filled the air and a red tractor drove around the corner and pulled up in front of the trailer. The man behind the wheel nodded his head at the hermit. "You ready?"

"In a minute." To Zee he said, "You think I am a foolish old man, and you may be right. But I ask you to consider this—how long have you hated the dragons? And how deep does it run?" He hitched the rope belt to ride more comfortably over his belly and brushed the crumbs from his beard. "Well, there's my mover. Take care of yourself. I shall leave you some supplies."

"Wait—you're moving right now?"

"She'll be coming for you soon, now. I don't wish to be here. You might want to be moving on yourself."

"But I have more questions . . ."

"Everybody has questions. Learn to live with them." The hermit clucked and shook his head, ran a hand over the top of his bald pate, and disappeared inside the trailer.

The farmer hitched up the trailer to the tractor without so much as looking in Zee's direction, then headed off in the direction he'd come from, hauling the trailer along behind. As it began to move, hands tossed items out of the windows.

Zee watched the tractor and trailer out of sight, waiting until the dust settled and all was quiet. In the center of the green lawn was now a rectangle of dirt and a few tough weeds. Scattered all around it were the items the hermit had thrown out the window.

Zee collected them, taking stock of his inventory. A pair of socks and sturdy leather hiking shoes. A sheath for the sword that ran over his shoulder instead of around his waist. A flannel shirt, and a T-shirt with a picture of a can of beer and a slogan proclaiming, *It's five o'clock somewhere.* A woolen blanket. An army canteen, full of water. A backpack, stocked with protein bars and a first-aid kit. And a battered copy of *Through the Looking Glass*, which explained absolutely everything and nothing.

He could feel the black dragon's presence. Not too close, not yet, but not far enough away. Much as he would have loved to slay her, he knew he wasn't ready. And so he put on the T-shirt and the shoes and socks, slung the sword over his shoulder, packed everything else into the backpack, and set out down the only road there was to follow.

Fifteen

Vivian tucked her chin into the neck of the sweatshirt she'd borrowed from Zee's closet and curled her hands up inside the too-long sleeves, seeking protection from the sharpness of a wind that smelled of snow. The streets of Krebston were still dark and mostly empty. In another hour there would be a trickle of traffic increasing to a steady flow as people headed out to school or work, but only an intrepid few were out at this hour. Her source of information, unless something had gone wrong, would be among them.

Tugging open the door to Sacred Grounds she found herself instantly enveloped in a steamy warmth, redolent with the rich smell of coffee and cinnamon.

"Hey, Doc! What are you doing here? Thought you'd gotten too uppity for the likes of us."

"Decided to come slumming." Vivian turned toward the speaker, the knots of tension loosening a little with relief as she saw Cal was there with him. Thank God for gossipy old men and unshakable routines. She'd hoped they would be here, sitting in the corner by the window and working through the crossword, but she'd feared that maybe even this reality had been altered. At least twice a week over the last year she had stopped here on her way home from a long night of work for a cup of coffee and participation in the communal crossword puzzle.

"Where've you been?" Cal asked.

"Took a little leave of absence. Personal stuff."

"Need a five-letter word for bring upon oneself," Rich said, not looking up. "You gonna help us or what?"

Cal just grinned. He'd left his teeth at home again, his collapsed mouth giving him a deceptively foolish look. He wasn't. At eighty-five he might be slipping a little, but he'd started with a towering intellect that left him still smarter than the average Krebstonite.

"Let the girl get her coffee," Marta said, rolling her eyes at Vivian. "Before she falls asleep on my counter. What can I fix you, hon?"

"Just coffee, in the biggest mug you can find. And one of those cinnamon rolls. They look amazing."

"Calorie content to last all day, and worth every crumb," Marta said, patting her comfortably rounded belly. "Room for cream, right?"

"Always."

Almost light-headed with the mingled aromas, mouth watering with anticipation, Vivian carried plate and mug over to the table where the old-timers had already shifted to make room for her.

The two were constant companions—where you saw one, you saw the other. Weekday mornings at Sacred Grounds, lunch at Café Michelle, afternoons at the library in winter, outside in the park on sunny summer days. Rich was shrunken down to nothing but bones, an old scarecrow with a few strands of white fluff on his bald head, blurred brown eyes behind thick glasses. Cal, on the other hand, was fat. He still had a full head of black hair, his brown eyes bright but almost buried, like raisins stuffed too deep into a gingerbread boy.

"Are you sure that's edible?" Rich asked, eyeing her cinnamon roll. "Looks like more frosting than bread." His voice was surprising coming from his thin body, a rich baritone made for giving speeches.

"That's what makes it edible," Vivian said, taking a bite. "You should have one. You're only young once."

"Abstinence," Cal said. "Fourteen down." His right hand, the joints red and swollen with arthritis, gripped the pencil and slowly added in the letters.

"I did. Yesterday I had two. What have you gone and done to your eyes?"

Vivian shrugged, and said lightly, "Wandered into an alternate reality and got poisoned by a dragon. They look like dragon eyes, don't you think?"

Cal's raisin eyes sharpened in a quick assessing look and then returned to the crossword puzzle. Rich frowned a little, his forehead puckered. "You're a little edgy, Doc."

Cradling the hot mug between her palms and breathing in the fragrant steam, Vivian thought about how to broach her topic. "Not sleeping so well," she said at last. "That business down at Finger Beach bothers me."

"No good thing has ever happened around that stone. They're keeping it real hush-hush this time. But I heard there were all kinds of suits down there the other night." Rich grabbed a fork and took a bite of her neglected cinnamon roll. "Damn, that's good. You should eat."

She slapped his hand. "I will, if you leave me any." She took a bite, gooey and cinnamony, an explosion of goodness so sweet it burned her throat. A swallow of scalding coffee to wash it down, and then she said, as casual as she could make it, "I've heard tales about the stone myself. Some guy named Jennings connected somehow, wasn't there?"

It was a guess, and a total score. Cal looked up from the crossword, actually putting down the pencil, his keen eyes peering deeply into hers.

"The old man was a mean old devil. Beat all the kids and his wife," Rich said.

"That fall his wife had maybe wasn't so accidental." Cal tapped the pencil on the page, but his eyes were no longer reading crossword clues, they were staring off into distant memory.

"Maybe so—but it wouldn't have to be the old man that pushed her."

"Weston mighta done it, you mean? He was only a little kid when she died."

"Some are born mean."

"He was nine. I hardly think—"

"Didn't he shoot the family or something?" Vivian broke in.

"That's what everybody said."

"My dad never did believe that story," Rich said. "He figured it was too convenient to blame the boy just because he wasn't around to defend himself."

"You saying the girl might have done it?"

"Why not?"

"A thirteen-year-old girl—"

"Like a woman has less murder in her than a man? Doc, I do believe our Cal might be a chauvinist."

"You both are," Vivian said. "Why do you suspect the girl, Rich?"

"Well, my aunt went to school with her, you know. Rose said Grace was downright unearthly, possessed maybe. Those were her words, mind. Hardly ever said a word, kept to herself but always watching. No friends. And they found her in that room with all the bodies."

"Never going to convince me a slip of a girl shot her whole family in cold blood. And it wasn't some stranger—no sign of a struggle. Had to be Weston."

"Well, whatever happened up there, it was spooky. The house is haunted."

"That's a fact, sure enough."

The two old men exchanged a grin that was suddenly all mischievous boy. "When we were kids we lived near the old place—what is it, twenty miles from here?"

"Round about." Cal shoveled half of Vivian's cinnamon roll into his mouth at one time, chewing with great enjoyment.

"Used to ride our bikes out there—take a lunch and make it a day. Dared each other to go through the house. Kitchen was allover bloodstains—nobody ever cleaned it."

"Could you draw me a map?" Vivian asked.

Cal stopped chewing.

"Well, I reckon we could," Rich said, slowly. "But why would you want to go out there? Less'n of course you took us along—"

"Some protection we'd be," Cal snorted.

"We're talking haunted, right?" Vivian made her voice clear, logical, and dripping with disdain. "Ghosts and such? Wooo and woooo? And you are going to protect me from that. You're not only old chauvinists, you're superstitious old chauvinists."

Rich unfolded a napkin, took the pencil from Cal, and sketched out a rough map.

"Does anybody know what happened to Grace?" Vivian asked.

The two old men exchanged glances, quiet for a long moment.

"Well, my old man said the neighbors took her in for a bit. But they shipped her off to an orphanage after only a couple of weeks," Rich said, finally.

"That seems harsh. Nobody in the community that would take her?"

"Probably would have done if she hadn't robbed her daddy's grave."

"She what?"

"Well, not the grave per se. Gotta be fair, Rich." Cal licked his fingers, then wiped them on a napkin. "Just the coffin. After the wake, before the funeral, minister come downstairs and found her rooting around in the coffin. Not kissing the dead good-bye, like, or weeping. Just cold and quiet."

Rich nodded. "That's what my mama said too. Couldn't have her here, going to school with the other kids, loose in the community. Even if she wasn't the one what did the killing, it must have turned her."

Vivian wasn't hungry anymore. The ancient tragedy, combined with her worry about Zee, swirled with cinnamon and sugar and dough in her belly. She shoved the plate and the remaining bits of the roll across the table.

"You not eating that?" Cal said.

"Feel free."

"So she never came back?"

"Never said that." Cal's mouth was full with the remains of the cinnamon roll. "Moved back to Krebston once she was all growed up. Lived down by the river."

"Died what—about forty years ago?"

"Near enough. Whole house burned up—poof. Didn't look so much like an accident."

"Suicide, if you ask me."

"No way of telling. Nobody went to the funeral."

"Let me get this straight. When she was a little kid her whole family got murdered, she got sent away to an orphanage, as an adult she was so miserable that she lit herself and her house on fire, and nobody in this community went to pay respects?" Vivian discovered that she was angry on behalf of this woman she had never met and knew nothing about.

The two old men looked surprised, then shrugged. "When you put it that way . . ."

"People want no truck with what they don't understand, Doc, and that's the truth. Something weird about that whole family."

Cal took back the pencil, tapped it on the crossword. "You weren't much help, Vivian. Twenty-one down, purchase price."

"Did Weston ever come back?"

Both old heads shook no at once. "Not that I heard tell," Rich said. "Never seen or heard of again. The rest of the lot is all buried in the old part of the Krebston Cemetery—not the one by the school, the one up on the hill. They found room for Grace in the family plot, so maybe you'll feel better to know that she joined them in the end."

Vivian looked at the map on the napkin, which seemed clear enough to find her way. "Don't suppose you two know whether this land belongs to anybody?"

Rich shook his head, his face suddenly serious. "Look, missy doctor, I don't know what you're up to, but I'm not kidding about that house. Laugh as you will about it being haunted, but there's an evil lingers 'round that place."

"Leave investigating to the cops," Cal added. "Go take care of sick people like you're meant to."

Rich yawned. "Damn, I'm tired and my brain feels fuzzy. Must be getting old."

"Ha, you were old when you were born."

Vivian left them bickering amicably, getting another cup of coffee to go.

When she stepped outside, she left all the warmth behind her. A slice of wind cut through her clothing, and she shivered, huddling into the sweatshirt and running down the street toward A to Zee.

Sixteen

Zee sat in the shade of a giant tree that reminded him of an unholy union between a weeping willow and a pine. The drooping limbs bristled with long, yellow-green needles that drew blood when he accidentally bumped up against them. But the sun had grown into a torment, and the cool darkness at the base of the tree was worth the price. He drank from the canteen and ate one of the protein bars. His body needed fuel for healing.

Just ahead the road he'd been following ended at a sudden line of trees. Three paths curved away into the undergrowth. He had no way of knowing which one he ought to take, which was another reason to just sit here for a few minutes, resting. He leaned against the trunk and allowed himself to drift a little, close to dream.

A shout roused him.

Heart thudding, he lunged out from beneath the tree, sword drawn and ready. All was quiet, except for a distant woodpecker and the crackling wings of a grasshopper in flight.

"Idiot," he told himself. "You're starting to hear things." His hasty exit from the tree had earned him a shoulder full of punctures, insult to injury.

Another shout, a man's voice sharp with a note of pain

and fear, came from the forest to the right. Still not entirely trusting his senses, Zee crossed the last stretch of gravel road and entered the path that seemed to lead toward the shout.

The trail meandered this way and that, taking him first away from the locus of the shout, and then back toward it, until a little voice in his brain whispered that maybe the path itself had shouted in order to lure him in, that he would die in its endless twistings and turnings with no chance to choose another way. His head ached with a vicious, stabbing pain, as if a hot prong pierced the lump on his skull and spiked into the brain tissue beneath. The lacerations on his arm and his rib cage throbbed. He was still weak from loss of blood.

The sun had moved rapidly across the sky, and shadows pooled thick among the trees. Little light was left to find his way, and he needed to rest; in fact, it would probably be smart to make shelter. Just a few more minutes, to be sure, and he'd stop for the night. He rounded a long looping curve and almost ran smack into a man standing at the edge of a small clearing.

The man's back was toward him, his legs braced in a wide stance. Around his feet patches of green slime bubbled, erupting into foul-smelling geysers. The man's pants—suit pants, Zee noticed, and expensive once-shiny shoes—were coated with the green goo, and the right pant leg was shredded and soaked with blood.

Facing him was a creature straight out of nightmare. Needle-sharp teeth as long as Zee's arm were set in jaws of blackish green, the texture of toad skin. It had no real face. Where its nose should have been there were only two black holes. Red-brown eyes goggled out of its head, independent of each other, the pupils spinning in opposite directions. It had an amphibian body, with powerful back legs, poised to leap. There were claws on its nearly human hands, but the arms were short and not well muscled. Batlike wings sprouted from its shoulders. A spiked tail twitched, catlike, hitting the ground at regular intervals and raising clouds of dust. Slime oozed out of its skin and rained down into the dust with a continuous plop, plop, plop.

Zee tightened his grip on his sword and stepped forward, putting himself between the creature and the wounded man.

"We wants no trouble with one such as you," the thing said, in a lilting, musical voice. "We only wants what is ours." Drool flowed in little rivulets from the corners of its wide mouth.

Zee's stomach twisted with revulsion. "I want no trouble, either," he said. "What is it that you do want?"

"Him what cowers there behind you."

"And what do you want with him?"

"We wants his death."

Zee could hear the man's ragged breathing, close to sobs. A sharp, acid scent, like vinegar, rose from the slime on the earth around his feet, crisping the tiny hairs in his nostrils and burning his sinuses.

Poisonous, most likely. Direct contact with either the creature or its slime would be a bad idea. "It's good to want things," he said. "In this case, I fear you'll have to go on wanting."

The toad's eyes swiveled until both of them were fixed on Zee. It clashed its teeth, more reflexive than threatening. "What has it done that you would come to its defense?"

Good point. Zee sidestepped. "What cause do you have to kill him?"

"Stomped on our children. Popped like fruit beneath his feet, they did, the beautiful creatures."

"They tried to eat me," the man gasped behind him. "For God's sake . . ."

The voice was familiar, but Zee couldn't quite place it, and he dared not take his eyes off the toad to look around. "That is a horror no mother should see," he said, "and yet I cannot let you have him."

"Your choice, it saddens us. You speak us fair and are a noble warrior. But we slays you, if we must. You are wounded already. Unfit for battle if I reads you right. Again we asks you, stand aside."

Zee settled into a fighting stance, adrenaline pumping energy into his body. Already his mind was compensating for the limitations imposed by his injuries as he planned both attack and defense.

"Let us have him," she pleaded one more time. "What matters it to you?"

He raised his sword in salute. "Defend yourself," he said, and lunged.

The creature sprang straight up into the air, hovering like a sickly caricature of a bumblebee. It dove, unfurling a long black tongue that wrapped around Zee's sword arm like Velcro. It burned wherever it touched and he twisted and pulled, trying to break the hold. Inch by inch the tongue recoiled, lifting him off the ground and forcing him relentlessly closer to the wicked teeth.

Zee opened his imprisoned hand and let go of the sword, catching it with his right as it fell. The wounded muscle in his arm pulled and strained against the weight, but he used his body to help him, flinging himself over and up toward the trapped arm, swinging the blade in a silver arc that sliced neatly through the tongue.

He landed on his feet, crouched and ready. The severed tongue still wrapped his arm, a ring of fire, but he ignored it, switching the sword back to his uninjured hand. Blood poured from the mouth of the toad, turning its teeth to crimson. An inarticulate cry burst from its throat and it flew in low, lashing its spiked tail.

The blow missed by a whisper. The tail lashed again, and Zee leaped into the air to intercept it. His blade bit into the bone at the end of the tail and stuck fast. The toad beat upward with its wings, trying to break free. Zee clung to the sword, throwing his weight backward toward the ground as it dragged him around, almost lifting him into the air.

He wasn't going to be able to hold on much longer. His right arm was bleeding again, the bandage he'd wrapped around it stained red. The other arm, snared by the venomous tongue, ached and burned. He couldn't feel his hands anymore, clenched in a death grip around the sword hilt.

There was a cracking sensation as the tail broke and the sword came free.

The creature croaked. It spun lopsided in the air just above the earth. Zee leaped upward, plunging his sword into the sickly white belly, then leaping to the side as the creature went limp and came crashing down. Its eyes spun madly and then went dark.

Zee scraped the tongue off his arm with the edge of the sword, revealing skin that was reddened and blistering.

"Help, would you?"

Zee was pretty sure what the trouble was, and when he circled the fallen heap of warts and slime, sure enough, the wounded man lay pinned with his legs beneath the carcass, unable to drag himself free.

One long look at the man's pale face, once clean shaven and arrogant, now besmirched with blood and slime, and Zee set one booted foot onto the heaving chest and laid his sword blade across the throat.

Throats were so vulnerable to a blade. No exertion required, no real strength. A little pressure, a twist and pull with the wrist, and jugular, carotid, and trachea would be severed. A man would choke on his own blood. And Zee wanted to shed the blood of this man with an intensity that nearly overrode his control.

It was a dream, he reminded himself. *A man cannot be held responsible for what he does in a dream. Cowardice, on the other hand, looking on from a distance while others are under attack . . .*

Green eyes stared up at him out of a face gone deathly white, save for the scarlet acid burns standing out in vivid and ghastly contrast.

"What happened to Vivian? What did they do with her?"

"I don't know. I swear."

Zee applied a little pressure. Blood welled. Each crimson drop held the promise of revenge. "Tell me!"

"I couldn't see. I was hiding!"

"Liar." A little more pressure. His hands were shaking,

torn between the desire to kill the man who had brought so much harm to Vivian, and the need to question him alive.

"I'm telling you the truth! They opened a door and threw her inside."

"What was on the other side of the door? Did you see?"

"No, I'm telling you. All I saw was the door. That's all I know. Please—get me out of here."

Zee's breath came in hard gasps; his heart was beating way too hard. How long did it take to recover from blood loss? Vivian would know. But Vivian wasn't here, had been thrust against her will through some doorway into who-knows-where. The very thought filled him with rage.

A battle waged in his breast. Was he really obligated to rescue one such as Jared? It was a coward's act to kill a wounded man, and yet some men needed killing. Deep in his soul he knew the right thing, much as he hated to admit it, and so he swung away and began to clean the globs of disgusting green goo off his sword blade by wiping it in the tall grass.

"Hey!" Jared called, an edge of panic in his voice. "You're not really going to leave me here. Please."

"Maybe I will, maybe I won't. Don't have much use for lying cowards." But he sheathed the sword, turning back only to see that his enemy had stopped struggling and lay perfectly still, eyes closed, arms flung wide. Acid burns filled with a greenish fluid marred his face.

"Jared," Zee said.

No response.

He nudged the fallen man with the toe of his shoe. No movement, no response. He shoved harder, shifting Jared's shoulder upward. The arm and hand trailed behind, limp and useless.

"Oh, goddamn it." Zee grasped Jared under the armpits and dragged him out from beneath the toad. Both legs were covered in green slime; the right was blood drenched, the pant leg torn to shreds.

Careful not to touch the slime with his bare hands, Zee sliced the remains of the pant leg open and shuddered in revulsion. Strips of flesh and skin hung loose and shredded. Retrieving the canteen, he poured precious water over the wound. As he sluiced the blood and slime away he caught a glimpse of bone.

The first-aid kit was useless; nothing in it even began to address the magnitude of this wound. Zee sliced a strip from the blanket with his sword. Not sterile, but it was all he had to work with. About the time he was done wrapping the wound, Jared's eyes flickered open, unfocused and fever bright.

"Where's Vivian?" he murmured, his voice thick and far away.

Awesome. Not only couldn't he kill the sniveling coward, Zee realized he was going to be stuck with playing nursemaid. A slight hiss off to the right triggered his reflexes and he dove to one side, dragging Jared with him, just as one of the patches of green exploded into the air. An acid smoke rose up that burned in his lungs and set him coughing. "We'd better get out of here. Can you stand?"

"I think so."

He towed Jared up onto his good leg, pulled an arm over his shoulder, and half-dragged him away from the clearing and into the closest path. Acid-tainted air burned in his throat and nostrils. Glancing back over his shoulder, he saw a wave of peristalsis ripple along the toad creature's belly, which had expanded into a tight balloon.

"Faster," he gasped. The path was rough going, laced with roots and stones, barely wide enough for the two of them. If they could just make it around a curve about a hundred yards ahead, they'd be sheltered if that thing blew. Jared was a weight dragging him back, limping and unsteady. A hollow boom shook the earth beneath their feet and he abandoned running and dove off the path and into the undergrowth, pulling Jared after him. They fell in a tangle of arms and legs and lay still, listening to the splat of thick slime dripping off branches to the earth below.

"What the hell was that?"

"Toad exploded," Zee said. "Come on, we gotta go before all that extra slime smokes us out."

"Don't know if I can—"

"You don't have a choice. Come on. Crawl."

The only thing to do was to work their way deeper into the underbrush. The path they'd been on was contaminated—he could see the puddles of slime already beginning to bubble and smoke—and there was no other path available.

Wounded and weary as he was, Zee goaded Jared deeper and deeper into the depths of the forest. What they would find there, he didn't know, but they couldn't go back and they couldn't stay still and it was the only thing he knew to do.

Seventeen

Morgan had no trouble finding his way back to the old homestead. It was a wonder to him that his body remembered, by force of habit, the things that his brain had cast aside, that there was no indecision or hesitation about where to turn, even without signposts or recognizable landmarks. For some reason, the county had kept the road open—not maintained, by any stretch of the imagination, but at least it was clear of trees and brush. Two rough tracks led through a forest of pine and fir, interspersed with tamaracks, bright gold still but beginning to shed their needles.

There were a few rough dwellings along the way—trailers, cabins, even a yurt. No evidence of telephone or electrical wires, and he saw a homebuilt windmill churning on a hill. These were the homes of people who liked the solitude, who were most likely off the grid entirely. And this was good, because as long as he left them alone they were unlikely to report on his activities to the authorities.

The old homestead lay at the very end of the road, in an overgrown clearing. Forestland had encroached, but someone had taken the trouble to beat back a healthy barrier between house and trees. It made a sort of sense—somebody must own the property. It would have been sold or taken over. Just because they hadn't chosen to rebuild didn't mean they weren't smart enough to maintain a firebreak between a tinder-dry old heap of lumber and acres of forested land.

As he got out of the truck a raven, hoary with age, glided over and landed on a nearby rock. It cronked at him, twice.

"Go away, would you?" Morgan snapped, but the bird cocked its head to peer at him out of one bright black eye and stayed precisely where it was.

Something about the bird was familiar, just as the turnoff and the road had been, and Morgan was pretty sure he had uttered that exact same phrase more than once during his childhood. Of course it couldn't be the same bird, even though ravens were long lived as birds went. Still, his fingers went of their own accord to the carved pendant he had worn ever since he could remember, a raven in flight, caught in a dream web.

There was no comfort in that pendant. It was a reminder of his guilt more than anything else. Guilt that he was finally going to confront despite the deep dread that weighted every step, restricted every breath.

The house was still standing. He had maintained a secret hope that someone would have demolished it by now. The windows were broken, the shingles green with moss. Apart from that, it didn't look much different than he remembered. His resolve failed, thinking about what awaited him inside, and he chose to allow himself a small grace and visit the barn first. As he made his way across the yard, the raven hopped and fluttered after him, never more than a few yards away, refusing to shoo even when he threw a pinecone at it.

When he reached the barn door he hesitated, eyeing the structure with some unease. The roof sagged in the middle, giving the whole thing a swaybacked look. The boards were gray and weathered and had warped and dried, forming cracks wide enough to slide fingers between. But it was still standing, and unlikely to come crashing down on his head.

The door scraped across the warped floorboards, creaking on its hinges. Small scurrying and fluttering noises signaled the presence of mice and swallows, hiding themselves from the unaccustomed daylight.

A thick layer of dust coated everything. Several of the floorboards were rotten, and he stepped carefully to avoid holes. Swallow droppings piled thick in places, clay nests above his head a varied sculpture of new, old, and broken.

To the right were the milking stalls where Morgan had sat on a three-legged wooden stool, half awake in the early morning and resting his head against the cow's warm flank. He hadn't been alone, though. Three stalls. Three people milking cows. Somebody else tending chickens, throwing hay out for the horses.

A memory flash showed him faces. It faded at once, taking the faces with it and leaving him only the irritation of having almost seen, a brain itch that made him want to peel back his skull and rake his fingernails across his brain. At the same time, his body responded with dread. His heart sped, his insides shook like Jell-O. He took another step into the barn.

At the center of the open space, not far from the feed bins, was a small hump of straw and dust. Again, for no reason he could think of, his entire attention fixated on that hump, with the same watchful respect he might have accorded a rattlesnake coiled next to his feet.

The raven hopped past, pausing once to poke his beak into what was left of an old feed sack, and then moved on to the looming thing. Morgan followed in spite of himself, a quiet horror darkening the edges of his vision. A memory flash assailed him.

He stood with the gun in his hands, his stomach knotted with guilt. Tears threatened and he blinked them back. He did not deserve the release of tears . . .

Dear God, what had he done? He didn't want to know, didn't want to look, but that's what he was here to do and he pushed himself forward. Beneath dust and cobwebs lay what was clearly a skeleton, the size of a small child.

He felt his gorge rise, clamped his jaw tight to keep his teeth from chattering against each other. Bending down, he brushed away the dust and straw that covered the bones.

Something wasn't right with the skeleton—the jaw was

too long, the skull too narrow, the leg and arm bones of equal length. Not a child, then, thank God. Long-denied tears wet his cheeks as he bent and touched a finger to the hole in the side of the skull.

Lady tries to get onto her feet when she sees him, but her hindquarters are flattened and refuse to move. Her tail can still wag and gives three whaps on the barn floor. Run over by the plow, his father says. Got in the way, no time to stop. She'll have to be put down, and Morgan's the one that will have to do it. But there's another option, his father says.

"You don't have to kill her, son. Just take her on into a Dreamworld and make a shift. She'll be running free and whole in no time. So easy . . ."

"No! When will you listen? I won't be the Dreamshifter, I don't want to. Gracie wants it—why can't you—"

"You're it, boy. I've already taught you, and rules say I can't teach two. Time to be a man and do what must be done."

He won't do it, though. He won't give in to his father's twisted games. He pushes the barrel of the gun against Lady's head and she wags her tail again, her brown eyes pleading.

Morgan pulled himself back from the memory. Why hadn't he buried her? She'd been a good dog.

He searched the barn and found what he wanted leaning up against the wall. The spade was rusty and the handle full of slivers, but it served his purpose. No more than fifteen minutes later he stood, head bowed, beside the grave he should have dug eighty-six years ago.

A soft squawk behind him, a rustle and flutter, and the raven landed on his shoulder. This too was familiar. Everywhere he went, the dog at his heels, the bird flying from tree to tree or sometimes alighting on his shoulder, always to be shooed away.

"Get lost, will you?" he said again, but the raven only dug sharp talons into his skin, a determined passenger. Part of his penance, maybe, and he let the bird stay. The business with the dog was bad, but he knew damned well there was worse to come. Images darted through his memory without any connection or explanation. Blood and death, terror and rage, and always the overarching guilt.

Whatever pain awaited in his memories he had most certainly earned, and it was about time he paid. Still, about halfway toward the house, as the first tendrils of memory reached out to pull him in, he hesitated. It was not too late. If he drove away now, if he directed his mind down other paths, if he stopped at the very first liquor store and bought a fifth of McNaughton's, he might be able to stuff this all back down into the place where he had kept it for so many years. He'd spent his entire life avoiding one thing or another; what was to stop him from continuing?

Memory of Jenn's desperate face at the last moment he'd seen her alive decided him. *Coward.*

Images of his brothers and sisters flicked through his mind, one after the other, Ellie, Jack, Will, Grace. Years since he'd seen those faces or allowed himself to think of them, and yet they belonged to him as surely as his own hands and feet. Bone of his bone, flesh of his flesh.

Tightening his grip on the shotgun as though it would somehow provide protection from his memories, he crossed the threshold into the house.

He was relieved to find the kitchen empty. No stove, no table, no chairs.

No bodies.

The kitchen window was broken, and glass shards mingled with a debris of dirt and leaves on counter and floor. A dead bird lay in the corner where the stove should have been. The rough plank table with the red checked cloth was gone.

Ellie would be appalled at the state of her kitchen.

Ellie is dead. Long dead.

A breeze flowed in through the broken window, rattling dry leaves into drifts in the corners, leaving bare patches on the dark, rust-colored floor.

Wrong color. It had been a lighter wood, scrubbed by Ellie's busy hands to an almost golden glow. The whitewashed walls, gray now with age and dirt, carried other, darker marks. A fine spray in places, solid color in others.

Morgan realized he was holding his breath; his blood roared in his ears like surf against stone.

Blood.

The fragile continuum that was time dissolved and he fell on his knees under the weight of blood and guilt, pressing the heels of his hands into his eyes to shut it out. But still he saw her, exactly as she had appeared in an endless procession of nightmares over the years. Grace, his little sister, his to protect, eyes wide and expressionless in a face splattered with blood.

Coward.

Morgan stops once to vomit as he walks back to the house. Lady needed to be put down; she was suffering. But guilt nags at him. All he had to do was give in. Take the dog to a Dreamworld and shift the dream.

All the trust in those brown eyes as he'd pulled the trigger. He wipes away tears with a hand that shakes with grief and rage and guilt. He did what he had to do. He will not be the next Dreamshifter. Will not become like his father. Ever.

He's late. They will all be at supper, waiting for him. So he stops to wipe his eyes again, to pull himself together, clutching the shotgun like an anchor. As expected, the table is set for dinner, everyone in their places. Except for his father, who stands waiting at the head of the table, his chair pushed back, the Winchester in his hands.

"I'm going to ask you one more time, son," he says.

All of them know that tone of voice and what it means. Every face in the room goes still; all eyes turn on the man about to erupt into violence.

"No," Morgan says. He's going to die, he thinks. Right now. Right here.

Instead, the old man swings his gun toward Ellie and shoots her full in the chest. Her chair crashes over backward and she falls to the floor, blood staining the front of her dress. Jack drops to his knees beside her, calling her name, pressing his hands against a red tide that will not be stemmed.

Before Morgan can think to speak or move, the back of Jack's head is gone and he slumps over his sister.

"No," Weston shouts, or means to. His voice comes out small and quavering. This can't have just happened, can't be happening. "I'll do it. Whatever you want—"

The old man's mouth stretches into a grin. "You're too late, son."

The gun swings toward Will, who has time to say one word—please—before he has no jaw to speak with.

"All I asked of you was for you to do your job," his father says. "You wanted one of the others to do it. Now there are no others."

But there is one, still. Grace. Blood in her hair, on her face, her dress drenched in it. She has left the table, is standing beside Morgan.

She lifts the shotgun, still clenched in his hands, aims, pulls the trigger. The kick startles him out of his shock as crimson blooms on their father's chest. The old man's jaw goes slack. The hand holding the gun sinks toward the floor. His mouth opens to say something and then he collapses.

"Coward," Grace says.

Morgan realized he was rocking like a small child or a man insane. He could have saved them all. One shot to take out the old man before he killed anybody. Grace would have done it, if she'd had the gun. She was only a child and she'd been able to think and act.

Or he could have just done as his father demanded and agreed to be the Dreamshifter.

People were dead because of his failure to act. His brothers and sisters. Carpenter and Jenn. It was time for justice, and he knew only one way to make things right.

Eighteen

V ivian white-knuckled the steering wheel of her old
Subaru, partly to stay on the road and partly to keep
from bouncing off the seat. Poe, making good use of his
flightless wings to keep his balance, made reproachful
noises that sounded human. She didn't blame him.

This couldn't be called a road; it was little more than two
tire tracks through the forest. Tall grasses swished along the
bottom of her car. Bushes and tree branches scraped along
the sides. Once she drove over something that made a long
metallic screech and she held her breath, waiting for the
radiator to explode or the smell of gasoline to fill the air.

At least one other vehicle had traveled here, and not long
ago. The grass was flattened in the tire tracks and had not
yet stood back up again. It worried her at first to think about
encountering a stranger in the middle of nowhere, but then
she began to notice the trailers and shacks along the way,
well off the track and nearly hidden in the trees. Civilization,
of a sort.

She hoped to God she'd read the map right, but even if
she hadn't she was going to keep on driving because there
was no safe place to turn around and she sure as hell wasn't
backing all the way out of here. At least it was early in the

day and she wouldn't get caught out in the dark. At least she had a full tank of gas.

These were small mercies, but she clung to them.

Time swirled around her ears, sang in her veins, whispered through every cell of her body with an urgency she could not ignore. Not the winged chariot of Donne's poem, merely drawing near, but right here and now, in your face, like a cat in the morning when you're trying to sleep.

Something was about to happen. Maybe she could stop it, but she didn't have much time.

Just as she was beginning to truly doubt her sense of direction and the map, the track widened and she drove into a clearing. As she had feared, she was not alone. There was another vehicle—a battered old pickup truck, dented and scratched, so mud-covered she couldn't figure out its color. It bore B.C. license plates, which meant someone was a long way from home, and the chances of ending up in this place accidentally seemed slim.

She stayed close to the car, looking around for movement. She had no weapon on her, not even a can of bear spray. No phone. Not that there would be a signal out here anyway. A raven flew across the clearing and settled in a tree not ten feet away, peering down at her. Other than the inquisitive bird, nothing moved. Nobody appeared from out of the bushes or behind any trees, and after a long moment Vivian eased the door closed and walked over to check out the pickup.

It was empty.

She opened the passenger-side door and rifled through the glove box. The truck was registered to a Morgan Weathersby, of Trail, B.C. A litter of receipts from grocery stores and gas stations for coffee and soda covered the passenger-side floor. A coffee mug, an empty chip bag. Nothing else. No wallet. No weapons, although there was a gun rack in the back window. In the bed of the truck a couple of gas cans, strapped down with bungee cords. A backpack, complete with canteen and sleeping bag.

The raven took flight in a burst of feathers. Vivian startled, pressing her hand over her racing heart. Poe stood beside her, his black eyes following the path of the bird toward the house. It lit on the eaves, scolding something out of sight.

A heartbeat later the target of the raven's attention emerged from around the corner of the house—a man wearing a red flannel shirt and faded jeans. Long gray hair hung in snarls over his shoulders; a grizzled beard cascaded over his breast. Vivian took an unconscious step forward. He was hurt in some way, moving in a shambling, loose-limbed gait as though something were broken and he hadn't realized it yet.

In his hand he carried a large container, fire-engine red. He bent over at the waist, pouring liquid onto the ground, splashing it up onto the walls of the house.

Vivian's brain registered slowly, making a delayed connection with the gas cans in the back of the pickup.

She broke into a dead run, but it felt slow-motion, like running in a dream. The man tossed the gas can toward the house, onto the sagging front porch, and stood up straight, both hands pressing into the small of his back as he stretched. He dug into his pocket and pulled something out, a small rectangular object. A motion of his right hand, and a flame burned. Matches.

Vivian found her breath and shouted, "No!"

The raven dove at the man's head.

"Shoo, damn it!" he yelled at the bird. Shielding his head from the onslaught with his free arm, he tossed the match with the other. Flames erupted up out of the dry grass with a loud whoosh, licking hungrily at the old wood. All around the perimeter of the house the flames shot up. The front porch flared into an instant bonfire, the fire reaching in through the broken glass of a window.

"Are you insane?" Vivian shouted. She stood at a distance, helpless, the heat already reaching out to sting the skin of her face.

The raven still fussed, diving over and over again.

"Tar and damnation, you blasted bird!" Continuing to cover his head with one arm, the man dug in his pockets with his free hand, drew back his arm, and hurled something toward the hottest part of the fire.

Vivian gasped, her heart twisting with helplessness and loss.

A small crystal sphere arced upward, splintering the light into a myriad of rainbows, falling with a soul-shattering chime into the flames. A dreamsphere. It would have taken her into Dreamworld, locked doors or no, and he had just destroyed it. Still the man wasn't done. He reached up and lifted something over his head, a pendant of some kind. Vivian was close enough now to see what it was, to reach for his arm and try to hold him back. Again, she was too late. He flung this too, directly toward the fire.

At the last possible second the raven swooped down, caught the thing in his beak, and flew to a nearby tree, where he perched, feathers ruffled, radiating disapproval.

"Damn you," the man said, "give it back." His body language changed with the outpouring of rage. He no longer appeared shambling or broken, but surprisingly vigorous and straight given his apparent age. Stalking over to the tree, he shook it until the dry leaves rattled and fell. The raven merely fluttered up a few branches higher and peered down, croaking disdainfully.

"I don't think he's going to surrender it," Vivian said. The raven reminded her of Poe and she knew that look. Stubborn.

"We'll see about that."

The man strode away from the tree and around to the side of the house, returning with a shotgun in his hands. Putting it to his shoulder, he aimed it up into the tree. Instinct told her it was essential that both bird and pendant be preserved, and she needed to stop this deranged idiot from firing his gun. But behind them the fire roared and snapped. A hot wind gusted in her hair. The hotter the fire got, the more her dragon blood responded. She could feel the change trying to take place—the dragon shape stretching her from within, her mind moving toward the angles and planes of dragon thought.

I am Vivian, I will remain Vivian. Her will was sufficient to hold back the shift, but there was none to spare for speech.

The raven took care of the problem. Almost lazily, dripping evident disdain, it took flight, keeping the tree between itself and the shotgun until it was well up into the sky, where it flew in tantalizing circles. The man lowered his weapon with a muttered curse.

Vivian heaved a sigh of relief. She could move away from the fire, ease the pressure to make the shift. But before she could take a single step, the lunatic dropped the gun and broke into a headlong dash, straight toward the fire.

It was already a raging inferno, flames shooting out through all of the windows, reaching toward the sky. Vivian wasted a precious instant frozen in disbelief before she raced after him. She was younger, but he was stronger and faster and was lengthening his lead. Head down, legs churning, arms pumping, his long gray hair blowing out behind him in the wind created by the fire.

The heat was intense, a solid wall of wind and energy that pushed Vivian's control to the breaking point. There was no time to fight it. All that existed was the man chasing self-immolation and her need to stop him. Everything turned into a blur. The distance between them shrank at speed. She intercepted his path and bowled him over backward, wrapping her arms around him and dragging him away from the flames. There was a muddle of air and grass and fire and flesh.

The next thing she was conscious of, she knelt over his body stretched full length on the ground. His eyes, coffee dark, were wide with fear and confusion. His long gray beard had been singed by the fire, his nose and cheeks slightly reddened. A scorched smell wafted off him.

"What the hell are you?" he asked.

This was not a good beginning to the conversation she needed to have with him, but the dragon flare was too recent for her to be able to invoke some therapeutic professional technique that might have de-escalated everything.

"Like you have a right to ask questions. Any questions.

You lit a house on fire. Then you tried to run into it. Are you sane?"

"No. Let me go."

His gaze turned back to the fire, and she read longing and desire.

"Oh, hell," she said. "Suicide? Maybe next time you could just use the gun like a normal person."

"Like a—did you just say *normal*?"

"Look—you feel the need to off yourself, fine, but first tell me why you just destroyed a perfectly good dreamsphere?"

"No such thing as a good dreamsphere. And you can't stop me from killing myself forever, no matter what sort of twisted mutant creature you are."

It dawned on her that they were a lot farther from the conflagration than they should have been. Also that her vision was extraordinarily clear and that the backs of the hands pressing on his chest were marked with a pattern of scales. Oh, shit. Mutant indeed.

"I need you," she said. "Needed that dreamsphere too, but it's too late for that."

His eyes narrowed. "I'm not helping a sorceress with anything."

"You will—"

"What are you going to do, kill me? Please, be my guest."

"Are you always this obnoxious? I bet you're not even Morgan Weathersby. In fact, you know what? I think you're Weston Jennings. So what I could do, here, is call the cops and get you arrested and then when you can't kill yourself, because you're on suicide watch in the jail, we'll talk about how you aren't going to help me."

"You think they're going to believe that I'm Weston Jennings? Still alive and kicking at a hundred and three? I think not."

Vivian smiled at him. Quite pleasantly, she thought, although his face reacted as though she'd just done something threatening. "So you do know about Weston? Do tell."

His jaw clamped tight. "I'm not telling you anything."

She shrugged. "Fine. You committed arson. And when I tried to stop you, you turned the gun on me and tried to shoot me."

"You wouldn't—"

"Try me."

He sighed. "And if I tell them that you grew scales and wings and carried me away from the fire, then I get locked up in a mental ward. Is that it?"

"I don't know what you're talking about." The scale pattern on her hands had gone. Her eyes felt normal; her vision had returned to a more ordinary level. "I'm a well-respected member of the community. Doctor who works in the ER."

"And I suppose every well-respected ER doc has a penguin following her around." He was looking over her shoulder now, and she could only guess that Poe had made an appearance.

The raven chose that moment to flutter down and land beside the man's head. In his beak still dangled the leather cord with the black pendant hanging from it. "May I?" Vivian asked, and the bird released it to her before running his beak tentatively through Morgan/Weston's fire-frazzled hair.

The pendant was much like her own, a raven rather than a penguin, and Vivian saw why this bird had reminded her so much of Poe. "You tried to destroy this too. Why?"

"Don't want it, don't need it."

There was more in his face, a deep despair that moved her despite herself. She thought of the scroll and the newspaper. Weston Jennings, gone missing in 1925. Weston Jennings, presumed to have massacred his family. A lot of years to live with that sort of guilt, to try to come to terms with the whole thing.

"Why did you do it?"

"What, burn down the house?"

"No—kill your family."

He had lain still and compliant, but now he began to twist and struggle. "Just let me go."

"Can't."

But he had both weight and muscle on his side and she

couldn't hold him. She looked around for something to sub-due him with. No sticks, no rocks; the gun was out of reach and even if she could get to it, what good was it to threaten somebody who wanted to be dead?

He flung her to the side and scrambled up onto hands and knees. He was going to run back into the fire, and she could not afford to let him go.

So she summoned up the Voice of command.

"Stay where you are."

His body shuddered to a stop, muscles quivering and convulsing with the effort to move on while the invisible barrier held him. Her own gut twisted in sympathy, but she held him with her will and did not release.

It only took a minute for him to accept the reality and surrender to his invisible bonds. "I knew you were a sorcer-ess."

"Only sort of. That's about the extent of my abilities."

"Bullshit. What about that whole dragon-woman thing?"

"Different scenario. By the way, I'm also a Dream-shifter."

"Oh dear God. A trifecta. What the hell do you think you need from me?"

"Knowledge. Experience."

He snorted. "You're asking the wrong man."

"Don't try to tell me you're not a Dreamshifter. Your raven and your pendant tell me otherwise."

"Yes, well. I had that foisted on me. The only Dream-world I've ever been in is the one inflicted on me by the Guardian in the infernal Cave of Dreams. And I've just thrown that dreamsphere into hell."

His words cut her to the heart. "But if you can't help me, it's all lost." She widened her eyes against an unwelcome welling of tears, staring straight ahead, biting her lip. *Don't blink, don't move, don't let those tears spill.*

"Hell and damnation. You're going to cry? What kind of sorceress does that?"

Vivian waited until she thought her voice would be steady, not looking at him. "The kind that isn't a sorceress and has someone she cares about trapped in the Between and no way to get there."

"You're a Dreamshifter—"

"Locked out. Somebody locked me out." All pretense of calm abandoned her and the tears came in a flood. "I thought I was the last of the Dreamshifters; that's what my grandfather said. He died and left me responsible without teaching me anything. I'm supposed to find the Key, but I don't even know what it does, or where to find it. And then I found something that made me think you were alive and I started looking but now you're telling me you can't help me and you've destroyed your dreamsphere and I don't know what to do."

It was impossible to weep and keep a hold on the command she'd laid on him. He wriggled out of her control and got to his feet. He glanced over his shoulder at the progress of the destruction he'd created but stayed put. "You've lost someone over there? Someone alive? That's what this is all about?"

Vivian nodded, mopping her face with her sleeve. "That and the Key."

"What key?"

"The Key to the Forever. Whatever that is—"

"Penance," he said, interrupting. He sank to the ground and the raven fluttered down onto his shoulder. "That's what you are. Death would have been too easy, so the fates kindly sent me you."

"For killing your family, you mean?"

"I didn't kill them." His voice was heavy with years and grief.

"But you said you were guilty."

"I am."

"So it was your sister, then."

He just stared at her, his face a mask of misery. "I don't want to talk about this."

"Okay, fine. You didn't kill them, but you are guilty of their deaths. You've lived with this for how many years now—why try to kill yourself today?"

His face darkened and his eyes turned back to the flames. "I also lost somebody in the Dreamworld yesterday."

"You're locked out too?"

"I never said that."

"Then—"

"I never said they were still alive."

Vivian pressed her face into her hands and rubbed her burning eyes. "I don't suppose you'd tell me what you were doing there in the first place?"

"Hunting."

"Of course."

"Look—a rogue Dreamshifter needs some sort of livelihood. When you're in and out of the Dreamworld and the Between all the time, you tend to find food. If it's not in the dreams you enter, you can shift it into being. And because you're so goldarn special, what you eat in dreams actually nourishes you. But if you're not going into Dreamworld all the time, then you have these basic needs for food, shelter, and cash."

This time she just looked the question at him, and he went on. "In the early years I also had to avoid the law. Everybody believed I did it. I wasn't educated, didn't have a trade, thanks to Father's persistent and deluded belief that I would give in and become the Dreamshifter someday. All I knew how to do was hunt. There was wildlife in my dream. Wolves, bears, cougar—and other things, a little more exotic. People paid me as a guide."

His voice trailed off and his face worked, fighting off some strong emotion.

"And the last hunt went badly."

"You could say that. Two dead—my fault. One was only a child." He turned to face her directly. "Please. I'm old. I'm miserable. All I ever wanted in this world was a normal life—wife, kids, to die when the time came. All I ever got was shit. Why would you hold me here?"

"Because there are other lives at stake—maybe everybody's. Not just the people I love."

"The Key," he said, bleak, watching the fire.

"What do you know about it?"

"Father mentioned it once or twice. I tried not to listen, but that I remember. He had a book that talked about the Key . . ." His voice trailed off, watching the fire.

"What else was in that book?"

"Mythology, mostly. About the first Dreamshifter and how she betrayed the dragons, or the dragons betrayed her. A bunch of malarchy about giants and sorcerers. The making of the Black Gates and a sort of pirate treasure map of how to find it."

"A map. There was a map of the Between."

Weston flushed. "Well, yes. Oh, and some sort of prophecy connected to the Key—when it would be found, who could use it, and how. I think there was some special incantation."

Vivian felt a strong desire to pick him up and throw him into the fire herself. "And that book was in this house and has just gone up in flames."

"I don't think so. There wasn't anything left in the house. Somebody emptied it."

"Oh, come on. Your father would have hidden something like that. Secret cubbyhole? Safe? Something."

"If he did, Grace would have taken it. She knew all the secrets in that house."

"When did you see her last?"

"That was it. That day—with everybody lying dead and a little sister who needed me, I got swept away into the Cave of Dreams for an initiation I never wanted. I came back to the house, once, to look for her. She didn't live here anymore."

"She stayed with friends for a few days and then went to an orphanage."

"Is she—oh, she'd have to be dead by now." His face creased and he rubbed the back of his neck. "Poor Gracie. I hope she died easy of a nice old age."

Mad as she was, still Vivian tried to protect him by keeping the truth out of her face, but he saw it in her eyes. "Tell me how she died. Tell me!"

"Fire. Her house burned down. She's buried in the family plot."

"Right next to my father. She'll love that." He rubbed both hands over his face. "You should have let me burn. It's the only justice."

"Why didn't you look for her? After the Cave of Dreams, I mean."

"The law was after me by then. What good would I be to her?"

There was no good answer to this question, so Vivian shifted on to action. "What would she have done with the book, if she had it?" A book could end up in so many places—used bookstore, library, landfill, fire. Trying to find it would be a hopeless task.

But Weston was taking her rhetorical question seriously. "Probably buried with her. That and my father's dreamspheres. If I know Gracie, she had the funeral all planned out and the coffin bought long before she died."

Vivian was quiet for a minute, aware of the extent of his pain and what she was about to ask.

"We really need that book, Weston. And if there were dreamspheres—"

"Now you're insane! Are you proposing what I think you are?"

She waited, keeping silence. It was something she'd learned early in medical school, effective on patients and staff alike. Just wait it out and let their own consciences do the talking.

"Oh, all right!" he said. "What difference does it make? I'll help you. And then you'll let me die."

"Do we need to call somebody about the fire?"

"It's a little late to salvage anything."

"I was thinking about fire risk. You know—the forest."

"No wind to speak of—trees are still well back, ground is damp. Should be okay. Anonymous tip maybe, when we get to town."

"Here. You might want this." Vivian held out the pendant.

He stood looking at it for a long moment, and she thought he would refuse. But at length he took it from her and slipped the leather thong over his head. "Guess I really didn't deserve to be free of it. Not yet anyway."

Vivian ached for her own pendant but managed a bleak smile. "Great. You're driving. We've got some digging to do."

Nineteen

Wishing was for fools and Zee knew it.

Nothing would be accomplished by wishing the winding paths of the labyrinth straight, or by conjuring up soft beds and healing hands and Vivian's face. Action was all there was, and so he put one foot in front of the other and kept himself moving forward.

He had spent the night lying on the forest floor, sharing the blanket with Jared. About the time the moon rose above the trees, the sick man began raving with delirium. His body burned with fever, and Zee had dribbled all of the water from the canteen into his mouth, reserving only one precious swallow for himself.

When the sun first came up and he'd willed himself to get moving, he'd collected some of the heavy dew from the leaves of the trees. Not enough to slake his thirst, but enough at least to wet his mouth. Knowing he needed energy he'd eaten one of the protein bars, but they were dry and went down hard without water. When he'd offered some to Jared, the sick man turned his head away, gagging.

By means of some serious goading, he'd managed to get Jared crawling, and they'd been lucky enough to come across another path. Or at least it had seemed like luck, until the sun changed from a pleasant source of warmth to a cruel and blazing heat. The trees thinned and vanished until they entered an endless prairie intersected by impassable hedges.

All through the morning Jared had grown weaker, his body heated by fever, his eyes dull. About the time they hit the open fields and the sun was directly overhead, he collapsed, unconscious, and could not be roused.

There was no water, no shelter, nothing Zee could do to help.

He thought about walking away. He had a job to do—find some way to get back to Vivian, find the one who had stolen the Key. Jared was holding him back. Who would blame him if he left the coward to fend for himself? Who would even know?

Bending down, he grasped the wounded man under the arms and tried to haul him up over his shoulder. He failed, the heavy body too much for his own decreased strength and wounded arm. Again he tried. Again he failed. On the third attempt he managed to stagger onto his feet with the unconscious man a dead weight over his shoulder, limp arms flopping, head bobbing.

He'd been walking for only a few minutes when the path he was on came to a dead end; nothing for it but to choose one way or another, which was not easily done. The hedges were tall and blocked his view. There was no rhyme or reason to the maze, and a nagging sense of familiarity prickling beneath his skin was not helpful. It never said, *Take this right and that left and the middle path when the way turns into three.* It just burrowed into his brain like a chigger, a thing he mentally scratched without ever shaking it loose.

At last he settled on a plan—he would take a left alternated by a right at every crossroads. If the way split into three or more, always take the middle. The goal was to go as straight as possible, although he couldn't say why. Only that he needed some sort of direction.

For the first time in his life he had absolutely no sense of either place or time. His wounds ached, burned, throbbed, and sometimes bled under the weight of the burden slung over his shoulder, inanimate and irksome.

A fly buzzed around his head, lighting on his bleeding arm, then Jared's leg. Another fly showed up, and then another, until the air around him buzzed with small black bodies. They crawled thick over Zee's head and shoulders, swarming over the bandage on his arm, buzzing around his side. At first he brushed them off, but they were too many and it took too much energy.

Time ceased to exist. No past, no future, only this step, and then the next. Always, there had been the buzzing of the flies crawling at the edges of his eyes and mouth. The sun had always beat down on the top of his head. There had always been pain, had always been the weight over his shoulder and the endless twists and turns of the paths he followed.

There came a time when he realized he had ceased all forward motion and was standing perfectly still. Not doing anything, not resting, just standing, with his burden still heavy on his shoulders.

He felt that there must be some reason for this.

His eyes sent back a message that the path in front of him was blocked by a hill of dirt, perhaps as high as his knees, reaching from hedge to hedge, with no room to pass on either side. As his attention focused in, he saw that the dirt was moving. Small red crawling things coming and going, in and out of a honeycomb of holes.

Ants.

Zee had a thing about ants. There were too many of them and they moved too fast. He'd read *The Once and Future King* in first grade, and the Wart's adventures among the ants had instilled a lingering fear of their ruthlessness.

There was a choice to be made. He could turn around and backtrack to the last turning and take a different route. Or he could wade knee deep through a nest of pissed-off ants. The balance of decision was skewed by the promise of shade. Beyond the anthill, not far in the distance, he saw trees. Nice tall, shady weeping willows. And beyond them, a glint of something that might be water.

As he stood in a stupor, unable to act on this simple choice, an ant separated itself from the nest and scurried toward his foot. He observed its single-minded approach. It stopped at the barrier created by his boot, indecisive, and Zee felt a sudden kinship with the tiny creature. To go forward, or to go back?

But the ant didn't share his problem with decision making, and it was only the matter of a single breath before it climbed up onto the toe of his boot. A tiny tendril of smoke followed behind it, along with a hot smell of burning. Zee watched its progress, mesmerized by the sooty trail it left behind as it explored this new territory. It was just beginning to register on him that if the ant could burn leather it would not be good to have it crawl up his pant leg, when the entire anthill exploded. Flying ants surrounded him, burning his skin wherever they touched. The hedge next to him began to smoke and then burst into flame.

Zee ducked his head low and charged forward, toward the fragile promise of water. Through the swarming ants, through the anthill, pumping his rubbery legs as fast as he could manage. A thousand pinpoints of fire covered his body. His clothes began to smoke. The smell of singed hair rose up around him.

He got clear of the nest, staggering down the open path, aiming for the space of trees and praying under his breath: *Please let there be water.*

The ants pursued him in a flying cloud of torment.

As he grew closer to the trees, a thick reek pressed against him, overpowering the smell of burning with a stench of stale water and rotting weeds. What he had hoped was a pond turned out to be a slough stretched between the trees, with a puddle of muddy water at the center. Brown algae floated on top. All around the edges sickly vegetation—grass, leaves, and weeds—fermented in various stages of decay. Something white and dead floated on the surface, a fish, its pale belly turned up to the sky.

Zee did not turn or slow his pace. When it came to flying fire ants, water was water. He reached the edge of the slough. It sucked his feet down into deep muck, slowing his pace. Ants whirred and clicked and burned. The world swam in front of his eyes; the stench of the rotten water overpowered him.

His feet were mired and he couldn't get them free.

The hem of his shirt burst into flame.

With a last burst of strength he managed a few more steps, which took him to the edge of the filthy water. He flung himself forward, throwing Jared clear as he did so. Zee closed his eyes and held his breath as the water closed over his head.

Cool liquid surrounded him, shutting out the ants, easing his burns. But his body was starving for air and he needed to get Jared's head above water, so he surfaced, preparing to face the cloud of insects.

The air he sucked in as he broke the surface was cool and sweet. All around him blue water sparkled clear and limpid, reflecting sky and trees fractured by the ripples on the surface. No slough. No algae. No smell of rotting. Just a round, perfect pool with water bubbling up at one side, spilling away into a crystal-clear stream on the other. Dead ants littered the surface, and Zee felt immense relief that the things could be killed. All around lay a space of soft green grass, dotted with wildflowers and overhung with green branches. A bird warbled high above.

A soft breeze touched his dripping face.

He didn't see Jared and was about to dive down looking for him, when the wounded man surfaced on his own, spouting water and coughing. Zee gave him an arm to support him at the surface. Jared coughed and spewed, eyes streaming. When the paroxysms finally stopped, he gasped, "Are you trying to drown me?"

"Right. That would be why I'm holding you up and letting you get your breath."

Despite the fact that his eyes were open and he was talking, Jared looked bad. The swellings on his face had turned from green to black, and there were more of the blisters now on his hands and arms.

"We were attacked by fire ants," Zee explained after a long space.

"The little biting kind?"

"No, the big, flying, light-you-on-fire-if-they-land-on-you kind. You have some burns. The water will be good for that."

Jared looked down at the swellings on his arm. "Looks like the burns are a minor concern."

Zee towed him to the edge and settled him with his arms and head resting on the bank, his body still immersed. Then he stripped out of the soaking backpack and his own clothes, noticing a network of burn holes in the clothing, and marks on his skin, as if someone had held him down and pressed lit cigarettes against his flesh. The clothes were near ruined but better than nothing, and he laid them flat on the grass for the sun to dry. As for the backpack, he'd see what could be salvaged later. Taking a deep breath, he ducked beneath the water and stayed as long as his lungs would let him before bursting back up to the surface.

Sunlight touched his upturned face. Already the fountain was clearing, the dirty water spilling over the edge of the basin and away in a small stream. No more floating ants. He could see to the flat stones at the bottom, and his own feet, distorted and ghostly through the water.

It was cold, though, and he had begun to shiver.

Jared was able to help a little when Zee dragged him out. They staggered out of the water and collapsed on the sun-warmed grass.

The wounded man propped himself up to look at his leg. In the course of the mad dash from the ants and the time in the water, Zee's rough bandage had come off. "That is revolting and disgusting," Jared said, shuddering. "What a way to die."

The wound had turned green, not any color that flesh should ever be, and even after the long soak in the spring it stank.

Jared sank down onto his back, eyes closed, asleep or unconscious or pretending to be. Zee knew he needed to do something—about those blisters, about the wounded leg. But he was exhausted and it felt good to just lie still, letting the sun dry the water droplets from his skin. The light was too bright and he let his eyelids close, his body relaxing into the softness of grass. In the distance he heard the low hum of bees. The sun warmed his aching muscles, eased the pain in his wounds. He would allow himself just one more minute. Just. One.

Twenty

T he cemetery gate was locked and chained, and Weston pulled the pickup off the road onto the grassy verge, deep into shadow and partly concealed behind a tree. They'd passed the time before sunset with preparations: buying tools, grabbing something to eat at a drive-through. Although Vivian was uneasy about leaving Poe to his own devices, the idea of him running loose in the graveyard at night had been considerably more alarming, so she'd stopped by the bookstore and run him a bath, where she'd left him looking reasonably content. As for the raven, the minute the truck door opened, it hopped out and vanished into the night.

Vivian was grateful that it was not only dark, but a deep black night. No moon to give them away, only the cold stars, which did nothing to pick up a glint of light on a shovel or a pick. They dared not even use the flashlight Weston had dug from behind the seat of his pickup, not out here by the road. People in Krebston were as likely to come in guns a-blazing as to call the police, and neither option was acceptable.

Weston climbed over the gate first, packing his shotgun, and she passed the shovels to him, one by one, and then the pick, reserving the flashlight for herself. Her depth perception was off in the pitch-blackness and she miscalculated the ground on the other side of the gate, falling the last few feet with an oomph of expelled breath. Weston loomed over her, little more than a shadow; she could hear his breathing, smell wood smoke and singed hair.

She expected a hand up, but instead he pushed her down and pinned her shoulders to the ground.

"I've been thinking. I need some answers before I go through with this."

"Weston, I explained—"

"I'm not a stupid man, if I am a little slow on the uptake. Last I remember Old George was still in business. If you're the last, as you say, what happened to him? Dragon? Pestilence?"

"Sorceress." She said it flippantly, not wanting to get into the whole saga.

It was a mistake. The cold barrel of a shotgun dug into her chest. "Maybe you're the sorceress. And if you try that voice trick on me again, I might just have enough gumption to pull this trigger."

"Oh for God's sake. I told you—I can do the voice thing, that's it. Think—why would I kill him and set myself up for this nightmare?"

"So some sorceress—not you—killed him. She after you next then? Going to show up here?"

"She's dead."

"A sorceress is mighty hard to kill."

"Trust me, this one's dead. She turned into dust and blew away."

She'd hoped this would relax him, but the pressure of the barrel intensified into a deep round ache between her ribs. "How did you manage that? Seeing as you can't do sorcery and all."

"If you think I can't be killed, why are you threatening to shoot me?"

"You might not die, but it would slow you down. Inflict a mighty big heap of pain. Now tell me how you managed to turn some sorceress into dust."

"Who said it was me?"

"Give me credit for half a brain. Who else could have killed her?"

"Well, I didn't kill her, precisely. She did some spell to twine her life with a dragon. We killed the dragon—"

"We."

"I don't want to talk about it."

"And I don't want any association with a sorceress."

"Look, I told you I am not a sorceress. And she's dead."

He used her own trick of silence against her, waiting. Vivian clenched her teeth against the words she must not say aloud. *All right, maybe I have the blood in me. Who knows what I might be capable of?* The thought made her shiver. "Please, can I get up now? It's cold and damp down here."

"You're not a sorceress, but you killed this Jehenna."

"Well—in a roundabout way, yes."

"And after you kill this sorceress, somebody steals your pendant and you get locked out of Dreamworld. Doesn't sound like a coincidence to me."

"I never said it was coincidence. We were ambushed in a Dreamworld."

He was quiet for a long time. The pressure of the gun barrel eased. "Who set you up?"

"That's what I'm trying to find out! Can we get on with it then?"

"Not quite. What about the dragon thing?"

"I don't know."

"What do you mean, you don't know?"

"I think I have it under control."

"You think."

"Look, Weston, you want honesty? Here it is. I'm a pitiful excuse for a Dreamshifter. I know next to nothing about it and I've had no time to practice. I have a tendency I'm not happy about to turn into a dragon, and I may have sorceress DNA. But I'm *it*. The last Dreamshifter. Unless you want the job. No? Fine. Then help me."

She counted to ten before he released her. As if he hadn't

been holding her at gunpoint he asked casually, "Where do you reckon she's buried?"

Vivian copied his tone. "Old part—over to the right and back."

"You sure she's here?"

"That's what the website said. They've actually cataloged the names on the headstones. There was even a map."

Dead quiet followed. A faint murmur of a breeze in treetops, a stirring of the grass, her footsteps and Weston's, the sound of her own breath.

"Trees will screen us now. Give us a light."

Vivian switched on the flashlight, which had far from the desired effect. The beam of light just made the dark look darker. It reflected off headstones with an illusion of ghostly movement. If Dreamshifters and sorcerers were real, there might well be ghosts. She'd seen plenty of strange things in the emergency room, enough to make her accept the possibility of lingering spirits. A fair number of dying people embraced the moment of death with a sudden joy, the name of a long-departed loved one on their lips.

Just because she accepted the idea didn't mean she had to like it. Grace had better not be a ghost.

Weston didn't look the least bit uneasy, even though they were on the way to dig up his sister's grave. He strode along like he was hunting, keen eyes prying into the dark, the shotgun over one shoulder, the tools over the other.

"Tell me what you know about sorcerers," Vivian said. Anything to shut out the silence and the gathering creepiness. The deeper they penetrated into the old graveyard, the thicker the air felt, as though something were trying to hold them back.

"Don't know much. They move and act mostly in the Between. Don't have access to the Dreamworlds unless they get hold of dreamspheres, or somebody else takes them in."

Lovely. There was a whole pocketful of dreamspheres lost out there somewhere. Her head hurt. "How many are there, do you think? Sorcerers, or whatever?"

"My father spoke in terms of nests. I have no idea what that means."

"Nothing good." She thought of ants, scurrying, and of *Star Trek* and the Borg. Her hand tightened around the flashlight. She felt numb, lost in a haze of unreality, and didn't trust that when she put her feet down they would rest on solid ground. She wished once again that she still had her stiletto. A gun. Any kind of a knife.

Weston walked on a few paces before realizing she had stopped. He turned back, moving into the circle of her flashlight beam.

"Any idea what this Key does?" She tried to make her voice casual, knew she was failing.

"Something to do with ultimate power and everlasting life. The old man went off on tangents about a war between the dragons, interference by the sorcerers, and the balance of the Dreamworlds. My childhood bedtime stories were an elaborate fairy tale. I always thought the Key was a myth—never gave it credence." He stopped. "You look like you've seen a ghost."

"I don't think it's a myth at all."

"Oh, come now. There were giants in these stories—giants who built gates that dragons couldn't open. Nobody believes in Jack and the Beanstalk."

"Jehenna believed in the Key. Mythical or not, she would have killed for it."

"You actually found this Key?"

"Yes," she said, guilt flowing through her. "And Jehenna stole it before she—died. I don't know where it is."

"Well, hell," he said. And then he shrugged. "All the more reason to get to the bottom of this. Reckon we're about there?"

"Over here, I think." Her voice didn't sound like her own, and she was surprised when her feet obeyed her commands and carried her between a line of old headstones. The light played over them as she walked, picking out bits of names and inscriptions.

A glint of the light on reflected eyes made her gasp, but the full beam revealed it was only the raven, sitting on a worn old stone that read:

GRACE JENNINGS
BORN 1912
DIED 1977
REST IN PEACE.

Vivian paused. Amen to resting in peace.

"This isn't right," Weston said, at the same time as Vivian shone the flashlight onto a rectangle of newly spaded black earth. There should have been grass growing here, thick and wild. Grace had been dead for years. Instead, this grave couldn't be more than a couple of days old.

"Weird," she said, her scalp prickling.

Weston shrugged. "It's been dug already. Best see what's still down there." His face had set into grim lines that emphasized the bones beneath his skin, and his voice sounded brittle when he spoke. "Set the flashlight on that stone across the way—it will free your hands and give us light to work by. Watch for anything else out of line."

He took the lead, thrusting his spade through the grass and into the soil beneath. He flung a shovelful of earth aside with a soft thud. Vivian joined in and the two of them fell into a rhythm. Strike into the soil, lift, turn, spill the dirt into the growing pile. Strike again. The reality of physical exertion became everything, past, present, and future. A blister burned and stung on her right palm. Her shoulders ached, her wrists stiffened. Breath sobbed in and out of her lungs, but she wasn't going to stop for a rest, not so long as the old man kept digging.

They were standing in the hole now, flinging the dirt up into the unseen dark. Between the two of them they'd marked out a rectangle they estimated as a foot longer and wider on each side than a coffin would be. Weston's unwelcome raven startled them at odd intervals, invisible wings flapping overhead, alighting on the side of the hole and sending little runnels of dirt skittering down at Vivian's feet.

As they'd gotten deeper she'd moved the flashlight to the edge of the pit. Weston moved in and out of the light as he shoveled, his face streaked with sweat and dirt. A strand of hair stuck to his cheek.

She tried not to think about Poe or Zee, but with every shovelful of earth that she dug they ran through her mind like a litany. Poe would be fine, she told herself, even as she imagined someone breaking into the empty store and carrying him away, or worse. Flashbacks of her last glimpse of Zee were even worse. Over and over she saw him wounded and fighting, falling beneath the onslaught of foes.

Thoughts of revenge kept her going.

Thunk. Her shovel hit something solid. She heard Weston's make a dull thud. Reality of what they were engaged in settled on her shoulders as she stopped to catch her breath. She, the doctor, the healer, the upstanding citizen without so much as a misdemeanor to her name, was about to rob a grave. And for Weston, this was personal. His little sister was in this coffin.

"You okay?" she asked.

"I'll do."

He wiped his face with his sleeve and turned away, back to what needed to be done. For the next few minutes they focused on digging a trench that would allow them to stand beside the coffin. They scraped the earth away until the wood was visible and then stopped once more, hesitating.

Weston's head was bowed, lips moving. Vivian waited, partly out of respect, but also out of dread. Whatever lay within the coffin would not be pretty. But they had to look.

After only a moment, Weston looked up and nodded. "Let's do it."

Vivian tugged at the lid. It was stuck tight. "You're going to have to help. Might have to pry it."

A new voice demanded, "What on earth do you think you're doing?"

Her heart convulsed and she looked up in alarm. The speaker stood above the grave, behind the flashlight, his face obscured by the dark.

"Put down the shovels." The voice was familiar, and Vivian's heart resumed beating.

"Deputy Flynne? What are you doing here?"

A heavy sigh. "What am I doing here? Put down the shovel and explain yourselves."

"We're kind of busy. You want to help?"

"You want me to help with a felony—"

"It's important. Related to things like giant penguins and dragons."

He paused, then said. "Doesn't matter. I can't allow this. For so many reasons that you ought to know, Dr. Maylor."

She wiped the back of her hand across her forehead, knowing she was leaving a muddy streak and not caring. "I don't have time for this. I'm sorry, Brett."

"I could arrest you—"

"Or you could make yourself useful."

"I am not helping you dig up a body."

"You don't have to help. Just go away. Pretend you didn't see anything."

"I can't. Do you have any idea how much trouble I've been in since the dragon thing? All those gaps in my report, combined with the fact that they already think I'm insane. FBI is involved, Vivian, do you understand? And Homeland Security. They're trying to hush it up, like it never happened."

"I'm sorry, but this is bigger than you. It's important, Brett."

"You can't just dig up a grave. Besides being illegal, it goes against nature—the dead should be left alone."

"I can't do that."

"You can't do that," he mimicked. "Of course not. Care to tell me why?"

"It's complicated."

"Of course it's complicated. You know what I wonder? I wonder why in all the years I've worked in this town there has never been a grave robbery. And now, not only are there two within a couple of weeks, they are apparently all interested in the same grave. You know anything about that, Vivian?"

She exchanged a quick glance with Weston and then shook her head. "Honest. I don't have a clue."

"What about him?"

"He doesn't know anything either. Who was grave robbing, Brett?"

"It's—classified."

"What—like FBI again?"

"No, like an embarrassment to the police force. If people find out and it comes back to me, I'll be tarred and feathered."

"We're not going to say anything. Right, Weston?"

"I can keep my mouth shut. Don't plan to be around to do much talking, anyway."

Deputy Flynne sighed. "I can't believe I'm telling you this. Round about a week ago—Mr. Lawrence was here visiting his wife's grave. Comes in every evening to tell her good night. That's over in the new part of the cemetery. He's a martinet, Mr. Lawrence—anything out of place bothers the hell out of him. So he saw a light over here, and he couldn't figure out who would be visiting the old cemetery. He called 911."

"And?"

"And Kim and Olivera show up, and lo and behold there's a mound of dirt piled up and a lantern in the grass. Not a flashlight, mind you, an old-fashioned hurricane lamp. Footsteps take off across the grass, but they're blinded by the light and can't see. They yell 'Freeze' and all that, but the person keeps on running. Olivera runs after the perp and does a tackle move from behind, and it turns out to be this nutjob old woman."

The dark seemed darker all of a sudden, looming outside the beam of the flashlight. Vivian's hand went to the emptiness at her breast.

"What did she take?" Weston asked.

"Is your friend okay?" Brett said. "You don't look good, buddy. She's a doctor, let her check you out."

Weston raised his voice. "Tell me what the woman took from my sister's grave."

"Your sister's grave?" Brett's face was still hidden, but Vivian recognized the tone. Obviously, anybody old enough to be Grace's brother should be lying in his own grave somewhere, not engaged in digging up bodies.

"We'll explain later," she said. "Please answer—what did she take from the grave?"

"Only some old book. Amazing, but it was still in readable condition, wrapped up in layers of what I'm told is oilcloth. Not that I've ever seen oilcloth, but that's what the tech called it."

Vivian's own knees went weak. "She dug up the grave for a book? That's it?"

"I know, right? Bizarre. Wasn't even a diary or anything valuable. Just some old book of myths."

"And this was a week ago?"

"Round about. One week, maybe two. I was still at Sacred Heart hallucinating penguins and freezing my ass off. My partner told me about it."

"Is there an investigation ongoing? Why isn't she in jail? Felony offense and all . . ."

"That's where the embarrassment comes in. She got away. Little old thing like that, and she escaped from two armed deputies."

"How did she get away, exactly?"

"Well, Kim and Olivera swear they had her in handcuffs and put her in the back of the car. You know, once she's in she's secure—locked from the inside and all. They swear they stood right outside the door for a minute discussing strategy. See, they figured there was no way someone of her age and weight could have dug that hole all by herself. They were wondering if maybe they should call in reinforcements to search the graveyard. Kim got in the car to radio for extra bodies, and she was gone."

"That sounds far-fetched," Vivian said, but it wasn't.

"Well, that's what the rest of the cops think, too," Brett said. "They figure one of those guys left the door open, that they turned their backs a little longer than they were letting on. Figure they're covering for each other. She could have slipped the cuffs; that's been done before. They deny it. But policy was to keep it hushed—doesn't do for the community to know the cops screwed up and let a criminal loose. Nobody's seen her since. Figure she must have had an accomplice and he or she helped her make the slip."

Weston broke the silence that followed. "So, where's this book, now?"

"Safely locked away in evidence."

"I need to see it," Vivian said.

"Oh, now you're asking me to break the chain of evidence. I can't do that."

"Sure you can."

"Vivian—"

"I've got to have a look at that book, Brett. Just a look. Time to see what it is, and then you can put it back."

"Can't be done."

"Can it be done if I threaten to let everybody know you told me?"

"You wouldn't do that."

"You think? A word or two to Rich and Cal tomorrow morning at Sacred Grounds and it would be all over town by nightfall."

"Come on, Vivian. I'm already hanging by a thread. The entire force skirts around me like I'm crazy and it's contagious."

"Which is why you're going to let me see this book."

For a minute she thought she'd misjudged him, and that his sense of honor would win out even over this threat. She knew she'd use the Voice again to compel him if she had to; prayed it wouldn't come to that.

She heard the surrender in his voice, along with the anger, carefully contained. "Oh all right. Where will we meet?"

"A to Zee. But give us an hour."

A moment of silence followed, broken only by the sound

of breathing. Just long enough for Vivian to worry he would change his mind, radio in for help, arrest them both. "Fine. I'll be there."

The shadow, all she could see of him, moved away.

"You gonna live?" she asked Weston.

"I'm fine."

"No, seriously. Are you having chest pain? I don't want to leave an extra body in this coffin."

She jammed the edge of the pick into the space between coffin and lid and leaned all of her weight on it.

"My heart is fine. Give me that." He worked at the lid, one side and then the other. With a creak and splintering of wood it came free.

He tossed aside the pick, blew a puff of air out through pursed lips. "Ready?"

She nodded. "You?"

He shook his head.

"Only bones. They can't hurt you." She was talking to herself more than to him. The horrible manner of Grace's death would be in their favor now. Little flesh left for putrefaction and decay. She hoped the part about only bones was true.

"Feel like I'm in a horror movie, cast as Old Guy, First to Die," Weston muttered. "On count of three?"

"One, two, three—"

They stood side by side, holding their breath, staring at the thing in the coffin. As Vivian had hoped, the remains were skeletal and the smell not overpowering. The bones were blackened, evidence of the severity of the burns.

"Maybe smoke inhalation got her first," she said, seeking some sort of comfort.

"Doesn't matter now," Weston said roughly. "Shine that light in here, will you? Book's gone, but there might be something else."

Reluctantly, she did as he asked, illuminating every corner of the coffin. No hidden compartments, as he seemed to expect. She just wanted to get out of here—fill in the dirt, leave the dead in peace. The whole scenario made her skin creep on her own bones. Weston, on the other hand, was businesslike and curt, directing her to shine the light here or there while he tapped and prodded.

He took the bones of the right hand in his and lifted. Vivian cringed as the connective tissue gave way and they tumbled out of his grip and into the coffin with a dry rattling sound. But when he held up a piece of paper she forgot all about that and tried to decipher the words.

"It makes no sense."

"It's our old code—the one we used to exchange messages so the old man wouldn't know what we were doing."

"What does it say?"

"I'll decipher it at this bookstore of yours. Let's get out of here—gives me the heebie-jeebies poking around the body like this."

Something had changed in his own body language and in his voice, though, and she shook her head. She trusted him, to a point. But there was no telling what the long years of grief might drive him to.

"Tell me now," she said.

He hesitated, his trust also a tenuous thing, and then sighed. "In for a penny, in for a pound, I guess. I'm hoping you don't take it wrong."

Vivian listened, and shivered, wondering how there was a way to take it right.

Twenty-one

Zee woke in the dark, staring up at a sky studded with stars. A soft breeze flowed over his skin, not cold, but caressing, scented with flowers and the smell of fresh leaves. Hope came with it, a fragile emotion at first, tentative, feeling its way into his heart. This story wasn't over yet. It didn't have to end in darkness. Perhaps, by some twist of luck or fate, he could still put things right.

One by one he tested his joints and muscles, gauging the extent of bruises and injuries and finding that he was still functional. If anything, the wounded arm moved a little more freely, his side pained him a little less. He'd been going to do something before he fell asleep. Something important. For a moment he couldn't remember and then it all came back.

Right. Bandage Jared's wounds. Give him water. Keep the bastard alive when he really wanted to kill him.

But a delightful languor kept him where he was, relaxed and drifting between earth and sky. Anticipation of something unknown and wonderful crept over him, and when he heard a rustling of grass he sat up with expectation and without alarm. A woman stood looking down at him, dimly illuminated, as though by an internal glow. She wore only a thin white shift, the outline of breasts and thighs visible through the translucent fabric. Auburn hair curled over shoulders white and unblemished, her eyes were gray and soft with love and desire. So many nights he had dreamed her thus, so many nights she had slipped away from him.

"Vivian," he whispered, disbelieving.

She knelt and laid a finger over his lips. "Shhh. You'll wake him."

He knew, as one knows these things, that she meant Jared. He took her hand, so slender and fragile compared to his, and pressed a kiss into the palm. She made a small sound of pleasure and turned her face so that her cheek rested in his hand.

"Are you a dream?" Zee asked her, turning her face so that her eyes looked directly into his. He ran his hand over her shoulder, the skin like silk beneath his touch. "I'm sorry, about the dragon," he murmured, waiting for her to pull away.

"I was wrong to fault you. You did what needed to be done." Her lips were parted, her breath uneven and tremulous.

He dared then to bury his other hand in the thick fall of her hair. She smelled of cinnamon and spring, and his body roused to her presence with such urgency he could hear his own breath loud in his ears.

"Zee," she murmured, and her voice undid him.

Tilting her chin up to his he kissed her, lightly once, lips barely touching, breath mingling. She gasped, knotted both hands in his hair and pulled him closer. He felt the sense of two things long held asunder returning to a union always meant to be, and then he was lost in sensation worlds away from thought. Her lips pressed hard against his, opening for him to thrust his tongue into the heat of her mouth, her hands on his back stroking his bare skin.

He pulled away for a moment, breathing hard, his brain stumbling over something in the distance that might be important.

"Please," she murmured, her breath warm against his ear. "I've wanted you for so long. You were right that we should be together."

She pulled away from him and lifted the shift over her head so that she was clothed only in the fall of her hair. When she lay down and pulled him down beside her, he did not resist. She took his hands and guided them to her breasts. Her nipples rose and hardened beneath his fingers and she gasped, arching her head back to let him kiss his way down her neck. His lips lingered a moment at the hollow of her throat, moved down to take the erect nipple in his mouth.

Her hand encircled the heat of his erection and then there was no room in his thoughts for anything but the pleasure, so long denied. She pulled him on top of her and lifted her hips toward his with a low moan of desire.

"Please, oh please oh please . . ."

And he thrust at last into the heat of her center as she rose to meet him. The stars swirled around them as they moved together and climaxed with an intensity of pleasure that washed away all memory of pain or worry.

He held her, after, with her head on his shoulder, a treasure beyond price. "Tell me you are not a dream," he murmured into her hair, knowing what would come next. Always in his dreams, she left him. And still, he was unable to fetter the hope that beat in his breast. In all the dreams, through all the years, she had slipped away before he was able to claim her. Maybe this time it would be different.

She only smiled, and kissed him one more time, lingering.

He raised his right hand to her hair, flinching as the torn muscles cramped and burned. And only then did the thought come clear, the thing that had nagged at him before all thought was driven from his brain by pleasure.

Vivian would first have seen to Jared's wounds, and his. No matter what her wants or desires, dreaming or waking, her first instinct was always to heal. Always. Even an asshole like Jared.

With his hand still tangled in the woman's hair, his lips on hers, he froze.

"What is it?" she asked, pulling back to look into his face. Vivian's eyes, Vivian's voice.

He searched her face for anything about her that looked

wrong. It took a moment, before he realized: She looked as he wished Vivian to look, and not as she really was. Gray eyes, not gold, the shoulders free of the mark of the dragon. Guilt flowed over him in a flood of self-loathing.

"You're not Vivian. Who the hell are you?"

Her face—Vivian's face—crumpled, and she bit her lip. "Did I get it wrong? I thought you would be pleased with this shape."

"Only when Vivian is wearing it. Where is she, what have you done with her?"

"We don't need to talk about her right now—this is about you and me and what we can do together." She took a step toward him, and the mix of desire and disgust awakened by a stranger's soul in Vivian's body nearly pushed him beyond control.

"Stay away from me." His fists were knotted, his body thrumming with the familiar energy of violence. *Don't hit a woman, even an evil one.* Especially not in Vivian's body—it could have been hijacked or possessed.

She stopped and stretched out white hands to him. "I need your help, Warrior. I have been looking for you."

"Why would I help you? I don't even know what you are."

"I swear I don't come here as an enemy. The form I wear is one I thought would please you. See—I have brought you a gift." She held out a dagger, the bone hilt toward him, the blade concealed in a leather sheath.

"Thank you, but my sword is weapon enough."

Vivian's lips turned up in a smile, but it wasn't right, a crafty, sly expression that would never cross the face of the woman he knew. "But this is a special knife to be used for dragon slaying. You could kill them all, one at a time. Nights, this body will be yours to love and cherish. Days, you will kill dragons for me. All of your dreams fulfilled. Do you see?"

Zee took a step back, dismayed to find the words a temptation. She offered him a chance to pursue his two conflicting passions. In the real world he would always be torn between his hatred of dragons and his love for Vivian, because she was both things in one. Here was a solution, easy and clean, if he was willing to let go of reality.

But he could not love Vivian's body without her soul filling it. The desperation to find her, to see that she was safe, blazed into a flame of need and desire.

"Where is Vivian? What have you done with her?"

"She's safe enough. For now. Do we have an arrangement?"

"No. God, no! Tell me where she is!"

All of the ways he could kill the creature spun through his head, but on the chance that this was still Vivian's body and her soul was elsewhere, he couldn't harm it. He could do nothing but make empty threats. And he needed to know what he was dealing with. "Show me your true form, and then we will talk."

She hesitated, an expression of what might have been fear filling her gray eyes. "Will you promise not to kill me if I make the change?"

Zee stared at her. Rage filled him, drove him. If this—thing—was not Vivian, had done something to her, harmed her in any way, all he wanted in the world was to wreak vengeance. But Vivian's safety came before vengeance, and he knew nothing about where she was or how to find her. Cautiously, he answered, "I will not seek to harm you unless it is self-defense."

"Do you give your word?"

"I swear it."

"Very well."

A wavering and shifting of muscle and bone and her appearance began to change. The slim white body softened and sagged. The auburn hair turned white and the gray eyes went dark. Her face was hollow with age, her teeth yellow and broken. Around her wattled old neck hung Vivian's pendant.

It was the old woman they had run over with the van.

Zee lunged forward and grabbed for the pendant, but she eluded him, too quick and lithe for a woman of her apparent age.

"Give it to me." He had sworn not to harm her, and that promise was tearing him apart. His breath rasped in his lungs; his entire body trembled with the effort to hold his hand from lopping off her head.

"The pendant belongs to me, as do all things. So tell me—are you with me, Warrior, or will you be so foolish as to stand against me?"

Vivian's voice emerging from the old crone's body made him shudder with revulsion. She stepped forward, close enough to lay an arthritic hand on his arm.

Zee shoved her away from him, harder than he'd meant. The dagger spun out of her hand as she sprawled backward into the grass. She lay as she fell, bony legs spread, naked breasts empty bags hanging down her chest.

His stomach churned with sickness at the thought that his hands had caressed the creature's body, that he had kissed her lips. "Cover yourself, in the name of all things holy." He tossed the shift to her, but she made no move to put it on.

"Have you made up your mind then? No more kisses? I can take on many forms."

His hand clenched so tightly around the hilt of the sword that he could feel it digging into the flesh of his palm.

She moved as if to get up, and he extended the sword toward her. "Don't move."

"You said you would not harm me."

"And I'm trying to keep my word. Lie still and don't test me." She obeyed, the dark eyes not leaving his face as he bent and picked up the dagger. The handle was made of bone, yellow with age and worn smooth with use. Not uncommon, although he found himself hoping the bone was animal and not human. The blade, when he pulled it free of its leather sheath, was a thing of wonder. It was carved from an unfamiliar stone, dark bloodred. No tool marks marred its glasslike surface, and yet it had been honed to an edge so keen it seemed as if just the look of it could cut.

"Give that to me," the old hag hissed, and there was

clearly fear in her eyes now. She scooted backward away from him. "It was only yours on condition."

"Give me Vivian's pendant and I'll think about it."

"You promised." At last she was fumbling at the shift. Not to put it on and cover her naked old body, he realized too late. Digging something out of the pocket, something small and shining that she held up toward the stars.

She vanished. No slow dissolution, no cloud of obscuring smoke. She was there and then she was not.

Zee stared into the darkness until his eyes ached and burned. He thought he saw something large and serpentine, but when he ran after it there was nothing there. Only a trick of the shadows. He tried to tell himself that it had been a dream, but her scent and that of their lovemaking lingered on his skin. When he looked up at the sky, the stars no longer offered comfort. The constellations were subtly wrong. An unfamiliar planet hung low in the sky, pulsing red and ominous.

Zee lifted his arm to hurl the dagger into the pond, but at the last minute he held back. A good throwing knife was invaluable. And the old woman had clearly feared it. He would use it to survive now—for hunting and protection, and when he found her, as he would do, then his promise would no longer be binding and he would kill her with her own blade. The thought gave him pleasure, though it did nothing to assuage his guilt.

A low moan of pain drew him back to the moment and his responsibilities. He pulled on his cotton breeches and the T-shirt, slightly dew-damp and full of holes but clean at least, shoving the knife into a pocket for safekeeping.

Jared was worse. Heat radiated off skin dry and so hot to the touch it seemed one tiny spark would send him up in flames. When Zee called his name, his eyes flickered open but there was no recognition in their depths.

Zee knew he had been a fool. But he had wanted so much to believe, had made it so easy. And since Vivian wasn't here, it fell to him to do what she would have done, which meant trying to keep Jared alive even if he couldn't heal him. Holding his breath against the ungodly stench of the wound, he grasped his enemy under the armpits and dragged him into the pool, hoping it might cool the fever.

Twenty-two

"What do you mean, the book is missing?" Weston demanded.

Deputy Flynne rubbed a hand over his jaw and then back over his head. "It was locked up in evidence. I have no idea how somebody could have got to it."

Vivian felt like an emotional pressure cooker about to explode. Enough already. The locket, the spheres, the Key, and now some book that held valuable information. All stolen. She was tired of being considerate, tired of trying to think the best of people. And the evidence pointed clearly in one direction.

"Grace took it."

Both men stared at her. It was Brett who finally answered. "Grace? As in Jennings, deceased, whose body you just dug up?"

"Grace, as in Jennings, who was not the body in the coffin."

"I thought we weren't going to tell him—"

"You're saying there's an unidentified body in the coffin? That's not possible." Brett's face belied his words, and he ran both hands over his head as though it ached.

"You don't know what you're saying." At any other time, Weston's face might have frightened her. The only evidence she had that he hadn't murdered his family in cold blood was his own word on the subject, and at the moment he looked sufficiently like a wild man of the mountains to be well outside the law.

"She had access to your father's dreamspheres, and plenty of time to study sorcery. She left you a secret message to let you know that she was using the dreamspheres."

"Goddamn it, Vivian, Grace is not a sorceress. They're born, not made." But there was doubt in his voice, and Brett jumped in.

"The woman was burned up in a house fire. I saw the body."

Vivian fixed him with her full attention, not missing the way he took a step back under the pressure of her gaze. "How could you have seen the body? How old were you?"

"I had a habit of sticking my nose in where it didn't belong. The fire was an obvious point of fascination, and I was seventeen and already obsessed with crime. Fire trucks, cops . . ."

"And the scene wasn't off limits?"

"Please. This is Krebston. I shoved in with an offer to help. They knew me, were happy for an extra pair of hands. I saw her body—"

"It wasn't hers."

Brett sighed. "Oh come on, Vivian—if it wasn't her, then who was it? No missing people in Krebston."

"Could have been from anywhere. She has access to dreamspheres, do you hear me?" The rage was fire in her veins now, heating her body from the inside out.

"But when did she get them?" Weston sagged into a chair. His face looked old and haggard. There were smudges of dirt on forehead and cheeks, flakes of it in his beard.

"From your father's coffin. She was found with the body before he was buried. From what you told me, I doubt she was grieving."

The old man shook his head, but Vivian pressed on. "Her behavior that night made people so uneasy they sent her off to an orphanage."

"I should have gone back for her."

Brett looked from one to the other. "You guys seriously expect me to believe your friend here is what—a hundred years old?"

"A hundred and three."

"Right. Well, you'll understand if I have a problem with that."

The room had shifted into sharper detail. Vivian could see into all of the shadowed corners, could smell Brett's fear and Weston's grief.

"Read him the note we found in the coffin," she said. She wasn't asking, and after a brief hesitation Weston complied.

"'I tried to wait for you, but then the cancer came and I had to go. I took one of the dreamspheres—hope you didn't need it. There are giants in it, so we'll see how that goes. As for the body, I didn't kill anyone so don't fret. Come find me.'"

"Perfect," Brett said. "Thank you so much for sharing. What am I supposed to do with that? We can't take her word for anything—now I have to try to place this body."

"I wouldn't," Vivian said, closing her eyes. "You have no idea where that body has been."

"Might not even be human," Weston added.

His voice sounded distant, the words close to meaningless.

It could be so simple, really. Allow the dragon fire to spread and grow, to bathe her cells in transforming heat. Give permission for the shift that was always there, always waiting. There was more to being dragon than scales and wings. There was power and a trick with doors. As dragon, maybe she could get through the doors and into the Between. Once there, she could track down Grace and take back the Key by force. That, and her pendant.

Simple.

And dangerous.

Mellisande, the dragon corrupted by Jehenna, had killed how many humans over the years? Even the young dragon, the one Zee had slain, had killed. Dragons were glorious, beautiful engines of destruction. Just considering the possibility, predatory thoughts flickered through her mind. A thirst for blood sent saliva flooding over her tongue.

Maybe she could exert control where the others had not, maybe the rest of who she was, Dreamshifter and sorceress, would make a difference.

But there was one more thing.

Zee. The look of hate that came onto his face when the word dragon *was spoken. She remembered the paintings upstairs, lined up side by side. If she shifted again, she would lose him forever, if she hadn't already.*

But if she didn't find a way to rescue him, he was also lost. And the dragon self was powerful beyond expectation.

"Vivian!"

The voices calling her name were distant but insistent. Her tongue felt thick, her skin tight. Inside something laughed. While she'd been debating the point her blood had escaped her control, had begun to make the change without her will and consent.

Freedom. A chance to shed the responsibility she'd been carrying since she was a small child parenting an unstable mother. Wings and a wide sky. Maybe she could be dragon, not for any noble purpose, but just to be, to fly. Voices whispered. Still she could not hear them clearly, not with the doors closed, but that too was a freedom. She could be power. Nothing and everything.

There was human flesh in the room, exuding the scent of fear. She could smell their blood, hear the beating of their hearts and the flurry of their breath. They backed away, slowly, edging for the door. As if they could escape her. What were they, other than prey—

No. They were men, with souls and with names. Brett Flynne. Weston Jennings. Human beings, with all the nerve endings and emotions, the burden of life and the fear of death. And what was she, that she should have the right to hunt them, to hunt anybody? With an extreme effort she focused on the kernel at her center that remained Vivian, clinging to all of the details that defined this collection of nerves and cells and made her like and unlike all of the other humans in the wide world.

Vivian drew a deep breath, and then another, feeling the coolness of the air, the small frailty of her bones.

"What's with you guys?" she managed to say, clasping her hands together, surprised by the fine movements of fingers, the smoothness of skin on skin.

Brett stayed where he was, backed up against the door, his face shadowed with horror and disbelief.

"You might want to just forget what you saw here tonight," Weston said, casual. "Or remember it as a dream. That would ease things for you."

Brett looked down at Poe, who had decided to be friendly and stood pressed up against his leg. He shifted his gaze to Vivian and opened his mouth to speak. Then, with a jerk of his shoulders and a shake of the head, he turned and walked out the door.

"He'll forget," Weston said. "Men do. What the mind can't encompass turns to dream, or this weird bit of daydream, or even hallucination. You know all this."

"I know." But she sank into a chair and sat without moving, looking at her feet side by side on the floor. One was a shade ahead of the other and she aligned them, toe and heel, as if it mattered deeply to the state of the world. Out of her peripheral vision she was aware of Weston plopping down in a chair across from her.

"Do you want to talk about it?"

"What is there to say?" A weariness had come over her, and a deep and abiding sadness. She felt stripped to the bone.

"How bad was it?"

"You didn't change, not all the way. Your eyes started to glow, the scales popped out on your skin, there was steam on your breath. Pretty impressive. Thought Flynne was going to have a heart attack."

"I noticed you didn't look comfortable yourself."

"Are you losing control?"

Letting her head fall into her hands she whispered, "I don't know."

"How long have you been dealing with the shifting?"

"Only a couple of weeks. It started soon after I found out I was a Dreamshifter, as if that weren't enough."

"Tough stuff," he said. There was no irony in his voice, or pity. Just a quiet understanding. It made her feel better.

"I don't think we have a lot of time," she said. "I might be able to open the door as dragon, just so you know. I was thinking maybe I should, but I am worried about losing control, about hurting somebody."

"Well, might just be a thing or two we could try before that."

"You'll help?"

"Penance. If Grace is a monster, I'm the one that made her into one. Only way I know to make amends."

"Seems like maybe your father carries some blame for that."

He shrugged. "I stood by while he killed everybody. My little sister had to shoot him to make it stop. What do you think that did to her? I could have saved her that, at least."

Vivian had no words for that. A moment of silence, and then she flung her arms around his neck and hugged him. His body was stiff beneath the embrace, long enough for her to feel awkward and begin to pull away before one of his arms came up and patted her back. "Don't expect too much, mind. I don't know what I'm doing."

"That makes two of us. Where do we start?"

"A door. I've had little practice with calling them up, but I can find one." His face creased into what was meant to be a smile, but it didn't reach his eyes.

"You're taking me to your usual spot. Where you lost your people."

"I didn't lose them. I know exactly where they are. I also know exactly where the door is. And if that doesn't work, I have plan B."

"What's plan B?"

But he only shook his head and would not say.

Twenty-three

*D*eath, Zee thought, but did not say. *Decay, despair, the end of all things.*

The way ahead slanted sharply downward between walls of tangled thorns, thick as his arm, covered in spikes. A dank wind blew up into his face, carrying a fetid scent of refuse and rot. No trees ahead, no grass, not even dirt. The path turned to bare, harsh rock, riddled with gaping cracks and jagged stones.

Going forward was walking voluntarily into hell. Going back would be nearly impossible. Staying still was not an option.

He'd chosen a path that started off innocently enough, a grassy track between trees, sun dappled and almost airy. He had even scouted a little way along it and chosen it from all other possible options as the easiest way to travel with a wounded man.

There was also a small something inside him, a breath of dream memory that whispered, "Surmise is this way." Maybe he had even been here before, in the alternate existence of the Warlord of Surmise. If he trusted his instincts, there was a hope of help and shelter by dark.

Once the way was chosen, it had taken a couple of hours to plan and build a conveyance that would save him from carrying Jared. A couple of sturdy branches, the blanket, some strips of leather cut from the pack to use as binding, and he'd lashed together a makeshift stretcher. The earth supported much of the wounded man's weight, with Zee acting as packhorse between two staves, dragging his burden behind him rather than slung over his shoulder.

He filled the canteen with water, making sure that he and Jared both had a good long drink before leaving the clearing. Breakfast consisted of the last of the protein bars, wet from the dunking in the pool and falling apart, but still edible.

It wasn't enough, though. Not nearly enough, and hunger sat tight and hard in his belly.

Jared seemed marginally better. He'd eaten a little, and drunk plenty of water. A long soak in the pool had brought his fever down and cleansed the wound. The blisters on his body seemed to be healing. Zee used up precious cleaning solution from the first-aid kit to clean and bandage them. He'd needed the blanket for the stretcher and ended up cutting his own flannel shirt into bandages to wrap around the leg.

With one thing and the other, it had been noon before they got under way, but they made good time at first, the conveyance sliding smoothly along a path that was mostly grass. Twice Zee had stopped to clear away scrub bushes, and once to move a fallen log, but at first he'd felt somewhat hopeful.

The change happened gradually. A thickening of the trees, so that the sun no longer filtered through. Underbrush closing in on the path, which became increasingly steeper and more narrow. Always in the Between there had been crossroads and branching paths everywhere, so many that it was hard to chart a course. Now there were none. No options but to keep going, or retrace his steps.

He felt Jared stir, the movement traveling through the wooden poles and into his hands. "You can't be seriously considering going down there."

Zee didn't answer. Hours of walking, dragging the stretcher behind him, had left his muscles rubbery and trembling. His hunger was a constant pain now; the canteen was nearly empty. The sun would vanish over the tops of the trees soon, and it would be dark. They needed food, shelter, water.

The thought of retracing his steps felt like despair.

It would be all uphill, some of it gradual, some of it steep. And to what goal? If they went back, it would be to discount this one hope he had—that his dream memories rang true, that Surmise was to be somehow reached at the end of this dark road. And if all hope was gone, then there was nothing left but to lie down and die, a thing he had no intention of doing.

"Hang on," he said, picking up the crossbars of the stretcher. "Gonna be a rough ride."

Rough and dark. As he descended farther down the path, the sun was lost to view. Occasional rays of light filtered through the thick wall of thorns, just enough to let him see how treacherous was the way ahead. Every footstep was a tentative act of faith that there would be solid ground to hold him, that he wouldn't go tumbling away into some deep chasm. He worked his way across cracks and fissures and around obstructing rocks, manhandling the stretcher behind him. Jared cursed and muttered at every jolt.

Zee's arms ached with the weight of his burden. Thirst burned in his throat, dried by a cold wind that blew constantly against him, searching through skin and flesh and probing his bones. His face hurt and his teeth ached and he choked on the stench of bitter emptiness. It brought to his mind all of his darkest days—the first time he had looked into his mother's eyes and seen the unlove and indifference, not quite recognizing it for what it was but feeling it through every cell of his four-year-old body. The first time he was arrested and dragged off to juvie after beating another kid senseless. Sitting in a cement cell behind bars and knowing he had lost control of his life and the ability to come and go with freedom. The moment in Surmise where the whole world had disintegrated around him as he hung by one arm from a fracturing doorway, whispering Vivian's name. The other memory, the darkest one, of Vivian's body morphing into that of an old hag, was too fresh and he pushed it back with all of his will.

"Death would have been more merciful than dragging me into hell," Jared muttered. "You should have killed me."

"Don't tempt me."

He stopped to rest, sinking down to the ground. The stone beneath his palms felt hot, as though the earth itself were stricken with fever. He needed a drink, but the water was almost gone. He heard a rustling from the stretcher, a dry cough.

"We're going to die here," Jared moaned. "You should have left me in the clearing; at least there was water."

Zee's fingers tightened around the sword hilt. It would feel so good to slip the tip of the blade between Jared's ribs. Give the man what he asked for. Straight into the heart. Blissful silence would follow. Call it a mercy killing and be done.

When he was a kid, the neighbor's dog had killed a chicken once.

"You need to kill that dog," Zee's father said. "Now he's got the taste, he'll never stop."

The old farmer disagreed. "There's better cures than that." He'd tied that dead chicken around the dog's neck. Left it there until it was so rotten it was falling apart. The dog understood the punishment and the shame. He crept around, belly low to the ground, meeting nobody's eyes, carrying his odious burden.

Apparently, Jared was Zee's chicken, and he hadn't learned his lesson yet. Dragging himself back up onto his feet, he handed the canteen to the sick man. "Here. Drink."

Trying to swallow past the desert in his own throat, he listened to the sound of precious water being swallowed and waited for the inevitable comment.

"It's empty."

"Astute observation. Buckle your seat belt."

"You're insane. We can't go down there. Can't you smell the evil?"

Zee could. Or he smelled something, at any rate. The

stench of decay grew stronger the farther they went. And with the increasing stink the darkness increased as well. No more patches of light. The stretcher jolted and tipped and caught on stones.

Jared cursed and moaned by turns.

At last they were no longer descending but on a level. The path widened and smoothed. Dim light filtered in from above, enough to see that they walked on a wide road, with high stone walls on either side. It was much easier going, but the sense of danger and death increased and the smell became so bad that Zee pulled his T-shirt up over his nose and mouth to provide a filter. He heard Jared begin to retch and couldn't help thinking of the waste of good water.

Something blocked the path ahead.

At first he took it for stone, but then it began to take shape. A long, sinuous neck. A broken wing. Ridged back and spiked tail. His hand tightened reflexively on the sword, but the creature was long dead, the curve of ribs visible through decaying flesh, and there was no longer any question about where the smell was coming from.

"Is that what I think it is?"

"Just be thankful it's dead."

Zee wasn't really thankful, though. He wanted to kill it all over again. For the first time he asked himself why he felt such hate toward the dragons. Maybe because his other self had suffered much on their account in Surmise. But he didn't think that was all of it. This went deeper, a primal antipathy of warring races. The impossible tale the old hermit had told nagged at him. Why couldn't it be true, considering all of the other impossible things he had come to accept?

It didn't really matter. The dragon was dead. And the path he needed to take lay over its inconvenient and very smelly body.

"Tell me we're going back," Jared said.

Zee laughed, a sudden and inexplicable burst of adrenaline flooding through him at the insanity of this entire situation. "Hang on tight," he said.

Gathering his strength, he took a few running steps to

gather momentum. His feet slid in a litter of scales and he lost traction for a minute, but he kept moving. Tightening his grip on the stretcher poles, he leaped up onto the neck and let his weight carry him down the other side, pulling Jared's weight up and over behind him.

Instead of continuing on down a clear path, he was forced to skid to a halt. A skeleton lay directly in his path. It was human in shape and composition but nearly double his own size, in both height and breadth. Scraps of flesh still clung to the bones.

No human could be that big. Some sort of giant monkey, maybe. The skeleton would look pretty much the same to his untrained eyes. But then, here in the Between it could be anything. A dream door stood in the stone wall a few paces away, tall enough to admit a creature as big as the one lying dead beside the dragon.

His first thought was that dragon and man-thing had killed each other in combat, but this theory didn't sit right. The skeleton showed no evidence of fire and was intact. No dragonish eating of heads or limbs or other body parts. There was no indication of any struggle. The straggling plant life was untrampled. No scorch marks. Nothing but a lot of bloodstains. Some of it was the thick black sludge he recognized as dragon blood; the rest looked human.

The idea of something roaming around that could kill both a giant man-thing and a dragon without a struggle was enough to push Zee forward into a slow jog. His immediate goal was to put as much distance between himself and this place as possible. He didn't trust that dream door to stay closed, wasn't at all sure he wasn't being tracked by the black dragon he'd encountered at the well.

Two paths branched out, at last, from the one he was on. Briefly, he paused. They looked identical, leading into old-growth forest. He chose the one on the right for no other reason than a vague familiarity coupled with the sensation that he was prey, and that the predator was never far behind. Run he must, and his gut told him this was the path most likely to help him survive.

Twenty-four

Vivian sat on a fallen log by the campfire Weston had built, toasting her front while her back turned to goose bumps with the cold. Poe stood across from her, his white patches glowing reddish in the flickering flames, the crimson mark where a sword had once pierced his breast seeming to move and change into different shapes. No stars tonight— the sky was opaque blackness. Weston had been muttering about the need for rain, the forest so dry that they shouldn't really be making a fire at all, but she prayed to all the powers that be to leave well enough alone. Bad enough to sleep on the cold hard ground without rain to make matters worse. Maybe that made her a wimp, but she was bone weary and not inclined to further misery.

Weston's tried-and-true door had not worked. Vivian couldn't even see the damned thing, although she sensed it clearly enough. A small buzz of energy when she was near it gave her its essential size and position. But she couldn't open it. And when Weston opened it, or said he did, he simply vanished from her view and she was unable to follow him.

A long time she stood, eyes closed, hands moving over the current of energy that eluded her, searching for a way through. It felt like trying to shift the course of a river, and she gave it up at last as a lost cause.

"Maybe if I shift," she'd said, staring at the bushes and rock that she knew marked a door into Dreamworld. But she felt cold and empty, the dragon fire far away, and she couldn't seem to remember why shifting had seemed to her a tenable idea in the first place.

Weston pulled supplies out of his backpack and set up a rough camp. He got a small fire going, explaining that he didn't dare make it any bigger because of the need for rain. He dragged over a length of fallen log for her to sit on.

She watched the fire rise and fall, the flames making ever-shifting picture patterns as they consumed their fuel, dying away in one place to arise in another. Poe pressed up against her and she laid one hand on his head. She startled some time later to find Weston standing at her side bearing a tin cup full of something steaming hot. Expecting coffee or maybe tea, she accepted it thankfully, but when she raised it to her nose to inhale the fragrance she sputtered and almost flung the cup away. A greenish wave washed over the side and burned her fingers.

"What the hell is this?"

"Plan B."

"Poison?"

"No, peyote."

"What?"

"Peyote. You know, the sacred medicine that allows you to see into the otherworld."

"You mean the hallucinogenic drug that makes you crazy." She tried to hand the mug back to him. "I'm not drinking this shit. Where did you get it, anyway?"

He shrugged. "You ask a lot of questions for a woman out of options."

"You drink it."

Weston laughed. "Yeah. I get high, see some pretty colors, and that's about it. But some people—not even Dreamshifters—have been known to have real dream quests on peyote."

"You're actually serious."

"I am. Don't give me that law-abiding holier-than-thou

look. The natives were doing this stuff years before you were born, all as part of spiritual journeys. Their version of dream walking."

"It's still a drug. A hallucinogen. People get stuck and can't find their way back to reality."

"For real? You're telling me you killed a sorceress in the Between and now you're afraid of a little peyote?"

She sniffed at the tea again, skeptical. "How do I know I can trust you?"

"Do you have a choice?"

"What if—I drink your peyote tea, and then I turn into a dragon while I'm high? What then?"

"Well, that would be quite a trip, I'd think. One for the books." His face was tight, belying the lightness of his tone. "Look, there's a ceremony that is supposed to go with this. I don't know the whole thing, but I can try. Maybe it will help."

He pulled his cooking pot out of the backpack, turned it upside down in front of him, and started beating out a rhythm with his hands. His voice rose in an odd, wavering chant that ran a shiver down the center of her spine.

"Where did you learn that?"

He paused in the chanting, but his hands kept the rhythm. In the firelight his face had taken on a remote, mysterious look. "I have a friend who brought me in to the ceremonies. I always sat in the corner and listened, which is why this won't be quite right. Well, that and the fact that I'm playing a pan instead of a ceremonial drum. Play big or go home, right?"

Vivian looked into the cup and back at him, believing despite herself. If there were Dreamshifters, why shouldn't there be shamans, and who was to say what mysteries existed in the spirit world?

"But if it matters—if you get it wrong. I mean, couldn't the spirits or whatever take offense? They might not take kindly to us messing around."

"If your heart is pure and your intentions clean—"

"But what if it's not?" A few minutes ago she'd felt beyond

emotion, even fear. Now something very close to panic set her heart to fluttering. Pure? She hadn't been to church in years, and she didn't think *pure* was an adjective that would have ever fit. An image of Jared came to mind again, his hands on her unwilling body. *Not your fault,* she told herself reflexively. But no amount of logic served to wash away the lingering shame and loathing that was always waiting, just below the surface.

"Either it works or it doesn't. If not, I figure we're shit out of luck. Take a few deep breaths, clear your thoughts, and drink the damned tea."

He went back to chanting, his voice rising high and quavering into the night. She'd heard native chants and knew he didn't make the mark, although his efforts definitely qualified as eerie. The shadows seemed to thicken and coalesce around the fire, as if other presences were moving in, crowding her a little. Poe puffed up his feathers. Somewhere in a tree branch close by the raven croaked, softly. It sounded like encouragement.

Vivian took a sip and gagged.

The brew was bitter and a little slimy; not a beverage made for pleasure. Maybe if she thought of it as medicine she'd do better. Holding her breath she drained the entire mug in several long gulps, shuddered, and waited. Too late to back out now. For a time nothing happened. Weston continued to beat his makeshift drum and sing.

And then the nausea struck. Her stomach cramped and convulsed. No time to move away from the fire before her body rejected the tea with a vengeance. "You poisoned me," she muttered, as soon as she could speak, but Weston didn't hear her. Pushing her hair back behind her ears with shaking hands, feeling limp and fragile, she resumed her seat beside the fire, watching the flames expand and contract to the rhythm of the drum.

Mesmerized, she breathed in the melody of smoke and pine, the scent of warm orange flame filling her ears. The shadows stretched and turned inside out, transitioning into color while the flames went dark.

Her brain insisted that this was all wrong. The fire was orange and hot, it flickered, it made the shadows by casting light. In response to the logical thought, the music lurched, the shadows bent and twisted, and nausea squeezed her stomach again. A deep breath, and she let the logic go, let the music and the fire and the color do whatever it was they wanted to do.

"It's beautiful," she murmured, lifting a hand to pluck at a strand of yellow light. It quivered beneath her hand, making a sound that smelled of lemon and sunlight. With both hands she played with the symphony of light and sound and fragrance, lost in a purity of sensual pleasure she could never have imagined.

A voice scattered the music, sending the color dancing away and out of reach. At a little distance from the fire a door appeared, hanging in midair. It was not like any door she had ever seen before—it glowed with translucent color. If stained glass were alive, it might look this way with a light behind it. Getting up from her place by the fire she paced toward it, solemnly and in rhythm with the steady beat that permeated the air. As she drew closer, she slipped off her shoes. Her feet sank into a maelstrom of light, currents of color that swirled and eddied with every step.

Holy ground.

In front of the door she paused, awestruck. She could see the atoms moving, electrons circling and shifting, changing allegiance from one partner to another. The dance expanded—planets circling stars, constellations revolving around constellations, one universe flowing into another. Cosmic wind blew against her, pushing her back and away, even as she stretched her hands out trying to touch the wonder. Farther and farther she blew, growing ever smaller until the door was the size of the universe and she was the size of an atom, tiny, flung adrift in the winds of empty space.

At first she thought she heard her own voice sobbing with loss, but light flickered around her, thousands of tiny fireflies, and as the light grew brighter she could see that each light was a human soul surrounded by multihued auras, their weeping creating a great choral flare of a dull greenish black, like a bruise on the surface of the universe.

Above, in a velvet-black sky, one bright spot shaped like a keyhole glowed with promise.

Vivian sprouted wings and flew toward it. There was a squeeze, and then she was through and flying over a land where the rivers were made of molten gold and precious stones the size of boulders were as common as granite.

Dragons everywhere—sleeping in the sunlight, swimming in the golden river, flying free and wild. And then they turned on each other and began to fight and kill. Fire swept across fields and forests and a great smoke rose up into the sky. Dragon blood, black and corrosive, fouled the golden river.

From out of the earth a thick black substance rose up like smoke, drifting and coiling above the scarred earth. It frightened her more than the clash of the dragons, although she couldn't say why.

A dark cloud boiled up out of the hills, growing bigger and bigger until it filled the sky like a wall. Lightning bolts shot through it; thunder rumbled and crashed. As a mighty wind came up that drove her back through the keyhole, helpless as an autumn leaf, she heard a baby crying, a lost, abandoned sound. She struggled against the wind to get to the child, but it was too strong, tearing at her body, dashing her about without mercy. Still, she could hear the wailing of the child, and she too was crying with helplessness and loss.

The darkness gathered and coalesced, took on shape and substance. Wings. A long body, a graceful serpentine neck, a horned head with eyes that shone like molten gold. Wherever the black dragon went, darkness went with her and she left a trail of darkness behind her. Stars were blotted out of the sky. Grass and flower and stone were sucked up into her shadow.

Let there be nothing, a voice said, and it was so.

After that it was a long time before Vivian came to herself. It took her a moment to remember the name of the man sitting across from her, silent and watchful, to remember the word for the thing around her shoulders—*blanket*—and the warm glowing light in front of her—*fire*. Despite both fire and blanket she shivered, her teeth chattering, and Weston walked over and pressed a tin cup into her hands.

She shook her head, *no, no more*, but when he pressed it to her lips it was not bitter but hot and sweet. Her hands shook too much to hold the cup. Even with his help it chattered against her teeth and hot liquid dribbled and slopped down the front of her, but Weston was persistent and for every mouthful that she swallowed she felt a little better.

"Now you will sleep," he said. Words sounded strange spoken aloud, twining with the smoke and the flame and drifting up into the night sky. She obeyed his guiding hands, though, climbing into a sleeping bag laid out for her by the fire. A gentle hand touched her hair, then brushed her eyes closed and she slid into a deep dark slumber.

Twenty-five

Surmise. Zee's instincts had been right, after all. Not far past the place where the dragon and the giant had died, he'd found an open door that led right into the grassy field in front of the castle. Prince Landon had come out to personally greet the new arrivals, and within moments Jared was whisked off to the healers. Landon had tried to get Zee to go too, but he had refused.

"No time," he'd said. "Vivian's in danger. I need your help."

He'd been conducted to the private garden where he now sat beside a fountain on the stone bench that had once been stained by the Chancellor's blood. No penguin lying dead now in the grass, no Vivian bruised and frightened, but these images lodged in his memory like stones in a shoe.

He was safe here, for the moment, but this did nothing to ease his sense of urgency and impending disaster. Safety meant nothing as long as Vivian was in danger.

He was hoping that Landon and Isobel could help him think of what to do next.

"Vivian will be a little lost without the pendant, I'd think," Isobel said, one slender hand dabbling in the clear water of the pool where the fountain endlessly played. She wore a white dress and her hair fell loose over her shoulders.

It made her look young, Vivian's sister more than her mother, and not possibly a woman of over a hundred years.

Zee watched her hand dip in and out of the water, the forearm marked by a network of thin white scars. The fountain and the garden around it was a Dreamworld of its own, somehow sewn onto the fabric of Surmise. Time did not exist here; as long as Isobel and Landon stayed in this small space they would not grow old, no matter how many years passed in the world outside.

A sense of unreality set his teeth on edge. His journey through the maze of the Between, dragging Jared behind him on a makeshift wooden stretcher, seemed a story from a distant past; perhaps something that had happened to another man. The sense of the surreal felt too much like enchantment, made him want to leap to his feet and run.

Which would accomplish absolutely nothing, of course, and so he held himself together and sat, his mind hammering his body into submission.

"What benefit would someone find in stealing the pendant?" Landon asked. The Prince had changed since Zee and Vivian walked out of Surmise, hand in hand, only a few short weeks ago. His shoulders were square, no longer rounded in defeat. His face held a restless energy, the eyes quick with intelligence. Already he had men out mapping the roads of the Between that led directly into the kingdom so he could better understand the risks and resources that were out there.

Isobel's hands fluttered, then stilled. "That depends. It would give the carrier some power over Vivian, perhaps."

"The old woman who stole it was crafty and stronger than she looked—overpowered Vivian and then opened a door and vanished." Shame kept him from telling them about his encounters with either the dragon or the temptress, although he knew he should.

"Sorceress," Landon guessed.

"A plague of sorcerers, a pestilence of usurpers, a contagion of evil. There must be no communion between them and the Dreamshifters, lest evil befall," Isobel chanted, in a voice that did not sound solely her own. A silence hung in the air, punctuated by the continual flow of falling water from the fountain. Isobel traced a line of scars with a finger still dripping from the pool.

"But what does that mean? You must know something that can help me find her."

Isobel's smile was sadder than tears would have been. "And you must understand, Zee, that anything my father said to me was long, long ago and that . . ." She paused. "Did Vivian tell you? About what happened to my mind?"

Landon trapped her restless hand in both of his, raised it to his lips.

"So much is lost," she said, with a sigh. "It comes to me, like this, in phrases remembered but not understood."

"Forgive me, if this is painful," Zee said. "But your mother was Jehenna?"

"Yes, and my father, as you know, was a Dreamshifter. And much evil did befall."

"He and your mother are both dead—"

"But the Key is in play," Isobel said. She rubbed her forehead like a fretful child, her brow furrowed in concentration. "It's a very powerful object. Jehenna thought it would open the Gates for her, but it did not. There are prophecies of doom and destruction connected to the finding of the Key."

"Jehenna said she wouldn't need the dragon blood anymore," Landon said. "That she would live forever. And then, in the end, she came running back saying it was the wrong key."

"Somebody believes otherwise. Somebody with enough power that she can't be new to the game."

"Hanging out in the background then," Landon said, "smart enough to bide her time, wait her chance."

Powerful enough to venture into Wakeworld and transform herself into an old hag. Crafty enough to borrow Vivian's shape, to know how to tempt Zee with his own desires. "But the question remains—what is the Key for? What does it open? If I know this, maybe I can find this sorceress and stop her before she acts."

"It was made by the giants, it is said. Back in the mists of time."

"Why?"

"To lock the doors and preserve the balance. There was a falling-out between the dragons and the first Dreamshifter, Allel. Their war threatened to destroy all of the Dreamworlds and the Wakeworld. In that time the giants alone had discovered the way to leave their world and walk in the Between; they had deep secret knowledge and took it upon themselves to correct the balance. The Gates were locked with a spell so that even the Key cannot open it until wielded by the hands of one in whom dragon, Dreamshifter, and sorcerer are joined together."

"But if that's true—then whoever this is who stole the Key won't be able to open the Gates . . ."

"Unless she's figured something out. Like the pendant. Could she have come by skin and hair and maybe even blood?"

Zee went cold, remembering the marks of the chain around Vivian's neck. The scratches on the backs of her hands. He nodded. "She could have all of these things."

"Well then—if she knows magic, she could work any number of spells." Isobel pressed the back of her hand to her lips, and Landon put a hand on her shoulder.

"She'll be all right, my love. She is strong."

"I saw a giant on the way here," Zee said. "Dead. Alongside the body of a dragon. Are they at war?"

Isobel and Landon exchanged glances, before the Prince answered, slowly, "The envoys. I'd wondered."

"What envoys?" Zee demanded.

"We sent messages to the giants and to the dragons, seeking a meeting to discuss the best interests of all. There was no response."

Isobel's brow puckered, and again she rubbed the scars on her forearm as though something itched. "And yet, although there was no response to our overture, the giants have been drawn to Surmise in greater numbers within the last few weeks."

"They are healers," Landon said, but there was uncertainty in his voice. "They offer no threats of violence."

"It is the timing I don't like. So many of them coming here, where the Key was found. If they know—then the company of the sorcieri will also know."

"With all due respect, this is all riddles and guessery and not much help." Zee's voice was sharper than he'd meant. Fear was an unaccustomed feeling, one that made him itch for an opponent he could fight. Give him a dragon or even a giant and he could accomplish something. This business of sitting around with insufficient information and trying to guess what was going on made him want to break things.

Landon gave him a look of sympathy, and Zee remembered that this man had stood by, helpless, for a hundred years while his love was caught in a morass of madness, far beyond his reach to help her. "Neither of us has the power to open or close the dream doors. We can't help you find Vivian or get back to Wakeworld."

"I may be able to help you find the lost Gates," Isobel said, "although I don't know what you will do should you get there." Eyes still closed, her movements detached as if someone else were in control of her body, she pulled a small dagger from her pocket and freed it of its sheath. Both men, conscious of the marks of scars on her arms, held their breath, waiting to see what she would do. Sinking down on her knees, she carved a line into the turf. This she intersected with another line, and then another. Zee watched, marveling, as her delicate hands cut away the grass to form an intricate maze, a complex tangle that twisted and turned in on itself.

At last she traced a path from one side to the other with the tip of the dagger, murmuring, in a voice so low Zee bent down to hear, "Let the one who seeks the Forever take care to walk true and not stray, for one misstep may lead to torment and dreams beyond the reach of death. Here is Surmise. Here lies the Cave of Dreams." Tracing another path, she stabbed the dagger into the earth and left it there. "And here are the Black Gates, that bar the way into the Forever."

Her eyes opened and she blinked three times, looked

down at the image she had made, and then up at the men. "What is it?" she asked, her voice edged with fear. "What have I done?"

Landon held out his hands to her and helped her rise, drawing her close and holding her against him, smoothing her hair as though she were a frightened child. "You've drawn a map. Did you not know?"

She shook her head, her face buried against his chest. "I don't remember. I'm scared, Landon. There was something—" She shivered, and he drew her closer.

"A glass of wine for you," he said, "and then a chance to rest." His eyes over the top of her head dared Zee to say a word.

But Isobel pulled away a little at that, and smiled for them both, though her face was deathly pale. "I am well, my love; the madness will not come to me again." She bent and looked at her handiwork. "It makes me dizzy. Are you able to read it?"

Zee nodded. "You explained it. I think so. If the two of you don't mind, I'll stay here a little."

"Take as much time as you need," Landon said. "There will be a hot meal and a bath for you in your room whenever you are ready. And the healers will do what they can for your hurts."

Isobel uttered a small cry of distress at that. "We should have tended to that already. Forgive us, Zee, we were worried about Vivian . . ."

"As am I. This was the greatest of my needs, and I thank you." He tried to smile, but the hurts that most needed tending lay beyond the skill of any healer, and his heart was a weight in his chest.

Out of respect, he waited until they were out of sight. Then he knelt on the cool grass and retraced the paths of the maze with a finger, over and over again, engraving the map on both his brain and his heart.

When he could trace it blind, eyes closed, without hesitation, he stretched out the muscles cramped from bending over the earth and retraced his steps to the castle.

His was not a large chamber, nothing too fancy, and he was grateful for this. Several windows let in what remained of the daylight. A warm fire crackled on the grate, with a comfortable chair pulled up next to it. The bed had been opened for him, a puffy goose down coverlet, soft pillows. Through a half-open door he saw a bathtub and thought with longing of his aching body immersed in hot water.

Crossing to the table where a cold repast had been laid out, he drained the goblet of wine and poured another from the stone decanter. Moving swiftly, then, before temptation had time to work on him, before the healers came and insisted on treating his wounds, he made his preparations.

The feather coverlet on the bed was too bulky for his needs, but he removed the warmly woven blanket underneath it, folded it, and put it into the backpack. Then he knotted the bread and cheese and cold meats that had been set out for him into a clean pillowcase and added that as well. He filled the canteen with cold water.

One more quick look around, and then he let himself out of the room, closing the door behind him. Careful not to make eye contact with anybody he passed, hoping not to be recognized, he worked his way downward through the winding corridors. After a few wrong turns, he found his way at last out of the castle and across the field to the path that had led him from the mazes of the Between into Surmise.

A strange anomaly, Surmise, woven into the fabric of both Dreamworld and the Between by the dark sorcery of Jehenna. George had shifted the weaving somehow, but it was still a thing that ought not to be. No door should stand open between Dreamworld and the Between, lest beings cross from there into Wakeworld. Only evil could come from such breaches of the doorways—as had been proven by the dragon that had found its way into Krebston.

In this moment, though, he was grateful that Vivian hadn't had a chance to figure out how to reweave Surmise so that the breach would be healed. It was an easy matter to find the path, a winding way through old-growth forest. He consulted the map now etched in his memory, marking the next series of twists and turns that he might not miss them, and set out in a long, swinging gait.

If his guesses were correct, the sorceress would also be headed for the Black Gates. Very likely she would arrive long before him, might already be there. Even so. He must do something, take some action, and it was the only thing he knew to do.

Twenty-six

"N o." Jared infused as much authority as he could into the word and tried to summon up a forbidding glare, but he was at a disadvantage. He lay flat on his back on a large four-poster bed. Most of him was discreetly tucked beneath a clean coverlet, but the wounded leg was stretched out and exposed like a science specimen, with three healers hovering over it. Vultures. Greedy, garrulous birds of prey, feasting on his misery and rotting flesh.

This was, he'd been told, Castle Surmise. The information rang true with certain dim recollections of dreams that he was attempting to suppress. What he didn't know, no matter how hard he dug into his brain, both conscious and subconscious, was how he came to be in Surmise and under the care of the healers in the first place. His last clear memory was of lying on a dirty blanket on the makeshift stretcher Zee had cobbled together, jolting and bouncing over what he wanted to think of as rocks. But the shapes and colors were all wrong and the stink of decay still lingered in his nostrils. Bones, flesh . . .

"No," he said again, tugging at the covers to twitch them up and over his leg.

Hands prevented him, and two voices said, in unison, "My Lord, the leg must come off."

"If we do not amputate," said the third voice, in the condescending tone of a long-suffering teacher to an unusually stupid pupil, "the contagion will spread and you will die."

Jared shuddered at the thought of the disfigurement. There was an attorney in his office who was an amputee— had lost a leg along with a wife and child in a car accident. Jared had always been repelled and slightly sickened by the sight of the empty pant leg, would find himself imagining what the stump looked like, and then wishing he hadn't.

"If I'm going to die, it will be with all of my limbs intact," he said.

"Your leg is hardly what I'd call intact." The youngest of the three, a curvaceous little blonde who couldn't be more than eighteen, wrinkled up her nose. "It reeks of putrefaction. The muscle has melted away from the bone."

In response, the dream memories forced their way into his consciousness. *I would have owned her once. She would have done my bidding in all things, would have come into my bed at a single command and would not dare to complain if my whole body reeked like a corpse.* Jared blinked as the thought went through him, foreign and familiar at once, leaving a trail of cold on the back of his neck that made him shiver.

One of the older healers, the woman, laid a work-worn hand on his forehead. The touch was soothing and cool, a gesture he'd seen repeatedly throughout his life and envied. No one had ever touched him that way, certainly not his mother. Vivian had come closest, but even Vivian, who so easily fell into a caretaker mode with everybody else, had never touched him in that way. She'd approached him cautiously at first, almost reverently, acolyte to priest rather than healer to patient. He'd liked that, the way she deferred, let him guide and direct and shape her.

Until something went wrong. In part it was medical school, and then working as a physician in the ER. She tasted power, leading her team, making decisions. Bit by bit she slipped away, finally moving to that godforsaken little town and telling him it was over. Jared knew he could have fixed it, though; he would have won her back given time. If Zee hadn't come along and spoiled everything.

Jared's hatred flared at the thought of Zee. It was bad enough that he'd stolen Vivian's love, that he was fearless and strong and adept with a sword. The fact that Jared now owed the man his life was insufferable; he would rather die than look up in Zee's face and see pity for his disfigurement.

"Fever," the older woman was saying. "Treating it will do no good as long as the source of the infection remains." She looked familiar, and he caught her hand and clasped it in one of his.

"Do I know you? Have we met?"

"Of course, Chancellor. I'm Nonette. I dealt with your— knife wound."

Chancellor. Flashes of memory, blindingly vivid, then gone. *Bowing deeply to a woman both sorceress and Queen. A black-and-white bird skewered on his sword. A fountain and the fragrance of roses in the dark. Vivian's body beneath him on a stone bench, unwilling. Vivian stabbing a knife deep into the flesh of his buttocks.*

Jared rubbed his forehead, fitful and confused. That couldn't be right. Vivian would never hurt anybody. As for himself—an image of the Chancellor, blood spurting from his throat, hands grasping at nothing—turned his limbs to water.

It made no sense. He had clear memories of a regular life—his house, his office, the courthouse—normal activities for a law-abiding man. That's what he'd really been doing. Not running around some fairy-tale kingdom with a bunch of magic rocks, raping and pillaging and feeding people to dragons.

On the other hand, he'd known exactly where to look for the spheres and the Key. And he recognized the healer, Nonette, clearly recalling every torturous spike of the needle as she sewed up the wound in his buttocks while he lay facedown on a hard mattress, humiliated and furious.

Make it stop. Please, make it stop. He twisted both hands in his hair and yanked until the pain made his eyes water, slamming the back of his head onto the bed, over and over.

"It's the fever," a voice said. "Sedate him."

Strong hands took control, one holding his head still, others disentangling his fists from his hair, binding his hands to the bed.

When a cup was pressed to his lips, he sealed them together and tried to turn his head away, but somebody pinched his nostrils shut and when he opened his mouth to breathe, the bitter fluid poured over his tongue. It was a choice of swallow or choke and his body made the choice for him, over and over as the draught continued to flow.

A moment later, a soft warmth spread through his muscles and he slumped back into the pillows. A gray fog of silence drifted over his churning thoughts and muffled them, one by one, shrouding them in forgetfulness except for one, the last one, so real that he chewed it between his teeth even as he faded into sleep: revenge.

Hours later he surged up out of dream as though he were drowning, hands groping at his leg before he was fully awake. His fingers found a swath of bandages and an utter lack of sensation. Before he could cry out his distress and outrage a clear voice said, "Nobody will take your leg without your consent."

Managing to get his eyes fully open, he blinked up into a face that he knew, only now the eyes were focused and keen.

"Isobel. What—how did you come to be here?"

She smiled, but there was no warmth in it. "Jared. Small worlds after all, yes?"

"You know me, then?" He hoped to all the gods there might be that she would not remember.

"I was crazy, not stupid. I saw you well enough."

Isobel pulled up a chair and sat by the bed, her hands folded quietly in her lap. She was a beautiful woman, he realized. He'd never really looked at her before. She carried herself with grace and a quiet reserve that spoke of power.

He tried to smile. "I had hoped you would be my mother-in-law someday."

"You hoped that Vivian would lock me up permanently

in a facility somewhere. Don't try to lie to me, Jared. When I say that I saw you, I mean that I saw what you try to hide beneath the looks and the money and the charm. It's easier to see these things when you are broken."

He swallowed, hard. "Look, Ms. Maylor—I was trying to do what was best for Vivian. You were not as you are now."

"True. I was not. What you are, remains to be seen. As for Vivian, that is what I am here to discuss. You have done her much harm."

"But it wasn't me! Whatever happened here, whoever the Chancellor is, he isn't me! Only a dream, however that works. Besides, he's already dead. Do you have any idea what it is like to have your dream self die in front of your eyes?"

She sat and looked at him, not answering, eyes so much like Vivian's that he felt an odd disconnect to see a different intelligence looking out through them. It was one of Vivian's tricks, that silence, to just sit and wait until you spilled something to fill it.

"Let's look at the evidence, shall we? You've met Zee."

Yes. He had met Zee. Anger burned his throat and chest with acid. "What about him?"

"Well, he too had a dream self here, the Warlord. He saved as many people as he could, even when Jehenna tried to control him. He helped Vivian. Your dream self raped her and killed her companion out of jealousy."

Beneath the anger, fear began to grow. A guard stood at the door to this room. He couldn't feel his leg. They all believed he was this Chancellor, or that at least he shared the guilt for the man's behaviors.

"He—the Chancellor—he tried to help her. He took off the silver bracelets so she had a fighting chance."

"And left her to confront the dragon alone. The Warlord gave his life for her. At best, Jared, you are a coward. At worst . . ." She paused and looked deep into his eyes. He wanted to turn away, to close them, to flee, but he was not capable of movement. "At worst, you are the Chancellor. Now tell me, what happened to Vivian in the Dreamworld?"

"I—she—"

"You stood by while she was forced through a doorway. While Zee was attacked and overcome. And you did nothing."

There was nothing he could say. Shame bubbled somewhere in the depths of him, overwhelmed almost at once by fear and rage. Zee again. Always the hero.

Freed from the searching, he closed his eyes to hide his own emotions. He heard the clink of a pitcher against crystal, the sound of liquid being poured.

"Drink."

A hand behind his head, something pressing against his lips. He turned his head away, used his hands to shift himself more upright in the bed, and opened his eyes to look at the glass. Clear liquid. He sniffed at it.

"It's only water."

"How do I know that?"

"Because I have told you it is so. You do not trust me, but I have been nothing but truthful with you. Here, does this help?"

She lifted the glass to her own lips and took a long swallow, then held the glass out to him again. "You should drink—it will help to wash away the poisons."

Jared licked his lips, feeling them cracked and fissured beneath the dryness of his tongue. A bitter, poisonous taste was in his mouth and he was deeply thirsty. He accepted the glass and drained it in several long swallows.

"Very good. I'll fill it again and leave it here where you can reach it. If you need anything else, or feel you could drink another glass, ring this little bell and someone will come to you."

"I'm afraid."

"The healers won't harm you."

"And the Prince?"

She smiled. "It's not the Prince you need worry about."

Twenty-seven

Vivian's eyes opened on a bleak gray sky. Cold air crinkled the skin on her face and the inside of her nose, and her body felt chilled and stiff. Her mouth tasted foul. A chickadee called not far away, and another answered. Even that slight sound hurt her head, grating on her skin like a physical irritant. Still, she was grateful that she wasn't tasting sounds this morning, and she pushed herself up to sitting. Poe stood at her feet, eyes black and unreadable as always.

Weston sat by the fire where she'd left him. He looked weary. There was still dirt in his beard from their grave-digging adventure. His face was creased with worry and fatigue, but he smiled at her. "I swear that bird is monitoring for dreams. He doesn't blink. How are you feeling?"

She got up, moving carefully, as though her limbs were glass and might break if she set her feet down too harshly or made a move too sudden. Weston dragged a fallen log a little closer to the fire. When she'd lowered her body into a sitting position, he handed her a steaming tin mug full of coffee.

Grateful, she inhaled the fragrant steam and took a careful sip to see how her stomach would react. It remained quiescent and she gulped down a long hot swallow, already feeling her blood stir and waken, sending warmth to muscles cold and stiff. A few more swallows and she began to feel human.

"Well?" he said, back in his place across the fire, his own cup cradled in his woodsman's hands.

The air was an affront to her skin, which felt extraordinarily sensitive, as though the top layer had been peeled away, leaving nerves exposed and vulnerable to the lightest sensation.

"I don't suppose there's an outhouse," she muttered, trying not to shiver, which hurt, but clamping all of her muscles tight to stop it made her head ache and increased the pressure on her bladder.

Weston snorted. "Yeah. I built it with my bare hands while you were tripping." He dug in his pack and tossed her a roll of toilet paper. "There's a likely spot in the copse over there. I promise not to look."

Despite her reluctance, the short excursion was good for her. The walk stirred her blood into warmth, loosened her muscles, reminded her of the gift of clear, untouched mountain air. Back at the fire she sat long in silence. It was difficult to find words, and Weston seemed to understand this. He silently refilled her mug and she drank the coffee black— bitter and bracing. Her eyes gazed into the flames and then flinched away; they were too bright.

The peyote had taken her to the border of reality and dream, had tipped her over the edge, and she hadn't been back very long. Her usual rigid control was weakened. Against her will she slid into a dream memory so vivid it was flashback. It possessed her, held her, pulled her under.

It is dark but this is no barrier. Vivian's eyes can see like a cat's, into all of the shadowed and unlit corners. She is hunting. Her prey has taken to its heels. She waits. She is faster, her senses better tuned. Let the frightened thing run a little, let it experience what it thinks is deep and abiding terror and then she will show it what fear really means.

Enough waiting; she begins to follow. Her movements are ponderous and slow at first; it takes time to get the

momentum up so that her heavy body will increase in speed.
Flying is easier, but her prey is on foot and so she proceeds,
alternating her poison-clawed feet, faster and faster. She
can smell the sweat and the heat, the blood and the fear.
No matter where the hunted one might hide, tonight she will
search it out.

As if sensing this, her prey stops at last and makes a stand.

There is a clearing in a grove of trees. Somewhere
nearby there is a door; it is closed and locked. The door is
insignificant. What matters is the woman at bay, her big
gray eyes in a face so white it is bloodless.

Vivian opens her dragon jaws, scenting both the clear,
sweet wind and the agitated blood.

The gray eyes stare into hers, hopeless and dull, done
with trying to escape. She strikes, engulfing flesh and bone,
her teeth tearing, crunching, swallowing the hot salt of
blood. She is sated, leaving nothing but a pendant shaped
like a flightless bird; strong wings lift her skyward and there
is no regret, no moment of sorrow for the one who has been
consumed . . .

"Vivian?"

She shuddered, pressed her hands against the rough bark of the log to remind herself that she still had hands. Within, the dragon stirred and stretched its wings in a movement that reverberated through every cell in her body.

Jung believed that every character in a dream is a part of yourself. If there was any truth to this at all, the battle with the dragon-self ended with no more Vivian. The dragon was hungry; the woman was tired.

"Vivian?" Weston said again. There was acknowledgment in his voice; maybe he could see that she was slipping away.

"I don't know what's going to happen when I shift," she said, as though he could follow all of her thoughts and knew where they had carried her. "I think I can get the door open. But I may not remember you."

"Yes."

"If I don't—remember myself—promise me you'll take care of Poe, and look for a man named Zee—"

Her voice broke and she turned her face away. For just a minute she let herself remember Zee as she had first seen him, sitting at the counter in the bookstore with a ray of sunlight illuminating his face. She remembered his eyes— clear agate rimmed in umber—looking into hers with that first shock of recognition, the collision of Dreamworld and Wakeworld vibrating between them like a plucked string. Whether he still lived or not, she was about to take an action likely to separate them forever.

She was about to voluntarily become that thing, the monster, that she had hated, feared, and run from all her life. The thing that she had also, against her will, longed and wished for. She was shaking now in good earnest, not with fear but with recognition, at long last, of this desire. All of her life she had been endlessly responsible—the caretaker, the protector and healer. The wounded child within had bided its time, all the while nurturing rage. It wanted to burn and destroy, to fly free and unencumbered, to eat what it wished and sleep where it willed.

The dragon heat flickered and flared and she focused her attention on that, building it, letting it grow and spread. Her senses deepened. She could hear Weston's heartbeat, as well as Poe's, smelled the heat of their flesh, and beyond that the trail of a deer that had passed in the night.

Prey.

Saliva welled in her mouth. Her body turned inside out, expanding, hardening, and this time she did nothing to hold it back.

A new awareness sang through her, a web of minds made up of a whole constellation of dragons. For the first time she truly understood the structure and hierarchy that made up the voices she had heard so clearly in Surmise. The individual dragon belonged to a Flight. Each flight belonged to a Consensus. And at the head of all there was one presence, stronger than all the others, that imposed order and structure and exacted punishment for those who strayed too far.

Vivian felt the will of this creature pulling at her, calling. All she needed to do was open a channel and the connection would be crystal clear. She resisted, and as she did so became aware of other, fainter signals scattered throughout the Dreamworlds and Between. Rogue and solitary entities, dragons without a governing body who performed their own will and went their own way. She understood now that the dragon on Finger Beach had been one of these. Mellisande had been ripped away from the others against her will, cut off by the web of enchanted silver with which Jehenna had bound her.

The voices that had been muffled since Vivian had been shut out of the Dreamworld and Between were clear again now, like radio channels. A little experimentation with focusing and she realized she could tune in or out, even to the overall command of the Queen, and for the moment she shut them off.

Distant memory said there was a reason she was in this place, this forest, that there was a task she needed to do, but she couldn't remember what it was, or why it would matter. The sky was calling. She unfurled her wings, stretched them high, scented the air.

"Vivian," a creature on the ground said. A two-legged. Afraid but standing his ground. "You are Vivian," he said, and memories stirred of herself as also small and naked and two-legged. She lowered her head on the long neck to see him better, watched the blood flee his face, smelled the sweat on him turn to fear. He smelled also of blood and smoke, but there were other scents not far away, other bodies of heat bigger and better to eat.

Her wings moved, lifting her above the earth, above the trees.

"Vivian!" the man-creature cried again. His voice tugged at her, but he did not have the right or the power to command her, no strength of will that she should have to listen to him.

She wafted her wide wings, feeling the air flow around her, watching the wind blow back the man's hair. He bent over to shield his face from the wind and dust and then she was so high above him that even to her eyes he was tiny. In the keen cold of the upper air her body was no longer heavy and awkward, but aerodynamic and free flowing.

She swooped and soared, lifting into a spiral and diving down toward the green earth so that it rushed up toward her, the trees, the grass, the stones, in a kaleidoscope of color as she flipped onto her back and then upright again. Almost brushing the tops of the trees with her belly, she watched the branches bend and sway.

From the man she still sensed fear and she dove down and shot a blast of fire toward him, teasing, just to watch him duck and stumble backward. The flames missed him, but a tree blazed up like a huge torch.

Then she was up and away, traveling fast and far over the forest. Her vision, crystal clear, showed her nests and birds and small moving things and then a larger four-footed creature.

Another dive, this time not for play, curving her wings for control and speed and aiming to intersect at the place where the creature's frantic leaps would bring it and then there was only warm flesh filling her mouth and throat and belly, the taste of blood and the pleasure of satiating hunger. A contented drowsiness came on her then and she settled with her long left flank protected by a sun-warm rock and let herself slip into an almost sleep.

In the place between sleep and dream, when her defenses and will were also at rest, fragments of Dreamworlds came to her. She sampled them, tasting them as if they were flavors—dark and light, with and without animals and people. One of them called to her more strongly than the others. There was a man with a face she knew, eyes like agate, and a voice that had once called her back from dragon to Vivian.

Vivian.

She was a twin soul, joined in this body. The giant, powerful force of destruction driven by desire, and the small and frail being who defined herself as a healer.

All of the Dreamworlds were before her still. All of the

dragon connections open for her to tap into. But she was free to choose whether to listen to the voices. Could choose whether to be Vivian or to be dragon.

She remembered the door she had seen with her vision altered by peyote, and found herself airborne once more, wings beating a deliberate course to the place where the two-legged calling himself Weston had said there was a door.

Smoke curled up into the air below, the forest obscured by its haze, bright flares of fire licking through as one tree after another incinerated. Where there had been a camp last night there was nothing but charred and smoldering black. No Weston, no Poe. The part of her that was Vivian sorrowed for this and hoped they'd found safety, but she was only a small spark of consciousness within the dragon who did not know or care anything for the loss of this human.

The door was visible as a shimmering in the air. Untroubled by the white-hot coals, she set down before it, heavy and cumbersome again now that she was earthbound. It should have been an easy thing to brush the cobwebby light aside with her mind, to open the door. An airy thought, a burst of power, and easy access. But there was something else at work, a dark shadow weaving through the light and locking the fabric in place.

She pushed against the black weave and felt it give a little. Spouted fire against it and saw the fabric of the weaving glow silver-white, except for the black, which remained obdurate and unchanged. She remembered the vision of dancing atoms making up the door, understood their fragility. The black thread held them together, an adhesive beyond her power to break.

Perhaps that would not be necessary. If she were to adjust the atoms *so*, unravel the threads enmeshed in the binding, like so, like so. At last the black weaving stood alone, a lacework trellis of negative space. She blew a breath of fire on it, and it collapsed and dissolved in tendrils of hissing steam.

And just like that, there was no barrier between her and

the Between. The door was too small for her clumsy body, but it expanded easily to let her through. There was a thing she wanted, a thing that should belong to the dragons but had been torn away and lost, then stolen. Lofting her wings high into the air she set a course for the Cave of Dreams, the only real landmark she had in the winding mazes of the Between. Deep within, the part of her that remained human whispered, "Zee," a faint thread of sound that hung in the air like smoke, and like smoke dispersed into the atmosphere and was gone.

Twenty-eight

Weston ran for his life.

Even with the fire roaring behind him, the wind it created breathing down his neck like a giant beast of prey, the irony of this was not lost on him. Mere days ago he'd planned to throw himself into an inferno, would have welcomed this turn of events as a gift of the gods and turned to embrace the flames. Now he had things to do and the idea of a death by fire did not appeal to him.

A trio of deer plunged past, not bounding gracefully but blind and panicked. Smaller animals scurried by on all sides, the fire sweeping everything ahead of its destruction. All of the creatures were faster than he, even the snakes.

So far he'd been able to keep ahead of the flames, but he was tiring, could feel himself slowing as his breath grew shorter and his heart beat harder. Poe, clasped against his chest, slowed him down. Not that the penguin was heavy, but he was an awkward shape and his feathers slick; it took both hands to hold him. This left no way to balance himself on the uneven terrain. Twice he'd stumbled and only just barely caught himself from falling.

Damn flightless bird. It was easy for the raven, flying far ahead, growing ever smaller and more distant. The odds were all against him, Weston thought. If the wind shifted, the flames would easily overtake him. Or if the fire jumped to the canopy it would leap from the crown of one tree to the next, far faster than any man could run.

No matter which way he looked at it, his chances for survival were grim.

For the first time in his life, Weston wished he had a dreamsphere and could walk into another reality. He wished he had honed the ability to create and open doors. He wished he hadn't tossed his dreamsphere into the fire.

The raven had circled back, flying low, demanding attention. It croaked twice and veered left. Weston followed, hoping that the bird had some sort of knowledge he lacked, because he wasn't going to be able to keep up the pace much longer. The fire was gaining. Heat played over his body with increasing intensity. Smoke choked him. His legs felt odd and lifeless, as if they'd been injected with Novocaine.

Wrong, wrong, wrong, he thought, even as he made the turn. It would take him slantwise in front of the wall of flame, increasing his need for speed even as he was tiring. Poe slipped again in his grip and he slowed his steps a little while he shifted the bird back upward. The fire gained on him.

But then he saw his salvation in a wide sweep of water. In the mad dash and panic he'd forgotten about Halcyon Lake. If he made it, he might just survive this after all.

He had to survive.

And so he flailed onward toward that liquid gleam, his body barely under his control, wild animals dashing past him, all with the same goal. His lungs were going to burn up with the heat. His hair was stiffening and lifting from his scalp, the fire wind swirled around him. And then his feet were slowed by some strange, cold encumbrance. He overbalanced and was falling, falling.

Water.

Poe wriggled out of his arms, and Weston dove beneath the surface, swimming as far as he could before coming up for a breath of air. It wasn't far; his body was oxygen starved and the water was icy cold. He bobbed up to the surface for another breath, lungs cramping, heat of the fire scorching his face. Black ash rained down.

Again he immersed himself beneath the saving grace that was water, shutting out the roar and crackle and snarl, forcing his arms and legs to move. When he came up again, he had gained enough distance to stay safely on the surface. The fire had slowed as it neared the lake—less fuel, fewer trees growing close to the rocky shore. The raven circled high overhead.

A loud splashing to his left drew his attention—a bear swam by, fixed on its course and paying him no attention. The water was full of other animals, all seeking safety, all on a temporary truce from the usual hunt-and-be-hunted in their common goal to escape the force of the fire. The penguin swam in circles around him, staying close.

Reality of the new dangers settled in: hypothermia and drowning. Already he was shivering, and it was hard to draw a full breath. His boots and heavy clothing weighed him down, and he realized there was no hope of making it across the lake.

And he couldn't go back.

All of which made it crystal clear that he was simply going to have to figure out how to be a Dreamshifter after all of these years of avoidance. *Step One, make a door.* Right. Easier said than done. So many years of forgetfulness lay between this moment and the far-distant childhood in which his father had tried to share the lore. It was hard to focus when he was descending into the numbness and confusion of hypothermia.

Grace would know about the doors. She was always listening, storing away knowledge. The thought of her was a knife to his heart. All those years ago he had done nothing to protect his family, to protect her. Had allowed her to do the thing he should have done. If she had turned to the dark arts as Vivian believed, then that was another sin resting on his own head.

He choked on a mouthful of water. He hadn't even noticed he was sinking. The hiking boots felt like rocks on his feet; his soaked clothing was a weight he didn't have the strength to fight. He should take them off, he thought, but it was a distant and vague idea. He was barely moving, his arms and legs circling in a slow paddle that barely kept his head above water. He tried to renew his efforts, but his body didn't respond to the directions from his brain. A deer approached, swimming hard. Maybe he could catch a ride. A few kicks, grab it around the neck, hold on.

But his feet did not kick, his hands did not move, and he slipped below the surface.

Something pulled him back up, a black-and-white bird, swimming like a fish. But it was small and he was heavy and again he slid below the surface.

Drowning, his brain said. *Interesting.* His body had enough sense left to hold its breath and he drifted, eyes wide open, peering through the murky green light, letting everything go because there was nothing else to be done. In a moment he would fill his lungs with water. A momentary panic of the body seeking oxygen where there was none, and then his brain would turn off and it would all be over.

A vague regret drifted through him, that he would die before he made things right. All he needed was a door into a Dreamworld.

In the instant before he opened his mouth to accept the burden of water pressing against lips and nostrils, the door he'd been imagining appeared directly in front of him. A tiny pressure of his mind and it opened. Water poured through it, carrying him along on the flood. The penguin followed, easy as a fish. Once through, his head was out of the water and he gasped in a great gulp of oxygen and then another. His brain cleared enough to command one last wish. The door closed behind him.

Through vision hazed by cold and fatigue, his body shivering so violently it felt like muscle would wrench away from bone, he sat up and looked around. Barely conscious and far from rational thought, he pictured in his mind the things he needed. Warmth. Dry clothing. Something hot to drink.

And for the first time in his very long life, he knew the pleasure of a Dreamworld shifting to accommodate his need.

Twenty-nine

When Jared woke again, the fuzziness of the fever had retreated. His head felt clear, his body light and easy.

Maneuvering himself into a sitting position, he checked out the leg, which was still numb. He supposed he should be grateful for the absence of pain, but it worried him. The only evidence he had that it was still attached was the shapeless lump of bandages stretched out on the bed in front of him.

He was thirsty and drank another glass of water. His own skin drew his attention—dry, stretched tight over his bones. His scalp itched, hair tangled and slicked with oil. Beard growth stubbled his jaw. Healing ulcers pitted the skin of his arms. And when he breathed he could smell himself, the stink of sweat and the permeating sweet reek of putrefaction.

Disgust overrode his fear and he rang the bell.

When the door opened a moment later, he wished he hadn't. He'd expected a serving woman or a page. Instead, a moving mountain lumbered into the room, literally shaking the floor with each step. Over ten feet tall, as wide as three men, but without an ounce of fat. The face looked like it had been carved from granite by an inexpert hand—a low, bulging brow, a slash of a mouth, cheeks and jaws that jutted in sharp and jarring angles. The eyes were deep-set and black enough to reflect the light in shards of blue and green fire. The voice matched, hard and uninflected.

"What do you need?"

Jared stared up at the thing looming over him and shook his head. "Nothing. I'm—it was an accident—"

"You have the bell in your hand."

Dismayed, he looked down to see that this was true.

"I'd expected one of the healers . . ."

"I am Kraal, apprentice healer. What can I do for you?"

"More water, please," Jared said. He would have felt safe maneuvering a serving woman into getting him a bath, a shave, and a peek at his wound, but he wasn't about to make requests of a slab of granite that could crush him without even trying.

Gnarled hands, each as big as Jared's head, picked up the pitcher and glass, pouring water with surprising delicacy. "It is good that you drink. The fever has burned the water from your body and it must be replaced. Could you eat?"

To his surprise, the question brought saliva flooding to his mouth; his stomach felt cavernous. "I could."

"I will bring a light repast, as your body is not accustomed to food. And then I will carry you to the baths."

The heavy footsteps thudded out of the room, making the water in the glass Jared was holding vibrate. "I've landed in fucking Jurassic Park," he muttered under his breath.

But his gigantic nursemaid turned out to be efficient and gentle. He returned in short order with a tray of fresh bread, cheese, and fruit. Jared thought he was ravenous but was able to eat only a little before he pushed the plate away.

"That is well," Kraal said, setting the plate aside and covering it with a white cloth. "It will take the body time to be used to eating. Now, we will go to the bath. Can you sit?"

It was a good question, the answer not at all certain. Jared pushed himself up with both hands and swung his good leg over the edge of the bed, noting with some surprise that the insensate lump of bandages beside it followed the commands from his brain and slid over with its mate. It felt wooden and heavy.

"I don't think I can walk," he said, hating his weakness.

"No need," Kraal replied, scooping him up in his arms like a small child.

Jared felt himself flush with humiliation. Perfect. How could he ever hold his head up again after having been seen carried around the castle by this overgrown numbskull? On the other hand, the bath was sorely needed and struggling would be more undignified than quiescence, as well as futile. Kraal had arms like small tree trunks, if tree trunks could be corded with muscle. He could break a man's back like a matchstick if he took the notion.

Outside the door was a wide courtyard. Jared had assumed he was in the castle, high up, a prisoner. Instead, this was ground level. Sunlight filtered down through the screening branches of shade trees. Beyond the stone courtyard lush green lawns swept outward, intersected by flower beds abloom with a riot of color. White-clad invalids sat in small groups, both on the covered plaza and on bright squares of blankets out on the grass, soaking up the sunlight.

Healers moved among them, carrying trays of water, medicine, and food. There were several giants among them, filling the purpose of carrying the patients from one place to another. Wind chimes in soothing tones hung from the trees, creating a pleasant undertone to the quiet hum of voices.

Kraal took a left, striding along the side of the plaza, and then another left, through a covered walkway that would keep the rain off during inclement weather but allowed the fresh air to blow in. They reached a wooden gate in a stone wall tall enough that even the giants could not look over it. Kraal knocked twice with a dragon-shaped knocker, paused, then knocked three times.

The gate swung open, and they entered a geometric wonderland of pools and gardens. Here there were no flowers, although there was a wide variety of plants. A rich herbal scent permeated the air—pungent, spicy, bitter, acrid, sweet. In spite of himself, Jared found himself drawing breath after breath, filling his lungs with a heady invigorating sensation that was close to a high, only it smacked of health.

"Almost overwhelming at first, I know," Kraal said. "The herbs are carefully chosen for different purposes, as are the pools. We go this way."

He set a course that led along the edge of the complex, past pools of varying sizes. In some the water steamed; others appeared to be cooler. Some had herbs strewn across the surface, some were murky with sulfur or other minerals, others were crystal clear. All had giant attendants lifting people out or lowering them in, carrying them from one pool to another.

At last they came to a small space screened by privacy hedges and closed by a gate. Kraal pushed against the gate, and it opened into a small square of grass and a basin just large enough to accommodate a tall man. A stream of water ran into it on one end and flowed out again on the other. Along the inside of the sheltering hedge, a low border of green with tiny white flowers gave off a scent that stung Jared's nostrils.

Kraal lowered him onto a wooden bench and instructed, "Take off the robe."

"No privacy?" he muttered, hesitating.

"You have nothing I haven't seen before. Robe off. Then we will soak away these bandages. This pool will cleanse all infection that is near the surface—from your wound and from your skin. When you are clean we will move on to another, more restorative. The water cannot do its work if you are clothed."

Jared complied as far as removing the robe, but then said, "Just help me, will you? It's not far."

Kraal grunted something unintelligible but helped him up and supported him as he hopped over to the pool and slowly lowered himself in. The water was blissfully warm; it stung a little, an effervescent buzzing that was not unpleasant. Without asking permission, he tilted his head back and immersed face and hair, scrubbing at his scalp with both hands while his body floated weightless.

This was a far sight better than that damned frigid pool Zee had tortured him in. Thought of his enemy ruined the moment and he surfaced, blowing and snorting, tossing his hair back out of his face.

"There is a barber to tend to your hair," Kraal said, and Jared thought he heard a hint of humor, although the giant's face remained expressionless. "Here, drink this."

This time Jared accepted the glass without question. Some sort of wine, warmed and laced with herbs. As he drank he had the sensation that it cleaned the inside of him as the water scrubbed at the outside. Tension seeped out of his pores and the flowing water washed it away. Even his hate seemed a distant thing, not worth the energy. It tugged at its moorings, following the other toxins out of his body.

He might have let it go, but at that moment he felt hands on his wounded leg. Startled by the return of sensation, he opened his eyes to see Kraal kneeling at the edge of the pool, supporting the leg in one hand and unwinding the bandages with the other.

When Jared saw the pulpy mess of what remained of his leg, the calm fled. His gorge rose, and he pressed both hands over his mouth, swallowing desperately to keep from fouling the water. Strips of dead gray skin floated in the current. In places the bone was exposed, all muscle eaten away. What remained of the flesh was mottled green and angry red.

Either amputation or death. He could see it now, all the denial stripped away.

"It can be healed," Kraal said, in a voice almost below Jared's hearing. He thought he'd imagined it for a moment. The giant wasn't looking at him; there was nothing about either face or body language to indicate that he had spoken.

"How?" he answered, gambling that his senses still functioned and he wasn't delusional.

"Not by Aelfric's methods. But the giants know." There was an undertone of disrespect in the usually uninflected voice.

"What do the giants know?"

The black eyes fixed him with an acute stare that made his heart skip a beat. He had dismissed the giant as stupid, based maybe on account of old fairy tales and the flatness of his facial features. But what looked out of those stone-black eyes was a sharp intelligence, coupled with something dangerous and wild.

"Nothing is for nothing," Kraal said, in that voice that sounded less like words and more like a slow rolling stone. His hands continued winding up the discarded bandage. He tossed it into a trash receptacle and held out a fresh white robe. "Come, it is time to move to the next pool. Then we will put on new salve and bandages."

"Whatever it takes," Jared said, clinging to the hard hand with both of his and using its strength to climb up out of the pool. "I will give anything for the healing of my leg. Besides, I fear they will kill me if I stay."

"Do not promise lightly to a giant." The warning was clear.

"I would sell my soul to the devil," Jared said.

Kraal grinned. "This is good to know. Now, silence. Later we will speak of a visit to my Queen."

"I have nothing to trade—unless she really wants my soul."

"That could be arranged." The giant's face showed no sign of humor, and Jared shivered a little as he realized that this was not a game. Last week he would have scoffed at the idea that souls really existed. So many strange things had happened since then that anything could be possible.

"She sounds formidable, your Queen."

"Indeed. She is not to be trifled with. But she can heal you."

Jared looked down at his leg and shuddered again. There was no good option here, no safe and easy path.

"What would it take? What would she want besides my soul?"

"Information."

"About what?" But he already knew. What had happened in that garden. She would want to know who was there, who fought. About Zee and about Vivian. It wasn't a betrayal, he told himself. There was no reason to think this Queen of the Giants would harm Vivian or Zee, although he would have been more happy about the latter.

Kraal didn't answer right away. He picked Jared up and carried him to another pool, this one cooler. Only a short dip, and then out again, dried this time with a towel and bundled back into the robe.

Still he kept silence, not saying another word. Only when he had laid Jared down on a high wooden table covered with a clean sheet and was spreading a thick, cream-colored paste over his leg did Kraal speak again. His voice was low, meant for Jared's ears alone. "Tell me what you were doing in the Dreamworld, as a gesture of good faith, and then I will arrange to take you to the Queen."

And so Jared told him—about Vivian and the dream-spheres, the attack, the Key, and the black dragon. As he spoke, the giant's eyes glittered, but the big hands continued steady and gentle, swathing the ruined leg in bandages.

"You have done well to tell me," he said, when at last Jared was done. "Now you are weary, and will rest."

Jared's eyes were heavy, and it was all he could do to keep his lids open, to not let his head drift down and rest on Kraal's hard chest when the giant picked him up to carry him back to bed. Pride held him until he was laid on the soft goose down mattress, with the clean sheets pulled up to his chin. But as his eyes were drifting shut he heard the giant's slow voice say, "Rest well. When you wake, you will find yourself in the Kingdom of the Giants."

Thirty

All Zee knew of the Cave of Dreams was the little Vivian had told him. Dreamshifters were summoned here on the day they came into their power and were given a dreamsphere by the Guardian of the Cave. Vivian's voice had softened into near reverence when she spoke of it, and she would say no more than that.

Now, standing on the threshold, he had no idea what to expect. His senses told him that magic had been at work here. No natural forces—water, or fire, or even wind-driven sand—could burnish stone into a mirrored surface like the one on which he stood. But magic or no magic, the only way to reach the Black Gates led through this cave and he was going to have to enter it.

He drew his sword, testing his right arm. The wound was healing but not yet strong enough. The left hand would have to do. In the pocket of his jeans the stone knife of the sorceress weighed heavy. The blade shone in his mind's eye, lethal and hungry, the color of blood already spilled, but he pushed the thought of it away. The sword he trusted; the knife he did not. He would carry it until he had the opportunity to bury it in the heart of the enchantress, and that would be an end.

Taking a deep breath, he turned and entered. A dim light

for which he could find no source allowed him to see that the walls and roof appeared to be formed by natural forces, much like any other cave. Only the floor was polished smooth as glass.

He had walked for several minutes before he felt the cave repelling him, the way one magnet will push another away when the poles are not aligned. He pressed on, becoming aware a few steps later of a faint vibration.

At first he felt it under the soles of his feet, then on the skin of his face, and soon every surface of his body crawled with a low-level trembling. A few more steps and the vibration emerged as sound, an off-key, discordant chiming that scraped through his eardrums and assaulted his brain. A warning. *Go back. You are not welcome here.*

At the edges of his vision something moved. He froze, forcing himself to breathe to his own rhythm against the torment of the uneven vibration, trying to see into the dark. Lights flickered ahead—blue, green, violet, crimson—and all of the possible myriad shades between, flashing in time with the unbearable sound. Each burst of light stabbed into his eyeballs like a red-hot needle; the sound tore at his eardrums.

All of it intensified as he pushed on; only a very little more and his cells would burst under the onslaught, splattering his body over the cave as red mist. A sticky wetness tracked from his ears down onto his neck; an exploring hand came away wet with blood.

Still he moved forward, one step at a time. There was nothing to be gained by going back.

Without warning, the cave opened into a high-ceilinged chamber, illuminated by an array of flickering lights, emanating from small round spheres covering the floor. A moment later he realized these objects also created the sound. At the center of the cavern they rose into a great rounded heap. A massive shadow draped over the top of that mountain of spheres.

Tormented by the vibration and the noise, unable to see clearly in the infernally strobing light, Zee tightened his grip on the sword and moved forward one cautious pace at a time. As he shifted his position the shadow came into focus all at once: a huge horned head with blankly staring eyes, black blood pouring from its nostrils. Where the blood struck the spheres a steam went up, hot and acrid, further obscuring his vision.

One less dragon in the world was cause for joy, but it was newly dead, which meant a dangerous predator couldn't be far away. Wary, he approached the dead creature, taking in as many details as the erratic light, the steam, and the constant onslaught of pain allowed.

As he waded through the spheres the sounds altered as they moved and he gave them closer attention. Dreamspheres, he realized in awe. The entire chamber was full of them. Around the body of the dead dragon they looked different, opaque. Some of them had turned black. Cautious, but curious, he reached out and picked one up between thumb and forefinger. It burned with a freezing cold, disintegrating at his touch into fine black sand. An acrid, bitter smell hung in the air.

Sorcery. He had time to think the word before a shadow warned him of something moving on the far side of the mound. Light as a cat, Zee stepped sideways and back, careful where he placed his feet on the slippery, rolling surface.

Around the curve of the heap of dreamspheres, high above where he stood, a horned head appeared, great greengold eyes darting this way and that, sometimes spinning, as though following the movement of things he couldn't see. Zee held his breath, froze his body into stillness, and the eyes passed over him without awareness.

Another dragon, this one alive and on the prowl. It lowered its head, opened wide jaws and shoveled into the mound of dreamspheres. When its mouth was crammed full, it extended its long neck to swallow, and then came in for another mouthful. It shook its head and swayed, as if it were dizzy. Still, it scooped up more of the spheres. Again it swallowed.

Zee's ready hatred flared. The creature must be responsible for the black and dying dreamspheres, for the imbalance in the cave, for the terrible cacophony of sound and sensation that was tearing his body apart. Most likely it had killed the other dragon.

He waited for the head to lower again and lunged, scrambling up the heap of spheres so he could reach the kill spot just where the jaw met the neck. Time slowed. He felt his body fighting for leverage on the shifting surface beneath him. Saw the soft, unprotected spot that he must strike with the tip of the sword. Felt the stretch and tear of his wounds as he leaped upward.

The dragon blocked him. Almost negligently she twisted her long neck aside so that the sword struck broadside to scales instead of stabbing into the soft flesh beneath her chin. The effect was like striking metal. His arm numbed from the blow and sent him staggering off balance. He slipped on the unstable surface, tumbling head over heels. The sword escaped from his numbed fingers, sliding away in a cascade of spheres.

Dragon jaws snapped at where his head had been; a wind of hot dragon breath tore at his clothing and hair.

The dragon shook its head again, its eyes unfocused and spinning. Once more it reached for him with wide-open jaws, the teeth as long as his arm, razor-sharp. Its breath smelled of molten iron, of copper, of overheated stone. It was hotter than the last blast had been, and when the creature drew back a little, sucking in air like a giant bellows, making a wind that shifted the heap of spheres on which he lay, he knew that he was done for.

The dragon was going to flame. His sword was gone. The cave offered no place to hide, no shelter from dragon fire.

Zee twisted his body upright, his hand reaching for the blade in his pocket. The thing was too small to kill a dragon, unless he could get to the eye, but it was his last and only chance. His right hand closed on the hilt, his left tore at the protecting sheath. His arm drew back as the dragon's head stretched toward him, smoke curling out of her nostrils.

"Stop, both of you. In the name of all things holy!"

Improbable, impossible, but the dragon paused, mouth open to flame, and turned toward the voice. Zee released the knife. It arced through the air, a lethal, perfectly balanced weapon, hungry for blood. He'd been aiming for the great golden eye, but the target had moved. The blade struck where the right foreleg joined the belly, drove into the flesh, and stuck there, quivering.

Nothing more than a flesh wound, a fly bite to a dragon. Zee slid backward, putting as much distance as possible between himself and the monster, his eyes searching all the while for the glint of his sword blade. If it had been buried beneath the shifting spheres, he would never find it.

Of course, if he was burned to death he wouldn't need it.

The newcomer lacked the wits to run away. Instead, he strode forward, scrabbling up the spheres toward the monster. The dragon didn't strike, didn't flame. It just stood, mouth hanging open, neck extended. Its gigantic sides went concave with each breath and its black tongue stuck out. A strident wheezing sound filled the cave.

The stranger reached up, grabbed the knife with both hands, and tugged it free. "Dragonstone," he said, and his voice was sharp with fear. He put a hand on the dragon's neck, looked directly into a golden eye, and commanded, "Change back, at once! Before it kills you!"

The monstrous dragon crumpled and twisted and shrank into the naked white body of a woman, lying limp and still with a bleeding wound in her breast. In the continuously flickering light the red blood gleamed the same color as the blade still gripped in the stranger's fist.

Zee staggered back as he saw Vivian's face, her hair, her body. Tears flowed silent from beneath closed lids, but she didn't move, other than a slow rise and fall of her chest.

"Talk to me," the man said, kneeling by the body and pressing his hand over the wound. Blood welled up between his fingers and over his hand. "Wake up and tell me what to do. Can you hear me?"

Zee edged closer. He'd seen a glint of steel near where the man was kneeling. His sword. Exultation grew within

him. This was not Vivian, but the sorceress, at his mercy.
Fate had given her to him after all, led him to use the stone
knife when he thought he was fighting an entirely different
foe. And now here was her accomplice, distracted and an
easy target.

Another foot. Six inches. Slow and easy. There. His left
hand curved around the hilt, tightened.

He raised the sword, ready for the death blow, even
though his sense of honor clamored against it. *Stab a man
in the back, Zee? Unarmed, unwarned?*

The man is in league with her.

"Vivian, you can't die now," the man said, dropping the
knife and pressing both hands to the wound. "Wake up. I
know you can hear me."

Zee checked himself in midswing, overbalanced, and
almost fell. His stomach twisted, his heart hammered in his
ears. He'd almost murdered an innocent man, somebody
who had fallen under the spell. All too easy to do, as he well
knew.

Put things right, kill the enchantress, and the man would
come back to his senses. He circled around and stood over
the unconscious woman on the other side, putting the tip of
the sword to her breast.

"What are you doing?" The man's eyes were keen; his
bearded face bore lines of strength and grief and a quick
intelligence. He didn't look like a man under enchantment.

"You think it's Vivian," Zee said. "But it's not. It's a thing
that needs killing."

Strong words, but still he hesitated. So much blood. Her
face was dead white and so very still, except for the slow
tears that continued to well from beneath closed lids and
flow silently down her cheeks. Zee longed to gather her into
his arms and soothe her, to bandage the wounds and heal
her, but it wasn't Vivian, couldn't be.

He pressed the tip of the sword against her chest and
demanded, his voice harsh, "Where is the Key? Tell me, and
I'll ease your death."

The other man's hands withdrew and Zee heard the

familiar sound of a shell pumped into a shotgun, but he never looked up to see the weapon. Unwilling, disbelieving, his eyes caught the glimmer of scales on a white shoulder, noticed the absence of a carved stone pendant lying over this woman's heart. And then her eyes opened, wide and golden, bright with tears. Her lips parted to speak, her voice little more than a whisper. "Would you really kill me, Zee?"

His heart contracted in grief and dismay. In the next instant, a heavy weight caught him on the back of the head and he plunged forward into a darkness that was beyond despair.

Thirty-one

Weston's eyes felt like someone had scrubbed them with sand, leaving a liberal supply behind. His muscles ached from clenching against the chill. The rock he sat on had seemed smooth enough hours ago but had long since begun to dig into his backside. Soon enough the sun would be blazing down and he'd be wishing for the predawn coolness.

Discomfort kept him awake, and watchfulness was in order. Anything that had ever been dreamed in any nightmare since the dawn of time could show up in the Between. And what emerged from the mouth of the cave could be even worse. His shotgun lay across his knees, loaded and ready, for all the good it would do.

His prisoner was still unconscious, propped up against the exterior wall of the cave with his hands bound tightly in front of him, but Weston didn't trust him for a second. He would have killed the bastard, given him a face full of lead at point-blank range, if Vivian hadn't spoken his name at that last moment. Zee. Obviously not the man she'd believed him to be, but Weston wasn't going to kill him without her permission. Unless he had a damned good reason.

He was praying for a reason.

The raven stood on the stone only a foot or two away,

head cocked to one side, eyeing him. It croaked once, gravely, and flew off to a farther distance. How the bird had managed to follow him he'd never know. It certainly hadn't been with him under water, able to swim through the door. But there it was in the Dreamworld, waiting, when he came out the other side.

As for the penguin, it stood at Vivian's feet, black eyes never leaving her face for an instant. Weston watched her just as closely; it was all he could do other than apply pressure to stop the bleeding and make her as comfortable as possible. He'd wrapped her in a blanket, elevated her feet to counteract the effects of shock, made a pillow out of his own warm flannel shirt. He'd have given her the T-shirt too, if he'd have thought it would make any difference to her comfort.

Her skin looked bloodless, her forehead furrowed with pain, her breathing too rapid, too shallow. When he put his ear to her heart, it fluttered like bird wings, quick and light. At least she wasn't bleeding anymore, but that didn't ease his worry much. He'd heard of dragonstone—that was one tale he had listened to when his father told it, mostly because it also involved the legend of the dragon slayers, and an adventurous hero had appealed to him. But what effect the stone would have on Vivian in human form he couldn't begin to guess.

The prisoner stirred, a low groan escaping him before he was awake enough to contain himself. Weston watched him shift his position, sitting up straighter with his back against the stone, shivering a little, trying to rotate and ease the muscles in shoulders pulled tight by the bonds. Weston had stripped him out of his T-shirt after he knocked him out just to see if there were any fatal hidden wounds. There hadn't been. But his torso was a mass of bruises, his right arm bloody from a laceration running from shoulder to elbow. Another wound marked a line down his ribs.

Injured, bound, and weaponless, he still had a dangerous look about him. Weston didn't trust him for a minute. He cradled the shotgun, hoping for an opportunity to use it.

"No need for that," the man said, his voice rough with thirst and pain. "Not going anywhere."

"Can't see as I put much stock in your word. Zee, is it?"

A nod of assent, that was all. Not much of a talker, this one. "Vivian worried about you. All-fired set on your rescue. And when you find her, you try to kill her. What sort of man does that?"

"I thought . . ." Zee stopped, his face closing like a shutter, unreadable and self-contained. In a moment he said only, "How bad is it?"

"Bad enough." Weston didn't know the answer, not yet.

Vivian's eyes opened, as though she had been roused by the sound of their voices. Her hands reached out, grasping at something invisible to Weston, and she murmured words that sounded like, "I'm coming," but he couldn't be sure. "Hurts," she added. Her lips were dry and cracked. He tried to give her a sip of water, but she turned her head away and it only dribbled across her face.

Weston pulled the blanket and his makeshift bandage away to check the wound and gasped with dismay. The flesh of her chest wall, from collarbone to breast, had risen in a tight, irregular swelling. The edges gaped, although there was no more bleeding. To a gentle touch, the whole area felt rock hard, as though the flesh beneath the skin had turned to stone.

"Dear God, what is that?"

Startled, Weston looked up to see Zee, made awkward by the bound hands, kneeling on the other side of Vivian's unconscious form.

Weston reached behind him for the shotgun. At such close range there was little need to aim.

"The knife," Zee said. "You called it dragonstone. Would it do this?"

Weston's hands tightened on the gun, his trigger finger itching. "Don't try to play stupid. If you were carrying it, you know what it's for."

"I found it. What will it do to her?" Agate eyes stared into his with all the intensity of a hunting cat. "Tell me!"

Weston found himself answering, compelled by the need behind the demand. "I don't rightly know. It is said the stuff will kill a dragon, no matter how slight the wound. No way to stop the bleeding. Whether it will kill her in human form, I don't know. Whatever this is, she's not bleeding."

The raven fluttered down and landed on his shoulder, poking an intrusive beak into his beard. Weston shoved it away. "Shoo, would you?" The bird edged sideways a little but stayed firmly rooted to his shoulder.

Vivian shifted restlessly. One of her hands clawed at her chest and he held it back with one of his, the other never leaving the gun.

He looked up at Zee, whose eyes didn't budge from their focus on Vivian. "Get back where I put you."

"Can't. Look—you have to do something."

As Weston watched, horrified, the swollen flesh shifted on its own, the lumps moving as though alive. The wound stretched and gaped as something blood-colored and shining tried to push its way out. Weston touched it with a shaking hand and found it smooth and hard as polished stone.

"Whatever that thing is, you have to get it out." Zee's voice betrayed him in that moment, stretched to breaking with guilt and grief.

Weston applied pressure, ever so gently, to the skin on either side of the stone, watching the flesh tear and stretch to make room. A gush of blood stained her white skin. Vivian cried out, both of her hands grasping at his wrists, but he steeled himself to go on. Little by little he eased the stone free. She sighed and went limp.

"Vivian," Zee said, his voice sharp with alarm.

"She's just resting more easy." It was true. Her hair was damp with sweat and her lip was bleeding where she'd bitten it, but her breathing was more regular and her face looked almost peaceful.

Weston held the thing up to the light—as big as Vivian's fist, red as heart's blood and strangely beautiful.

"What the hell is it?"

"Feels like stone. I've never seen anything like it." He

turned back to Vivian. She was still breathing, slow and even, no longer muttering. He put his hand to the area around the wound and pressed gently at a smaller lump, manipulating it into the opening and out. Another stone, smaller. One by one he expressed more of the stones, easing them out until the flesh felt soft and there were no more swellings.

"Will she live?" Zee's voice sounded like broken glass.

"Time will tell. But she's better."

Already her face had gained a touch of color. When he put his ear down to her heart, it had slowed and steadied to a more even rhythm. Weston gathered up the handful of strange stones. They chimed as they shifted against each other, with a clear crystalline tone for all the world like dreamspheres. In all of his memories there was nothing to prepare him for this, nothing that even hinted at what they might be.

"When I found her in the cave, she was a dragon," Zee said. "The other dragon was dead, I still don't know how. Maybe they fought, and she killed it. The dreamspheres—the noise was mind-bending. I saw that they were dying. And she was—she was—eating them. Swallowing them. And then I saw—I thought I saw . . ." He broke off there and wouldn't say more.

Weston was wrung with a reluctant pity. Set adrift in such a maelstrom he could see how the mind would go astray, how a person might mistakenly turn on a loved one. And he had reason to believe that the man had seen more in the cave than he was going to be willing to mention.

Weston shook himself, jolted back out of the memory and into a now he wanted to escape. Zee was looking at him, apparently expecting an answer for some question asked and not heard. He jumped back to the last thing he remembered and assumed the topic hadn't wildly strayed.

"I remember a childhood tale about the Guardian . . . she is the dragon who guards the Cave of Dreams. There was danger once to the dreamspheres; some sort of blight had come upon them and they were beginning to die. The

Guardian consumed as many as she could hold, preserving them . . ."

"If the dreamspheres were to die, what then?"

"Perhaps nothing. Perhaps dreamers would die with them."

Zee caught the hint of something left unspoken. "And sometimes?"

"I don't wish to speak of it, not here. So close."

The other man's eyes appraised him, warrior's eyes, reading both the warning and the fear. "What—who—do you think killed the Guardian, then?"

Weston shrugged. "I suspect it was whoever took Vivian's pendant and set up the trap for the two of you."

"The sorceress?"

"Looks like it." *Oh, Gracie. What have you done?*

"We're not safe here, if that's true. She's not safe."

This was true, and not just because of the sorceress. And a shotgun wasn't going to be of much use against anything that would come against them. But Weston also didn't think Vivian should be moved.

"That's not your concern," he said to Zee. "Get back over there and sit, would you? She'll be mad if I shoot you, but I can live with that." Maybe. Unless she turned into a dragon again. Hell and damnation, he was in way over his head. He thought back to the flaming house with longing. A moment of pain, and then nothing. No responsibility, no guilt, no worry.

The man named Zee hesitated. "I know you don't have to tell me anything," he said. "But it would ease me to know who you are—what sort of hands she is in."

Weston wasn't entirely sure why he answered; something in the eyes, the tone of voice. "Name's Weston. I'm a Dreamshifter, but not a good one."

"George told her she was the last—"

"Yes, well. Never say I didn't try to make it so."

"So you know what to do then—how to get to the Black Gates. As soon as she's well enough to travel, anyway."

"Haven't a clue. There was a book with a map, but it's missing."

"I have the map."

Weston was on his feet, shotgun ready to fire, before the words were fairly out of the other man's mouth. "So you're in cahoots with her then, the one who stole the pendant and the book. Where is she? And give me the map."

"Whoa, easy. Vivian's mother drew it for me. In Surmise. It's in my head."

A few steadying breaths, and Weston lowered the gun. Just because he hadn't pulled the trigger when he should have so many years ago, didn't give him the right to get trigger-happy now.

"So which way do we have to go?"

Zee nodded toward the cave. "Through there."

Weston looked at the mouth of the cave and thought about what lay within. His stomach churned; his mouth went dry. He shook his head. "There has to be another way."

"There isn't."

"Well, then, I think we have a problem."

Thirty-two

Her body was made of glass, fragile and transparent. Surely she would shatter at a touch. Her fragmented heart must be visible through the wall of her chest to anyone who cared to see. And yet she was breathing. Alive.

"Vivian?"

A vague memory came to her of winging above a forest fire, a fire she'd started by tormenting a man for fun, and she opened her eyes and looked up into Weston's face. His skin was reddened, hair and beard frizzed; he smelled of wood smoke. But he, too, was alive.

"Oh, God. You're singed. I—didn't mean to start that fire—"

"Shhh. I know. How do you feel?"

"How transparent am I?"

"What?"

She raised her hand to her face, surprised that the joints bent where they were supposed to, relieved to see flesh and blood and skin. "I dreamed—so many things. I thought I was made of glass . . ."

Something in his face stopped her. "What is it? Tell me."

He held something up for her to see. A large stone, bloodred but crystalline clear. "It's beautiful, Weston. What is it?"

"Your blood."

"My blood."

The stone stirred a frail strand of knowledge, of dream, just a hint and then gone. No matter—there were more important things. "Weston—something killed the Guardian. The dreamspheres were all dying. I didn't know what to do, I couldn't think, but I had this instinct to eat them. It seemed right, but they made me feel so strange, all the dreams at once . . ."

Zee had tried to kill her. Surely that part had been a dream.

"That would explain the hallucinations."

"So I was hallucinating?" That was a relief. Zee would never, ever hurt her. But then how had she come by this injury in her chest? She raised her hand to explore the burning place, but Weston clasped it and held it aside.

"What happened, Wes? Tell me."

His sharp eyes glistened with unexpected moisture, and he hesitated, which told her what she needed to know.

"It's true then? It happened? Zee . . ." She broke off, unable to say the words aloud.

"I'm afraid that part is true. He had a dragonstone knife."

Vivian felt like the knife was in her heart, twisting, twisting. "Dragonstone? But I'm alive, still—"

"Yes, thank God. Because you were able to shift to human, I think. But, because of the shift to human, your body didn't know what to do with all of the dream material, and thus the hallucinations."

"Is this real, now?"

"Yes. Your body solved the problem—it made these."

He put the stones in her hand. They were heavier than they ought to have been. She held one up to the light, wincing as the movement pulled at her breast. "It's beautiful. And terrible."

"That it is."

Weston rubbed a sleeve across his eyes.

She tried to smile for him, past all of the pain and the fear. "You saved me."

And then, remembering. Jaws snapping in anger and hunger at the small figure with the sword. Flame.

"Oh, God. Zee. No wonder he tried to kill me. I was going to flame him, Weston. Tell me I didn't hurt him." She tried to sit up and he pressed her back. Had she roasted Zee, burned him?

"What do you care? He damn near killed you."

"Please tell me I didn't. Tell me I didn't hurt him."

"He's hurt some, but you didn't do it. Now rest, will you?"

"Let me up, I'm all right. Please, I can't breathe lying flat like this. I'm in my right mind, truly. Where's Poe? Tell me he didn't burn up too—"

"He's here, he's fine, he's keeping an eye on Zee. You've lost a lot of blood. Seems like you'd be best to just lie still a bit."

"Well, let me get dressed at least. Oh, shit. I don't have any clothes."

"You do. I've got a change for you in my pack."

"Wait—how did you get here, anyway? With your pack and a change of clothes. There was that horrible fire, I saw it . . ."

"As it happens, I'm a Dreamshifter, like it or no. I ran from the fire, made a door, landed in a Dreamworld that just happened to have everything we needed."

"But you're here—at the Cave of Dreams—"

"Only place I know in this maze, Vivian. I thought I'd start here. It was a lucky guess."

"Sounds like a freaking fairy tale, doesn't it? I'm sorry about almost roasting you." Gently she shoved away his hands, held the blanket to her chest, and sat up. Pain lanced through her body at the movement but eased as soon as she was upright.

"Give me something to wear, Weston. Please."

He sighed heavily but didn't argue. Sitting on the ground behind her, he supported her from behind, helping her get her arms into a warm flannel shirt. It was fully three sizes too large, but she wasn't about to complain. While she fumbled with the buttons, she looked around for Zee.

He was propped up against the stone wall beside the mouth of a cave. Her heart turned over at the sight of his face, so changed from that first glimpse of him, sitting in a ray of golden sunlight in A to Zee Books. All of the artist had been beaten out of him, nothing but the warrior remaining. His head leaned back against the stone, eyes closed, but his face was tight and hard even in repose. The scars left by the bear were healing into long red welts. Both eyes had been blackened, and a greenish swelling marred his jaw. His right arm was bloody. A laceration ran along his rib cage; his belly and chest were marked with vivid purple bruises.

The strong hands were bound together, resting in his lap.

Vivian's eyes blurred with sudden tears. "His wounds need tending. Help me up."

"You are not getting up. Especially to tend to a madman who tried to kill you. Tell me what to do, I'll take care of it."

She shook her head, no, grateful that this small movement didn't make the world spin. "I have to see."

"I don't see that there's anything else to be done, and you need to lie down and rest."

"There's no time for rest, Weston. Look—my pulse is a little bit rapid but not too bad. I'm not feeling short of breath. We need to be moving soon, anyway. It's not safe here."

Zee's eyes opened, those beautiful agate eyes, once light filled and now so dark. No smile at the sight of her, no softening of his face. "Rest," he said. "I'm all right. We'll try to move tomorrow."

But he wasn't all right, not at all. She could hear it in his voice. And she couldn't bear the sight of his hands, tied together as though he were a criminal. She tried to push herself onto her feet, but her legs felt like rubber.

"I'll not help with this madness," Weston said, but when she started to crawl he picked her up like a child and carried her, setting her down in front of Zee.

She reached out to touch his cheek but he flinched away, avoiding her gaze, his eyes and face unreadable.

He was so very hurt. It was more than the wounds, all of which looked painful but not life threatening. The cut on his side was healing. The bruises didn't indicate broken bones. But his arm was a mess. She kept her voice matter-of-fact and professional. "Looks like every time it starts to heal, you tear it open."

"That's been about the way of it."

When she laid her hand on the taut skin of his bicep, his flesh quivered beneath her touch. She began fumbling with the knots in the rope that bound him, but they were tight and stubborn and her fingers kept slipping off.

Weston put a hand over hers to stop her. "He's a danger-ous brute, Vivian. He tried to kill you."

"He tried to kill a dragon," she said, her voice level. "Any man could make such a mistake."

"And threatened the woman who replaced the dragon. Don't you forget it."

Vivian looked up into Zee's eyes, guarded and watchful, as though she were a stranger, an enemy. She knew full well how lethal Zee could be. If he had turned against her, if he thought there was reason to kill her, he would do that if she freed him. And she could not afford to die—there was too much riding on her success. She must find the Gates, the Key, stop the sorceress.

There was no room for love or mercy in this equation.

"Give me the knife, Weston," she said, never once break-ing the gaze that bound her and the dragon slayer together.

"Vivian, it's dragonstone."

"I'm aware of what it is. Give it to me." At the touch of stone against her hand she curled her fingers around the carven bone hilt, feeling the dragonstone respond to her blood. For the first time, emotion stirred in Zee's eyes. Stricken, she recognized it as hope. With a long, shuddering breath he closed his eyes and leaned his head back, baring his neck, his breast, asking for a death.

Vivian's breath came ragged and harsh as she shifted her position for a better angle. It was essential that she not slip or make a mistake. The blade was honed to a killing edge, and it sliced through the rope as if it were butter.

Zee's eyes flew open. He sucked in a breath as though he

were drowning. She was near enough for a kiss, to reach up and press her lips against his, but he might as well have been on the other side of one of the forever-locked doors.

"Why?" he asked her, and his mask had melted now, his face, his eyes, nothing but pain.

In all the worlds there were no words for this; she laid the back of her hand against his scarred cheek, and he trembled at her touch. "Please," he said. "Don't. I can't bear it."

One long moment they remained thus, Vivian knowing that her touch caused more pain to him than any of the wounds that marked him.

"Weston, give him his sword," she said.

"Vivian, surely—"

"If he's going to kill us, he can do it without a sword. It belongs to him."

"No," Zee said. He moved away from her, putting distance between them. "I swore an oath to protect you. I broke it. If you ask, I will go with you, but I will not carry a blade."

Vivian closed her eyes. In his voice she could hear all of the places where he was broken, and knew it was beyond her ability to heal him.

Thirty-three

❧

For three long days they rested.

Weston built fires and went on short forays seeking water and food. A rabbit one night, split between the three of them. Some sort of creature that looked too much like a giant squirrel the next.

The time lay heavy on Vivian's shoulders. She was not strong enough to travel; she knew this but chafed at her own restrictions. By the end of the third day, as the sun completed its arc across the sky and hung like a ball of flame just over the horizon, she could no longer endure the screaming of her nerves and the need to do something.

Despair gnawed at her courage. They would never catch up with the enemy. She would use the Key, if she hadn't already, and whatever evil was going to be unleashed would be unstoppable; but still Vivian would have to fight it. She would spend the rest of her life—if she survived this adventure—pursuing one hopeless quest or another.

Zee was yet another heartbreak, and the proximity to him was tearing her apart. He had shared his adventures in clipped, military tones—a soldier reporting necessary information back to the unit. He talked about waking up among the dead warriors, his encounter at the well with the dragon, the hermit, what he had learned from Jared and from Isobel in Surmise. Other than that, he remained silent and closed. He rebuffed her attempts to check his arm and rebandage it, saying only, "I'm fine, let it be."

"I can't take another minute," she said, finally, feeling like she was going to start tearing off her skin with her own fingernails if they didn't do something. "It's time. Let's get moving."

Weston looked up from the fire he was building. "It would be wise to wait until morning." But his face had sharpened into eagerness. Zee was already on his feet.

"I don't think so," Vivian said. "We need to move now. I feel it. Morning will be too late."

"Where?" Weston asked, his hands stilled in the act of striking flint to tinder.

"How do we get to the Black Gates? Any ideas? And if you don't know, maybe we can find Surmise. My mother might know. We can't just sit here."

The two men exchanged a look that shut her out.

"What is it? Tell me. I'm not ten years old."

After a long moment Weston shrugged and turned back to his fire.

"Isobel drew the map for me," Zee said, sounding as though the words were being dragged out of him.

"And?"

"Through the cave. The only way lies through the Cave of Dreams."

"We can't go in there," Weston said.

She looked from one to the other, confused. Zee's face pale and set. Weston's frightened. She had reason to know he was no coward.

"What aren't you telling me?"

Weston avoided her eyes, blowing onto his pile of shavings and waking a tiny flame. It edged its way upward, growing brighter and stronger as it fed.

"Weston! Talk to me."

He looked up then. "Have you thought about what happens to the dreamspheres that die?"

"Some sort of imbalance in Dreamworld, I'd expect. Is this really important now?"

"Deadly."

The tone of his voice caught her attention. "Dead dream-spheres. I guess—if you were in the dream when it died, it would be bad."

"To say the least. That's the good news."

Vivian followed his gaze to the mouth of the cave, felt the hairs on the back of her own neck rise with a sense of something lurking in the dark.

"Only the shape of the dream dies. It reverts back to raw dream material."

She still didn't understand, but Zee did.

"So that's what I saw, then," he said. "Somehow the stuff reflected what I have in my head."

"Sort of. It's more like—it reads the energy signature of what comes into contact with it. Not what's in your head, so much as the deepest fear or desire or love—"

"Or hate."

"What happened in the cave?" Vivian knelt down by the old Dreamshifter and put her hand on his shoulder. "What did you see?"

"It's not just seeing, you have to understand. It manifests. It can kill you."

"So how did you get out, then?"

"I knocked Zee out. You were unconscious. It couldn't read either of you, so it was just me. And . . ." He swallowed hard. "I don't want to talk about it. But if we go in there, what are we going to manifest? Either one of you care to tell me what is going to come up?"

All of them were silent. Vivian knew full well that she didn't want to face her own demons, and she suspected that Zee had already seen something in the cave and knew what his was going to be.

"A dragon might be immune to that sort of magic." Weston fed twigs into the hungry little flames. "Able to pass through the cave without triggering the dream matter."

Vivian shook her head. "I can't. It takes energy to shift. There's nothing there."

"I'm sorry. I just can't think of another way."

She rubbed her face with both hands and explored, tentatively, the place at her core where the dragon heat had been. Cold, empty. "I don't know, Weston. Maybe after I eat something. I'm so tired—"

"No." Zee was on his feet, eyes blazing. "Have either of you considered the condition the dragon was in before she shifted back to human? Have you forgotten the dragon-stone?"

Vivian's gut clenched around his words as though she'd been struck, and she saw Weston's face drain of color.

"Correct me if I'm wrong—but if she shifts, she dies. Yes?"

"Oh, gods," Weston whispered.

"I did that. It can't be undone. But I won't stand by and see her do something *on purpose* that is going to get her killed. Are we all clear on that?"

For an instant Zee's eyes met hers, and Vivian read the depths of the guilt and grief that marked him.

Oh Zee. Oh, my love.

She would have gone to him then, would have made him see that she knew, that she understood, that she still trusted him with everything that she was. But before she could act or say another word, Zee stiffened. His nostrils flared as though he had caught the scent of something that disturbed him. In the same instant Weston was on his feet, pumping a shell into the shotgun.

Only then did she hear the rattling at the mouth of the cave. She tried to pick up Zee's sword, but it weighed too much for her strength. She couldn't get the tip of it up off the ground. Panic loosened her muscles, weakened her knees.

But it wasn't the embodiment of her own fear that emerged first from the cave.

They shuffled out four abreast, despite all the laws of health and physics that decreed they shouldn't be able to move at all. Vivian had seen such mutilations in the ER—declared dead on arrival, covered with a sheet, and sent off to the morgue with all due haste.

These bodies were different. Despite horrific wounds, their eyes were open and all of them pointed the index fingers of their right hands at Weston, all of their eyes turned in his direction. "You owe us our lives," they said in chorus, even the one who was missing a jaw. "You owe us our lives."

Weston aimed the shotgun in their direction, but his hands shook so hard he would never hit what he aimed at. Vivian's brain froze in blank horror. Surely there was something she should do, could do, but she continued to stand there as the things shuffled closer, still chanting.

And then Zee was at her side. "I'll take that," he said, and the sword was out of her hands. He strode forward, already swinging, and struck the head off the closest figure. It sailed through the air and landed close to Vivian's feet, eyes wide open, the same dark brown as Weston's.

"Ellie," Weston moaned. "I'm so sorry."

At last Vivian recovered the ability to move and speak. "Weston!" She made her voice sharp to get his attention. "It's not Ellie. You know this. Only the dream things."

Zee's second stroke took off the legs of the boy with the missing jaw. Vivian shuddered. They were so young. And if these were what walked in Weston's memory, it was no wonder he had tried to kill himself.

She took a step toward him, but a movement from the decapitated head at her feet held her back. The eyes blinked. The mouth moved, soundlessly repeating the mantra. "You owe us our lives." And then the neck began to elongate, formed a chest. Arms sprouted, and grasping fingers reached out toward the old Dreamshifter, grazing his knees. Meanwhile, a new head had grown on the body and now there were two Ellies, both crying, "You owe us our lives."

"Zee!" Vivian shouted. "Stop! It makes it worse!"

But he had seen, was even now evading the second jawless boy that had grown from the body of the other.

"What do we do?" he asked, retreating, using the flat of

the sword to swat away the outstretched hands, careful not to sever any limbs.

"I don't know. Stay back. Let me think."

But there was no time. Another figure emerged from the cave—a creature mostly dragon, but with Vivian's hair and eyes. A familiar sword hilt stuck out between the front leg and the belly. Blood poured out of the wound, turning the earth black where it fell.

She stared at the thing, transfixed. But it had eyes only for Zee. It opened its mouth, not a dragon's jaws, but a woman's, *hers*, and Vivian knew it was going to flame.

"Zee, look out!"

He dove to the ground and rolled, coming up barely out of reach of the grasping fingers of the dead girl. But the Vivian Thing didn't flame. It stopped in its tracks, shuddered, and fell to the earth. Once, twice, the dragon ribs drew breath, and then it sighed and went small and still, shifting into the body of a woman who lay dead with a sword in her heart.

Zee made a broken sound, as though somebody had thrust a blade between his own ribs. Vivian reached for his hand, grazed and blistered now, the nails broken. She wanted to kiss it, but he pulled away from her.

"Only a dream thing," she said, but they both knew it wasn't quite true. The healing wound in her own breast was evidence enough.

And any minute now the other monster would come out of the cave. Already red eyes glared from the entrance, so big it was clear the thing could never fit through the existing space.

"We have to do something," Vivian shouted at the others, her voice shaking and desperate.

"What's coming through?" Zee asked her. Calmer now, the worst over for him and a worthy foe emerging.

"Like yours. Only bigger and meaner and full of rage. Also, not dead." She could sense it now, feel the tie with her own body. All of the pent-up rage of her childhood; the little girl who played mother to the woman and the anger that bloomed dark and quiet inside her soul. The fury about the hospitals and the blood and the insatiable, unfilled need to be loved and cared for.

That was it, probably. The way to stop it was probably to love it.

Which was, she knew, beyond her power.

The three of them retreated, dodged, evaded, did whatever they could to avoid the touch of the dream creatures already pursuing them. Weston clobbered one of his brothers over the head with his shotgun, and the thing slowed but did not stop.

The man with the hole in his breast and a face that was like Weston's, only so much harder and colder, grew bigger and stronger. His hands had been empty, but now he held a gun. He aimed it at Weston.

Meanwhile, back at the cave, rocks began to fall as an enormous head forced itself out through a too-small space. It opened a mouth full of teeth and roared, a sound that shook the earth beneath their feet.

Only minutes to act if they were going to survive.

No time to discuss plan B, as it had come to her. No idea of whether it would work. Because Weston's father was about to start shooting, and when that other Thing emerged from the cave, there would be no mercy.

"Give me the bloodstones," she said to Weston.

"Vivian, no—"

"Give them to me." She used the Voice. There was no time to argue.

He pulled a sock from his pocket, tied off to make a carrying pouch. The stones felt strange in her hands. Heavier than she had expected. Not quite inert, not quite sentient. Between states. Waiting.

For what? What would wake them?

Always retreating, faster now, she fumbled to untie the knot.

A shot rang out, spraying up dirt and rock to the left of them. Weston's family was gaining. A sound of grinding rock and another bellow echoed from behind them.

"Quick—behind that rock," Zee shouted.

They followed his lead, bent over, racing for their lives toward a large stone formation about fifty feet away. Another shot rang out, this time striking closer. But so was the shelter of the rock. Vivian reached it and dove behind it, knowing it would grant only a moment's reprieve, and hoping that would be enough.

Weston slid into place beside her.

She put her hand into the sock and drew out the largest stone. At its touch, memory came to her. A dream.

The bloodstone gleamed in a dim light, full of portent and power. A power waiting to be unleashed.

Zee's voice. "This is dark magic, are you certain?"

And then . . .

Zee. He was not crouched beside her. She peered out, to see that he stood directly in front of the approaching nightmare. Weston's father in the lead, giant-sized now, with the gun in his hands. The rest of his murdered family trailed behind him. The Vivian Dragon Thing still lay dead.

And the other monstrosity had gotten itself free of the cave. It was the size of a small mountain and stank of brimstone and sulfur. Steam and flame erupted out of its nostrils with every breath. Vivian tried to encompass one small loving thought toward this creature born of her own soul, but fear and loathing was all she could manage.

And the creature grew larger.

They were doomed.

Weston's father pulled the trigger. A crack like thunder from the gigantic gun. Vivian's heart suspended beating, waiting for Zee to stagger or fall, but he stood unwavering. Beside him now, a small black-and-white form. Oh God, Poe.

Another shot. Rock fragments flew through the air with a sound of an explosion. A line of blood opened on Weston's cheek.

Following an instinct she didn't understand, Vivian lifted the bloodstone close to his face so that a drop of blood fell on it. The color of the stone darkened to almost black and it pulsed, once, as though it were alive.

Memory stirred again. "Zee!" she shouted. "To me."

She feared he would not come, would have used the Voice on him at last, but there was only an instant's hesitation before he raced toward them.

"Poe!" she screamed, but the penguin held his ground, right in the path of the dragon.

Zee slid behind the rock beside her and saw what she held.

"Dark magic," he muttered.

"You know what must be done?"

"I remember." He held out the blade of the sword toward her, as needed. Without her asking, he ran the back of his wrist against the edge. As his blood struck the stone, it pulsed once more, glowing now with an ominous, lurid light.

"Wrong, wrong, wrong," Weston said. "This can lead to no good."

"Hush, we have no choice."

"What of Poe and the raven?" Zee asked.

"Poe!" she called again. He didn't move so much as a feather, but stood undaunted, staring down a creature that could roast him in the beat of a heart.

"Can't get rid of the damned raven, no matter how hard I try. They'll probably find us."

Vivian drew a deep breath and ran the heel of her own hand over the keen edge of the blade, watching the thin line of blood well up and spill over onto her white skin. She twisted her wrist, letting the bright drops fall onto the bloodstone.

The stone began to beat like an exposed heart, expanding and contracting, emitting an ever-increasing light with every pulse.

"Now what?"

"Hell if I know." Maybe she was supposed to talk to it or something, but the only phrase that came to mind was *Calgon, take me away.* She gazed into the center of the stone, taking a deep breath and letting go of all her rational thoughts and preconceptions. Listening.

And then she spoke to it her deepest need. "Take us to the Gates."

The world began to spin, the three of them at the center of a cyclone, whirling faster and faster, trees, water, walking dead, dragon monster, dark, repeating over and over until it was all one solid blur, all of the things joined into one and spinning around the beating heart at its center.

And then, darkness.

Thirty-four

Vivian was unable to see a single thing in a dark so intense that it pressed against her eyeballs. The bloodstone in her hand was quiet and inert. She shoved it into her pocket and reached out her hands to find Weston and Zee on either side of her. Poe pressed up against her leg. With a quick rush of joy to find him present and unharmed she bent to hug him but didn't speak, still trying to get a sense of where they were and whether there was danger.

Little by little, sounds began to trickle into her consciousness. The liquid flowing of running water. Not the babbling of a brook or the noisy rushing of a stream, but the sound of a large river flowing between banks worn smooth by its passing. A murmuring and rustling came to her next, like a large group of people, hushed and waiting. Shifting position from time to time, asking a brief question, uttering a reassuring word.

A light appeared in the distance. "Come, let's go closer." She meant to whisper, but her voice seemed loud and harsh. Zee and Weston took her hands, one on each side, so as to stay together, and she took courage from their strength. Measuring her steps, testing each before she set it down to be sure she remained on solid land, she led them right up to the edge of the river, still invisible in the dark.

The light drew closer and brighter, until her eyes could make out the shape of a boat with a man standing in the stern, a long oar in his hands. He was cloaked all in black, with a hood covering his face.

"If that is who I think it is, I'm going to kill you," Weston said.

"Hush. If this goes badly, you won't need to."

She should have been frightened, but she felt strangely easy.

The Ferryman's head swiveled in their direction. His chin lifted. Out of the dark his eyes shone green like a cat's. He altered his course, steering the boat around to come in close to where they stood, using his long oar as a pole to anchor him there while the boat swung about in the slow current.

"This is not the landing, nor are you the dead. What do you want of me?"

"Passage to the Black Gates," Vivian said. "Can you get us there?" Her voice surprised her, rolling out strong and confident. Downriver to the right she could see, thanks to his light, the people who waited on the landing, cloaked in gray, huddled together for warmth or comfort.

"Passage to the Black Gates? That I cannot give, even if I would. I owe nothing to the living."

"We have coin such as is hard to come by, in this land or in any other."

"Even so. I cannot take you to the Black Gates."

"You can tell me, though, whether there is a way to reach them across this river."

"I might be able to tell that, if the coin were of sufficient value."

She selected a small bloodstone from the sock bag and held it up to the Ferryman. "And this?"

His face went cold with desire. "Now that is rare coin indeed. Is it real?"

Vivian tossed it to him. He caught it neatly, held it up to look through, touched it with his tongue. His eyes glittered.

"Well?"

"There may be a way for one such as you. It lies across the river, and is dark and perilous."

"So be it. Will you take us across?"

"If you pay me."

"What is your fee?"

"Two of the stones for each human, one for each of the birds."

"Done. I will give them to you when we reach the other side."

"Or I can step ashore and take them now, and leave you stranded."

"Their value will be lessened if you take them by force. Heart's blood must be freely given. You know this, Charon."

The words came from deep within, beyond knowledge, but she knew they were the right ones. They rang out in that dark place with a power long dormant.

He snarled. "You delay my true work."

The throng of the dead pressed up against the river, sighing like a wind in the treetops.

"The dead you have always with you," Weston said. "Sooner we go, sooner you can get back to your task."

"A bargain then," Vivian said. "Passage across the river for the three of us and the birds. Eight bloodstones. And you direct us to the path that will lead to the Black Gates. I will pay you now, in full, if you give me your word to fulfill your end of the agreement."

"We have a bargain." She thought she caught a flash of sharp white teeth, lit by the glowing eyes.

Zee touched her arm, and she knew he too had seen it. The Ferryman was holding something back that gave him pleasure. He was not to be trusted, but there was no choice. Already he had brought the raft to shore. Weston shrugged, picked up Poe, and leaped aboard, holding out his hand to Vivian.

The moment her foot touched the deck, the Ferryman stood blocking her, hand outstretched. If she took one step back, if he pressed one hand against her, she would topple into the river. She shuddered at the thought of what that would mean, to fall undead into those black depths and be swept away. She felt Zee's hand on her arm, steadying her, knew if she fell he would do his best to catch her.

"Toll," the Ferryman said.

Vivian counted the bloodstones out into his palm.

"There are only seven here."

"I gave you one already."

"True."

He looked up, and she gasped to see his face. Not deformed or scarred, or ugly. A beautiful face, one Michelangelo might have used for a David or an angel.

"What will you do with them?" she asked.

He smiled, his lips a sensual curve over white teeth. "I have my own debts to pay. Keep to the center of the raft if you would not fall in."

Turning, he picked up his long oar and shoved the boat out into the current. Vivian took uncertain steps toward the center of the boat, Zee's hand still warm on her arm. A strange and silent trip in the wide dark followed, lighted only by the Ferryman's lamp and the glow of his eyes.

The light reflected on the water in a radius around the boat. The current rippled and flowed. No sound but the water slapping against the bow. Vivian was deathly cold, her muscles clamped tight, racked by shivering. Zee's hand on her arm ceased to be warm, and then she ceased to feel it at all. Frost glinted in Weston's beard.

How wide the river was, she could not tell. Neither bank was in the range of sight. There was nothing but the small island of light, the Ferryman's movements, Weston's and Zee's breathing, a small rustle of feathers as the birds shifted restlessly.

The change began as a kernel of warmth at her core. Cold as she was, she welcomed it without thought, grateful and encouraging it to grow. It did so, fist-sized, hotter now, until her belly was full of the growing heat. It flowed through her veins, throwing off the cold, expanding her senses, filling her with strength.

Charon turned as though he felt the change. The green glow in his eyes spiked and again he smiled that dangerous smile. "Ah, My Lady, I fear I did not recognize you. I should tip you into the river before you come into all of your power."

"I mean no harm to you."

"Not now, perhaps. Still, a bargain is a bargain. And you have a dark and dangerous way to go."

The Ferryman stopped paddling for a moment, lifting his lamp to look at them all more clearly. In the light of his lantern Zee appeared clad in chain mail, bearded and fell as though he had stepped out of a painting of one of the knights of old. Weston was in leather, a bow in his hand, a quiver of arrows slung on his back, hunting knife belted at his waist.

"So now I see. The River reveals what has been hidden. You, My Lady, are many things. As for your companions— you are well protected. The Warrior and the Hunter. The bird who does not fly, and the raven. All headed for the Black Gates. And there are bloodstones in play. Truly, time has moved apace in the world above."

The boat gave a little shudder. Vivian glanced up to see the light sparking against cliffs of glistening black stone. A narrow path wound like a gash up the side.

"There is the way," the Ferryman said. "It is steep. There are—barriers." A new respect had entered his voice and he swept his hood back and looked Vivian clearly in the eyes, with no mockery or treachery in his. "There is little I am permitted to say. Because of what you are, it is possible that you will find the way out into the land above. It is probable that your death awaits you."

"In which case," she said, "I will see you again very soon."

"Ah. There is much you do not know."

"What? What aren't you telling me?"

"Of this, I may not speak. Beware. Death has no favors for one such as you."

The boat bumped up against the stone wall. Weston was first to leap out, carrying Poe. Zee followed. They stood waiting for Vivian, but she lingered, shivering and afraid.

"You could stay with me," Charon said, lowering his voice. "You are the first in lifetimes of humans who would be fit to be a companion to me, and I would keep you safe."

"It is long to be alone in the dark," she said, "but I must decline. I have oaths to fulfill, if I can."

He nodded, and to her great surprise, bowed to her. "Go then, My Lady. Beware."

His last word echoing in her ears, Vivian turned and clambered off the boat to join the others. Charon lifted his hand in a salute and began his journey back across the river.

Thirty-five

He might have warned us," Weston said.

"He did warn us." Vivian sounded tired and frail, but Zee was not misled by that. The strength of will that drove her was a mystery and an amazement to him.

They stood at the very edge of a precipice beneath a sky not black but gray. As they had followed the path a dim light gradually emerged, enough to allow them to set one foot in front of the other, steadily increasing until now they could see the sheer drop-off at the end of their way, thousands of feet straight down to where the river flowed beneath them.

Here it was not the smoothly flowing entity that Charon had ferried them across, but rather a seething mass of white water, spiked by sharp spits of stone. It was hungry.

"Do you feel it?" Vivian asked, stepping up beside him.

Zee put out an arm to fence her in, to hold her back. "It wants us."

At his touch a shudder went through her, and she blinked as if waking from sleep. "Can't have us." Her head turned to follow the river's course to the place where gray light filtered in through the roof of the cave. "There's our exit."

"I still don't see how we're to get there." Weston had stepped well back from the edge and was clinging to a spar of stone, looking dizzy and sick. The cut on his cheek had bled freely into his beard, which contributed to a sort of mad-prophet look that might have been amusing at another time.

Here, in this place, even the memory of humor was hard to find.

Zee assessed the options. The path ended here; the rock between them and the opening downriver was nothing but a jumbled mess of sharp pinnacles and crevices that would be impossible to navigate without climbing gear. Even then, only an experienced mountaineer would be able to do it, and it would take time. Going back would accomplish nothing. There was only one path, and no way back across the river.

"What now?" Weston asked.

"There is only one thing we can do," Vivian answered.

Zee's heart twisted into a knot so tight he wondered that it kept on beating. Already his pain ran so deep he could scarcely contain it, and now there was more. He had known the moment they reached this point what she was going to do, although he had hoped to be wrong.

"We'll have to fly," Vivian said.

She glanced up at him, her eyes deep wells of hurt, and he wanted to say something, to tell her he was sorry, that he loved her for all the things that she was, but the words were all knitted into the pain and he held silence.

A grim smile twisted her lips. "It appears to be the way of things," she said. "Neither of us can argue with fate."

A glimmer of hope lit Weston's eyes. "I thought you couldn't shift."

"I can shift. The question is whether I will remember that you all are my friends and allow you to ride."

"Or try to roast us," Weston said.

"The question really is," Zee said, speaking the truth they were all avoiding, "whether the shift will kill you."

"There's no other option. This goes so far beyond my life, or yours, that they don't even weigh in the balance. We need to reach the Gates. We need to stop her. You saw what the dream stuff does—I don't even want to think about what will happen if that leaks into Wakeworld somehow. Grab

Poe, somebody, and step back. There's not a lot of room for the shift."

Zee needed to say something, to hold her, to press his lips against hers, but was blocked by memory of his betrayals. He wanted to wrap her in his arms and keep her there, safe and sheltered. But he couldn't protect her from what faced them, and much as he loved her, she deserved the right to choose the manner of her death.

"Weston, stuff my clothes in your pack, will you, so I'm not naked on the other side?"

"Vivian, there must be another way—"

"There's not. You know there's not. Please don't make this harder than it is."

She turned her back on them then and began to undress. Zee meant to look away, but his eyes lingered on the smooth curve of her back, the fall of her hair, the long lean legs; he had painted her so many times from dream that he knew the curves intimately. He had always hoped there would come a day when he would be given leave to explore them in the real world, but that was not to be.

Folding the clothes in a neat little pile, she turned and retraced her steps up the path, her white body almost like flame in the gloom. She stopped in a wide space, spread her arms wide, and closed her eyes.

This too, Zee had seen in dream, the shift from woman into dragon. It had hurt him every time, but he had earned the pain, it was all he deserved, and he forced himself to watch as her body bulged and changed and transformed at last into the green-gold dragon.

"Vivian," Zee called out to her, remembering that she must be named to be held to herself. He had no right to name her, to hold her, and yet it must be done.

"Vivian," he said again, softer now, noticing the blood that gushed from an unhealed wound between foreleg and belly.

"Vivian," he whispered, because his voice was breaking, but she must be called three times.

Weston came to stand beside him. "It won't heal. Not ever. We'll need to hurry before she grows too weak to fly."

Zee wanted to protest, to insist that she change back now, at once. But her words came back to him—*this goes beyond my life, or yours.* And so he said only, "How shall we climb aboard? I think the tail, yes?"

"If we can get there—we'll have to climb those rocks to reach it . . ."

But the dragon lowered its head to the ground, making a small flameless snort. Vivian, Zee reminded himself, not some stupid beast. She could hear and understand. "Or, we get up this way." He scooped up Poe and stepped onto the broad skull, holding to one of her horns for balance. The head lifted like an elevator until her long neck was level with her body, and Zee walked it like a plank and settled himself at its base. The scales were smooth and hard as stone, sharp edged. They could cut you if you weren't careful, but he was taken aback by the jewel-like brilliance of their color. He'd been too busy killing dragons to much notice the beauty of their scales.

Weston settled beside him, the raven on his shoulder. The dragon wings unfurled and beat once, twice. A thrust into the air as she pushed off with all four feet, and then the wings were lifting them all, carrying them out and above the river, heading for the dim light that offered hope of an exit.

Zee felt the pull of the river at once. It sucked them down in a sickening plunge, like a glider on a downdraft. The dragon beat her wings harder to gain altitude and carry them back aloft. A foot she gained, two, but no matter how hard she labored she could do no more.

They flew about a stone's throw above jagged rocks thrusting up out of the water, spray tossing so high into the air that he could feel it against his face. It slicked the scales beneath him, so that between the slipperiness and the pull of the river it was a battle to hold to Poe and keep his place.

Out of the corner of his eye Zee saw Weston begin to slide. The old man scrabbled with both hands on the dragon's back, trying to find purchase. There was nothing else to hold on to, no friction. Zee flung out a hand, but he was too late and too far. With a cry, the old Dreamshifter slid away into empty air.

An answering cry from the dragon echoed through the cavern. Her wings stopped beating and folded back, and she plunged downward after the falling man. The river rushed up toward them, rock spikes reaching, seeking. Weston was going to crash, and the rest of them immediately after.

Zee braced himself, wondering if it was possible to survive that foaming stretch of water without being impaled or beaten to death on the rocks. A small jolt, and then the wings were working again, faster and harder, straining to lift up and away from the rocks. Cautiously peering downward, Zee saw Weston dangling just above the water, his backpack snagged in a dragon claw.

One of the straps snapped, and the Dreamshifter's body jolted again toward the long fall. He flipped around and grabbed hold of the pack with both arms, clinging.

Zee stared, horrified, at what lay ahead.

There was no way they were going to make it.

The river dropped off in a falls that plunged a thousand feet into a swirling cauldron of foam and spray. Glimpses of stone teeth emerged and vanished again in the ever-shifting waves and white water. Beyond the falls, at the far side of the cauldron, a narrow ledge intersected the cliff. A faint light filtered in through a small opening in the stone—just big enough that a man might crawl through it flat on his belly.

No dragon would ever fit through that gap, nor was there room for her to land on the ledge. There was nowhere else for her to go, except back, and she would never make it. She was weakening, each wing beat more difficult and desperate than the last.

The cliff came at them with dizzying speed, and Zee knew they were too low to catch the ledge. He felt her intensify the effort, the great wings straining, beating harder and faster, gaining a few inches at a time. She had to see it, had to know there was no way there was room for her to set down there. Maybe the switches between human and dragon had disoriented her and she couldn't see.

Zee braced himself as well as he could for the crash, clutching Poe, ready to roll or leap or whatever had the slightest chance of bringing them to safety. But at the last instant the wings curved and checked. The dragon swerved. Momentum pushed Zee sideways with too much force for his tentative hold on the slick scales. Across the wide back, into the air over the wing, fingernails scraping for an instant at the last hope of gaining a hold. Then he was flying, the tumultuous water reaching up for him from below, on an arc that carried him onto the ledge with a crushing jolt that squeezed the air from his lungs and left him dizzy and winded.

Unable to draw a breath or so much as lift a finger to intervene, he saw the dragon roll in the air so that her talons were extended upward, still grasping Weston by the strap of his pack. He clung to it with both arms, embracing it as salvation, his beard and hair wild and windblown. Another roll, a twist of dragon legs, and Weston was dislodged and barrel rolling through the air toward the ledge, still clutching the pack to his chest.

He was coming too fast and at an angle that would take him along the edge and shoot him back out over the water.

Zee managed to get his body in motion and flung himself forward to catch the spiraling Dreamshifter, both of them crashing down and rolling to a slow stop against the cliff face.

Zee was up again in a heartbeat. "Vivian!" he shouted, knew he shouted because of the strain on his throat, but his voice was sucked up into the roar of the waterfall and made no sound.

The dragon's wings trembled once and then hung limp, doing nothing more than passively slowing her as she spiraled downward. He could see the hole in her breast, the black blood still falling, falling, to hiss into steam when it struck the water below. Her golden eyes were glazed and unseeing. She struck the water like an immense stone, without protest or struggle, creating a great drenching spray that rose all the way to the ledge. Zee's face was wet with the droplets, tasting of grief, bitter and sharp.

Poe joined him at the edge of the cliff, perched precariously with his webbed toes over the edge. He stretched out his flipper-wings as if he were going to fly, and then dove, free-falling into the dark water below without so much as a splash.

Zee huddled there, watching, hoping against hope. Maybe Vivian would come back up, despite all the odds. Dragons were tough and hard to kill. They had magic. Surely Poe, at least, would bob back to the surface.

But the penguin was small, for all that he was at home in the water, and Vivian had been sorely wounded by the dragonstone. His doing, his fault. If she was dead, it was because he had killed her. This was knowledge he could not endure. He would rescue her, or die with her, one or the other. He took a step back, prepared for a running leap out over the chasm.

"No!" Arms around his waist restrained him, pulled him away from the edge.

Zee tried to fight, but he was off balance and Weston was using all of his weight to pull him down and back. He hit the stone with a jarring pain in the injured arm that shot red-hot spikes through his vision, but still he struggled and rolled until Weston's shout stopped him. "Careful or you'll take us both over!"

"Let me go."

Stronger in spite of the injury, he twisted himself free of the Dreamshifter's hands. Weston promptly doubled up his fists and delivered strategic blows to one laceration, and then the other. The pain made Zee gasp, froze him for long enough to hear Weston shout, "You can't save her! Think! She's a dragon. What are you going to do, drag her to the surface?"

"Let me go—"

"No! You haven't earned a death! You have to save the Key. That's why you're here. That's why she saved you. Both of us. Well, that and because she's Vivian. We have to do this thing. It's the only way to make right the wrong."

A part of Zee stood here on this ledge, and the rest of him, the part that mattered, had plummeted into the water with the dragon. She had gone down never knowing how much he loved her, or how deeply he had betrayed her. And she had gone out of her way to save him, to save them all.

"Come on," Weston said, turning away. "If we survive, there will be time to grieve later."

Zee knew he was right. Still, he stood, head bowed, in a moment of silence for the sacrifice and all that was lost.

Thirty-six

The weight of the dragon body spun Vivian down through the black water, careening off stones, deeper and deeper until she knew that even a dragon could never hold its breath long enough to reach the surface. Especially a dragon weak from blood loss and poison.

This was it, the end.

Without any conscious agreement of her will, she shifted. Her bursting lungs were no longer dragon lungs; her frantic heartbeat was far too rapid. And she knew that what had been impossible for a dragon was beyond impossible for a human.

Sheer obstinacy kicked in. Impossible or not, she wasn't just going to accept death without a fight. She began to thrash with her legs and arms to stop the downward trajectory and thrust herself upward, even though it was impossibly far and the rocks would kill her if she ever did make it to the surface. Her lungs burned. Another few heartbeats and she would open her mouth and let the water flood her lungs, weigh her down. Her heart would stop beating. And that would be the end.

Just as all conscious will was fading, a black-and-white form appeared at her side, and then passed her: Poe, flying through the water. Mindless, Vivian followed him through a stone archway, but that was the end of her endurance. She could hold her breath no longer. Her mouth opened. Instead of the expected inrush of water, she gulped in air.

Stale, mineral-smelling air. Her feet touched solid ground and she realized she was standing in a calm pool, only waist deep. Poe scrambled up onto a flat surface, paved with red stone. Weak and exhausted, she staggered after him. There was pain in her chest and she remembered, a little dazed, the unhealed knife wound. It throbbed but wasn't bleeding.

Poe waddled away across the chamber and she dragged herself after him through yet another arch, which led out onto the edge of a flat plain. Mist swirled around her feet. A dim red light filtered down from an indifferent sky. She blinked. There should be no sky here, deep beneath the earth. Wonder gave way to an awareness of a throng of people, silent, waiting. She could feel the intensity of the eyes, all focused on her as though she were the single most important thing in the universe.

Naturally, she stood before them naked. Like everybody else, Vivian had experienced dreams of appearing naked at a crucial moment. This wasn't one of them. She had no need for a pendant to realize that this moment was real. Banishing the impulse to cover her breasts with her hands, to turn her back and flee the way she had come, she forced herself to stand tall and face them down. Only her knees were all wobbly and in a minute she was going to collapse, in which case she'd be naked and unconscious.

It was not to be thought of and she pushed away the encroaching darkness.

A figure separated from the mass and approached. An old man with a long white beard and eyes keen and blue despite his obvious age.

"Vivian," he said, his face alight with a fierce and savage joy. "I barely dared to hope, but you have found us."

Swaying, barely able to support herself, she clung to his proffered hand. "Grandfather. I'm in so much trouble. Can you help me?"

All the joy ran out of his face at her words, and he shook

his head. "I'm sorry, my child. Your burden is already heavy, I know, but it is we who need help from you."

"I won't be much help to anybody if I'm dead."

"Then you mustn't die."

She snorted. It was precisely the sort of thing he could be expected to say. And also an appropriate, if acerbic, response to her overdramatic words. At this moment, at least, she was in no danger of dying. Exhausted and hungry, maybe. But thoroughly alive. Poe pressed up against her side and she felt energy flow from him, strengthening her a little.

"What is this place—hell for Dreamshifters?"

"Close. We are trapped here when we die. Between life and the beyond."

"You've got to be kidding. Why?"

But there was no humor now in his blue eyes, or in the hard-set lines of his face. The Ferryman had warned her— *Death has no favors for one such as you.* She looked from him to the others, women and men of all ages and nationalities. Her grandfather wore blue jeans and a button-up flannel shirt. Those farther back wore homespun. Beyond that was a mélange of clothing styles that should never have been seen together in one place: ball gowns and animal skins, togas, armor; there was even a man wearing a Viking helmet.

"There is no joke, child, unless it is a joke of the gods."

She closed her eyes, remembering the people Jehenna had trapped in cattle pens to serve as dragon fodder. Some of them had been torn apart before her eyes. The rest of them had been freed, thank God, and now here she was again, being asked to do the impossible on behalf of a crowd of people she didn't know. Her shoulders ached beneath the familiar weight of responsibility, but she said at last, "What do you need from me?"

"Find the Key—"

"That? Get in line. Everybody wants that freaking Key."

"Find the Key," he repeated, ignoring her interruption. "Open the Black Gates, travel through the shadowlands into the Forever, and bring back a cup of water from the fountain at the foot of the throne of the Dragon King. Only when that water is spilled on this plain will we be released."

"You have got to be kidding."

He shrugged. "As I said, this is beyond a joke. Here we are trapped, and here we will remain until it has been done."

"And then what? If I succeed in this task—you all acquire eternal life and there's an army of indestructible zombie Dreamshifters loose in the universe?"

"No," he said softly. "If you succeed, then we will be able to truly die. Look around you. All are in some kind of hurt. Some for thousands of years."

For the first time she noticed the jagged, bloodstained tear in the breast of his shirt. Looking beyond, she saw a hard-faced old man with a crater in his chest. She'd seen an image of him far too recently, trying to shoot his son with a rifle.

"Edward Jennings," she said. "The man who destroyed his entire family. For you I have no compassion."

"I regret," he said. "I've had a long time to think on what I have done."

"We are able to see," her grandfather said. "To watch the struggle, but unable to intervene. He has been punished beyond measure already, Vivian. As have we all. If you do not help us, there is no hope."

"I have the will," she whispered at last. "I'm not sure I have the strength."

"You must find it, child."

"I need food, water—"

He shook his head. "I'm sorry, but we do not eat or drink. And I fear the water of this place would keep you here if you were to drink it. Now come. I will lead you to the path you must take."

A woman stepped up beside him and touched his arm. She had been drowned, Vivian saw, water dripping endlessly from her clothing, her hair. "Perhaps it would be permitted for us to carry her, as far as the path. She is much wounded. Surely this much we could do to help her."

"We will pay for it."

"Let that be on us."

The throng murmured, repeating "Let it be on us," until the words swelled and became a chant. Two of the stronger men came forward and bowed to Vivian. "If you will permit, we will carry you."

"I would be grateful."

The two of them made a chair of their arms and lifted her. She placed her hands on their shoulders for balance as they strode out across the dry, dusty plain.

It was a strange and ghastly procession. As they walked, the undead parted to allow them to pass, bowing as they did so. So many different injuries marked them, all beyond any hope of healing. Vivian looked over her shoulder for Poe and saw that her grandfather had picked him up and was carrying him. The crowd closed behind him and followed, most of them bleeding, many of them lame.

Uneasy at first, Vivian became increasingly grateful for the lift as her human conveyance walked on and on. She could never have walked so far, and with the time to rest she felt strength gradually returning. How long the journey continued she had no idea. There was no day or night in this place, only the same dull, red light from the unchanging sky. Perhaps time did not even pass. She dozed and waked and dozed again.

A terrible thirst was on her, parching her throat, turning her tongue to sandpaper, and still they marched across the unchanging plain. Same dull sky above, same flat dusty earth beneath their feet, same halting, shuffling walk.

Then, at last, rock formations rose in the distance. These grew upward into cliffs and in one of the faces of stone she saw at last an opening. Light—real, white light—spilled through it. A draft of living air brushed against her skin.

The company came to a halt and her bearers lowered her to the ground. This time her legs held her, steady enough. Hope stirred, sluggish and feeble but alive, as she breathed in the sweetness of fresh air and fixed her eyes on the light.

"We can go no farther," her grandfather said. "Do not

fear what you are, child, or what you shall become." He laid his hand over her heart. "This remains ever the same."

Vivian only nodded, and did not speak. He was smaller than she, wizened and shrunken and so very old. But his eyes were the color of summer sky and his smile dazzled her, as unexpected as sun breaking through the clouds.

Garnering all of her small strength she turned from him and set off toward the promise of the light, Poe waddling solemn at her side.

Behind her, weighing heavy with their gray hope, the undead waited for her to free them.

Thirty-seven

Aidan rode the wind currents above the black mountain, allowing herself a moment of fierce joy. In her belly the Warrior's seed had quickened into life, a white-hot flame that grew beyond the speed of any purely human child. Not long, only a few months, and she would bear a son.

It hadn't been a part of the plan, but it was better this way. Her son was of the blood; he would grow to be a dragon slayer who would follow her bidding. She would hide him away as her mother had once hidden her, and when the time was right he would kill the King and help her rule the others.

Which meant she had no need of the Warrior, who had shoved her away in disgust as though she were some slimy scrap of refuse. Rage filled her at the thought. She hadn't killed him at the time, believing she might still have need of him. But that was before she knew that she would bear a child. There was time to make him suffer, some special pain for him before he died. In the meantime, she ruled all of the dragons of the Between, and they would launch forays wherever she sent them. They were only pawns in this game, little more than primitive beasts after all of the years of inbreeding and the absence from the golden river. Their minds were full of nothing but hunting and flight. Docile and stupid, they flocked to her will like chickens in a farmyard. Most of them must die, of course, but once she had dethroned the King and taken her rightful place as Queen of the Dragons, those stronger and smarter would be allowed to live as slaves.

As for the giants, they too had fallen since the day they set the Black Gates in place and made the Key. Look at them—thousands upon thousands strong, just standing there on the plain before the Gates. Waiting. From this height they looked like rock formations, and would be about as effective. The sort of magic needed to create a containment like the Black Gates and the Key had been lost, long ago.

With the exception of Jehenna, the sorcerers—sorcieri, Allel had called them—had kept to themselves for so long that even Aidan had no idea what they were up to. Whatever it was, they were unlikely to interfere. Which meant there was nobody and nothing left to ruin her plan of destruction.

It had been so easy to kill the Guardian; she too had grown stupid and complacent over the years. Without the Guardian the dreamspheres would die, were already reverting to raw dream matter. People in the place called Wakeworld would die as their dreams winked out of existence. Any who survived would be unable to find a dream to enter. There would be chaos and insanity and war and the fools would destroy each other.

This was the deep desire of Aidan's heart—that all things would end. If anything was left alive outside the Forever, her reign could never truly be secure. And she deserved to reign supreme for all time because of what had been done to her mother. And to her.

All things were in place and accounted for. Only one thing rankled. Surmise had proved to be beyond her reach. Not really a Dreamworld, not really Between, and not subject to the rules of either. Her only hope was that since it was woven from the fabric of the Dreamworld, perhaps it too would fade out of existence.

There was nothing she could think to do about it, and so she chose to dismiss it from her mind. It was time, now, to put her plan in motion.

Spiraling lazily down through the air, she alighted in front of the Gates. Huge they were, even to her in dragon form. When she shifted so as to manage the Key, they seemed to grow taller and blacker. She felt small and vulnerable in her human skin, frightened all at once.

A new emotion, fear. A thing she hadn't felt since the time almost beyond conscious memory when she and her mother had fled from one place to another to stay in hiding from her father. No shelter for her anywhere in the world, then. She was not fully human or dragon, nor was she of the Dreamworld. Nobody wanted her, everybody feared her. But she had grown past that, learned to shift and blend and bide her time.

Fear would not stop her now, even though a sense of wrongness filled her with foreboding. Up close, the Gates gave off a subtle vibration that was at odds with her body. It pulled her heartbeat off its regular rhythm, made it impossible to draw a full breath. Her bones felt like they were being jarred apart.

Her hands shook too hard to hold the Key. It dropped to the ground and she bent to pick it up once, twice, three times.

She glanced at the giants. They could stop her now, if they chose. It would only take a moment for them to reach her. In dragon form she could easily elude them, but in dragon form she couldn't open the Gates. Her plan had been based on speed and had already failed.

The giants didn't move, but what they did was worse. They began to laugh, a sound that rattled across the plain like thunder, echoing off the impenetrable barrier in front of her. Louder and louder. As if they'd known all along that she was going to fail and had come to bear witness.

Aidan tried once more to navigate the Key, but the vibration this time dropped her to her knees. Involuntarily and without her will her body shifted back into her dragon form, and she unleashed a scream of rage that shook the Gates and stopped the laughter from the first ranks of giants. Tough as their hides were, they were not impervious to dragon fire and she felt it building, ready to flame.

But she held herself back. Oh, they would pay. They would all pay. But there was still a chance to get through the Gates. The One still lived, as far as she knew. Aidan wanted her to suffer, had locked her into Wakeworld for that reason. Dream deprivation would be a terrible death for a Dreamshifter. Long and slow, with the insanity creeping in and no means to beat it back.

But if she still lived, she could be made to open the Gates. Aidan not only had the pendant, she had also taken skin and hair and blood from the One, and a simple spell would serve to find her. Which meant that the plan had not failed. Not yet. Circling high above the plain before winging away to a quiet space to do the spell she had been taught long ago, Aidan's eyes caught unexpected movement on the mountainside across from the Black Gates, and she flew across to investigate.

As she looked down on all that moved below, exultation filled her breast. Perhaps there would be no need to waste time on a fiddly little spell. Fate had presented her with a much easier way.

Thirty-eight

It wasn't much of a passage. Through it Vivian could see nothing but daylight. There was no telling what lay on the other side, or even how much time had passed since she fell. Hours, days, even weeks or years. But the clean air drew her, along with the promise of finding water and food.

Poe decided the matter, as he had done so many times before. He slipped through the crack and out of sight. As always, Vivian followed. It was a hard scramble up a pile of loose stones that cut into her bare feet and scraped the palms of her hands. The crack itself was about the height of a tall man, and narrow. If she'd been heavier, she would not have made it. As it was, the sharp edges of stone carved into the skin of her shoulders and thighs as she eased through.

But then she was free and clear.

A cold wind blew against her and she staggered under the assault, naked and shivering.

She stood with Poe beside her on a narrow ledge, halfway down a sheer cliff with no obvious way either up or down. Her range of motion was restricted to about a ten-foot space. To her left, the ledge narrowed and ended. To the right, the cliff bulged outward. The shelf continued around it, but only about three inches' worth. Enough for an experienced climber, maybe.

Not for a small and weary woman.

Poe huddled against the cliff wall, away from the wind. Looking back to check on him, Vivian saw that the cleft she had climbed out through had closed behind her. Even if she had wanted to, there was no going back to the purgatory of the Dreamshifters.

A desolate valley spread out below—rock, sand, and sagebrush. On the far side another mountain loomed, its summit shrouded in dark clouds. Familiar. She had seen it in dream after dream, nightmare after nightmare. At its base, what could only be the Gates, made of a stone so black it sucked up all the light. Even in full sun, the area at their foot was in permanent shadow. All across the valley floor, tall shapes stood in symmetrical patterns. Standing stones, she thought at first. Giant chessmen, except that as she watched they moved, and her heart convulsed in a beat of fear as she remembered Zee's talk of giants.

They made the Key, she reminded herself. *They crafted the Black Gates. There is no reason to think of them as enemies.*

Dragons wheeled and soared above the mountain, for all the world like a flock of birds except that their wings made a constant thunder and raised a dust storm on the plain below. Vivian tried to reach out to them, but there weren't even murmured voices in her head, now, not so much as a faint response. Grief at this broadsided her; she had fought so long and hard against the dragon power, hating and loathing it, and now that it was gone she missed it.

Which figured. It would have been nice to fly down off this inconvenient perch, because she had no idea how she was going to get where she needed to go. Or anywhere, for that matter. It would be ironic to die of cold and hunger on the side of a mountain after everything she had already survived.

Closer than the dragons, another bird flew, large and black. She watched him, envious of strong wings and the gift of flight. Poe made a small sound almost like a whimper, and she wondered whether he felt the lack of wings. The bird croaked solemnly, as if in answer, and then fluttered down at her feet.

Weston's raven, she was sure of it. And if he wasn't with Weston, then something was wrong. *Not dead,* she told herself. *Just lost somewhere, or in trouble. As am I.*

The wind died down a little, shifted its direction. In the relative silence she heard voices from around the buttress.

"Strategy? Direct line across the center? Or circle to the left and try to stay out of sight?"

"First thing we have to do is get down. I can't see how we will do that unnoticed."

"And if they notice us?"

"They may do nothing."

"If they stop us?"

"We fight." Zee's voice was unyielding stone.

They were alive, and still fighting. Vivian's heart leaped with joy. She shuffled across the ledge to press up against the bulging place and called, "Zee? Weston? I'm over here!"

"Vivian?"

"How do I get to you?"

"Just a minute. Weston's got a rope."

Of course Weston would have a rope. It was a long way down, though, and the ledge was so very narrow and the wind so very strong. Even with a rope tied around her waist and secured to something, she was nearly frozen at the idea of making that trek. She was nearly frozen anyway from standing exposed in the wind. Hopefully Weston also had her clothes. Not that it mattered. Right now, she couldn't think past getting off this ledge.

A rattling sound drew her eyes to a small rock careening down the cliff face, and then Zee moved into her line of sight. His body pressed up against the stone as though it were a lover, arms spread in a wide embrace. He shuffled sideways toward her with his toes on that tiny strip of rock, one slow step after another. A rope was tied around his waist, along with the flannel shirt and jeans Weston had brought for her; shoes hung around his neck by the laces. Vivian held her breath, waiting for what seemed an eternity before he stepped down onto the wider ledge and turned to her.

She would have thrown herself into his arms in joy and relief, but his grim face stopped her. He was staring at her chest. Self-conscious, she wrapped her arms around her naked breasts, and as she did so her fingers automatically tented over the still-healing knife wound, protecting it.

"I nearly killed you." His voice scraped like stone on stone.

"You didn't."

"I don't understand how. Missed lung, heart, major arteries . . ."

"Zee. You have to let it go."

"Can't. Oh damn it, you're freezing. Here." He fumbled with the clothes tied around his waist and helped her into the flannel shirt. It served to cover her but provided precious little protection from the cold wind, which was as good an excuse as any. She wrapped her arms around his waist, laying her cheek against his broad chest. He stiffened, but she knew now what the trouble was and didn't let him push her away.

"If you don't want me dead, you'd best warm me a little or I'll be too numb to make it around that ledge."

His arms came round her then, enclosing her in his warmth. A moment later his cheek pressed against the top of her head. "I have pants. And your shoes."

"I know. I saw."

"You should put them on."

"In a minute."

"Vivian—"

"You didn't mean to kill me. It's the whole dragon slayer thing. You said I was wrong about you and me, that we could get past it."

She felt his chest heave and tightened her arms around his waist, afraid that he would try to pull away.

"There are things you don't know—"

"So tell me." She turned her face up to his, and saw his

resolve waver. He was going to kiss her, and everything would sort itself out from there.

His head bent toward hers.

"Are you guys lost over there?"

Vivian might have hurt Weston at that moment if he'd been in range. Zee kissed the top of her head and pulled away.

"That's not fair!" she protested. "You can't just throw something out like that and not tell. What don't I know?"

"We don't have time." He tucked a strand of hair behind her ear. And then the old smile broke out, full of mischief. "Besides, when I tell you I want to have plenty of room to run away and lots of shelter. All right? Ready to put those shoes on?"

She looked at the ledge and shook her head. "Why can't Weston just come here?"

"Because Weston is where we need to be. There is actually a path of sorts that will get us down into the valley." He untied the rope from around his waist and knotted it around hers.

"What about you?"

"I'll be right beside you."

"But—"

"The wind is blowing against the cliff. It holds you to the face. It's not so bad; only the fear is a problem."

"What about Poe?"

"Questions, questions." He knelt and tied a second rope around Poe, careful to secure it beneath his wings so it wouldn't slip. Then he carried the bird over to the edge of the cliff, and gave the rope a tug. "You ready, Weston?"

"Ready."

"One penguin coming your way."

Gently he eased Poe over the edge. The little bird swung out over the emptiness below, and then over to the left. Vivian's heart swung with him, but at once the rope began to shorten and Poe vanished from her view, presumably finding safety with Weston on the other side.

She delayed, slipping into the pants, putting on the shoes, but then she couldn't put it off any longer. Her hands checked and double-checked the rope tied around her waist as she stood shivering and reluctant to take that first step.

"Weston's got you. If you slip and fall, worst-case scenario you lose a patch of skin and collect another bruise. You can handle it."

"I'm a lot heavier than Poe—"

"And he's got you belayed around a rock. Come on now—we've got work to do."

Right. She was being a coward and there wasn't time for that.

Zee put his hands on her shoulders and looked into her eyes. "If I thought it wasn't safe, or that he would drop you, I wouldn't let you go. Understood?"

She nodded, feeling marginally better, and managed a feeble smile.

"Ready?"

She nodded, and he put his hand on her waist and steadied her as she edged first one toe and then the other out onto the ledge. Zee tugged the rope as a signal, and it instantly tightened. He was right about the wind, too—it pushed her face-first into the rock. She could do this. If she could bring herself to move her feet.

Don't look down. Slide one foot over, and then the next. Zee was beside her now, to the right. Doing the same thing she was doing but without the safety of a rope. *Don't think about that. Don't think at all. Just move your feet, cling to the rock, don't look down.*

Halfway. A few more steps and she should be able to see Weston and Poe and the place she was aiming for.

The rope tugged sharply, setting her off balance and almost throwing her backward off the cliff. Her fingernails scrabbled on sheer rock, found a crack, and caught. Not much, but enough to prevent her from falling away. She clung, not daring to move, breath sobbing in and out of her lungs. The rope slackened, then tightened again.

"Grace," she heard Weston say. "So it's true then."

Vivian caught her breath, in dismay. Grace here was not a good thing. Not good at all. But the thought steadied her. She wasn't going to allow the old hag to finish off Weston after all of this time. Besides, she wanted her pendant. And the Key, of course the Key and to save the world and everybody in it.

But first things first.

It wasn't far, not really. She felt the difference in the air, caught the change in light and perspective in her peripheral vision, but didn't dare to turn her head. Her arms burned with the effort of clinging to the crack; her calves ached. But then the ledge widened, little by little, so that it held her whole foot and not just her toes. Wider yet, and then she was on a level platform as big as a house.

A small house, anyway, not big enough for any sort of comfort. She could see the path Zee had mentioned, winding down the shoulder of the mountain. Steep, but not sheer. And between her and that path, an old woman.

Weston looked like he'd been carved from the stone of the mountain, his face etched in lines of grief. The old woman facing him had a face much like his, softened to the feminine. Her lips curved in a smile as she saw Vivian and Zee.

"And there they are. Unfallen after all. Depending on your definition of that word, of course. Hardly innocents, the lot of you."

"Give me my pendant." Deep down Vivian knew that the other things were more important, but the reaction was a primal thing that boiled up out of the depths of her.

"Or you'll do what? Take it from me?"

Vivian darted forward to do exactly that, but the old woman raised a filthy, gnarled hand in a casual gesture and she bounced off an invisible force field.

"Now, now, young one. That will never do. Remember what happened to your brain when you fought me before."

And with those words the pain began, Vivian's skull in a vise, tightening bit by bit; her brain was going to explode under the pressure like a ripe melon. She tried with all of her strength and will to fight back but found herself doubled over, gasping, both hands clutching at her head.

"Release her." Zee's voice.

"Or you'll do what, lover? Have you told her about you and me?"

The pain eased, enough so that Vivian could stand up straight and watch as the wrinkled old face smoothed and tightened. The bone structure altered. Brown eyes turned to gray. Her hair waved and curled and brightened to auburn.

A mirror image of Vivian's own face and body before the dragon marked her, except that the belly swelled out in the soft curve of pregnancy. Her brain still felt scrambled with the pain, the words and the visual not connecting.

"Don't even think about using the Voice on me," Vivian's own voice said from that other body. "It won't work now. I've got your pendant and your hair and skin. I have the power over you, and you will do as I say."

Zee had the sword in his hand. "Take whatever form you wish—I will kill you."

But he hesitated.

"Would you take the life of an unborn baby then? Your own child, Zee." One of the woman's hands went protectively to her belly.

"It's not possible."

"Blood of your blood, Warrior. Flesh of your flesh."

Zee's arm dropped to his side. "It's an illusion. It has only been a matter of days—"

"Time passes according to its own whims in the dark realms. And there are Dreamworlds where time passes even faster, if one has earned such passage. You're not going to kill your own child, no matter how you might hate the flesh that carries him."

Vivian looked up into Zee's stricken face and knew that it was true. He had made love to this *thing* and it was pregnant with his child. She shuddered in revulsion, pushing away the inevitable heartbreak for later.

"Stop this," Weston said. "Enough. This is cruel, Gracie.

There's no need to hurt anybody—there's been too much of that already. You of all people know this. What do you want?"

"You are wrong," she said, and the voice was cold as ice, neither Vivian's nor that of the old hag. "There can never be enough pain to make up for what I have suffered."

Silence hung absolute. Even the wind died away and a darkness seemed to hang over the sun. But then she shrugged her Vivian-shaped shoulders and held out a black cylinder, carved all around with symbols. Vivian felt herself step forward in response to an invisible pull from the Key, only to be pushed back again by the woman's power.

"What happens next is that the Chosen One is going to open the Gates."

"You've got the Key. What do you need me for?" The ongoing push and pull of both brain and body and emotion was beginning to produce a blessed numbness that was beyond pain. A little piece of Vivian's brain wormed itself free and began putting together one piece after another of the puzzle.

There were flaws in the image the woman wore. The shape of the face wasn't quite right. The eyes were a little too close together, the nose a shade too aquiline.

"It turns out that it's not only the Key that's needed. It wouldn't work for me, even in this body. So you are going to open the Gates for me."

"No," Vivian said. "I am not."

"Oh, I think you will."

Again the pain overwhelmed her. When she was able to focus her eyes, the woman's body was shifting again, this time to that of a child just on the edge of womanhood. Dark hair braided in two pigtails; an innocent face with knowing eyes. Worst of all, a rail-thin child body and the abomination of a pregnant belly. Vivian had seen that face before on the dream construct back at the Cave of Dreams. But again, it was subtly wrong.

Tears streaked Weston's cheeks. He didn't move, didn't speak.

"A lot of people are dead on account of you, Weston," the girl said. "Help me now, and you can make it right."

Vivian wanted to warn him, but she didn't yet know of what. Zee's knuckles on the hilt of the sword were white.

Weston gasped, as though he'd been struck. His face set in lines of determination. He took a step in her direction. "I owe you," he said.

Grace smiled. It should have been a sweet child smile, but it was too knowing, too calculating. "Kill the Warrior. Then we'll talk. Don't look at me like that—you have a gun."

In slow motion, as though he were sleepwalking, Weston bent and picked up the shotgun from where it lay beside him. He chambered a shell. Vivian stepped sideways to put herself between him and Zee, and Zee shoved her out of the way, hard enough that she fell to hands and knees.

The muzzle of the gun came up. Zee hefted the sword and launched himself toward Weston.

Vivian watched, helpless.

And then both trajectories changed just before they met at the middle.

Poe stepped directly into Zee's path and tripped him. A sharp curse, a tangle of legs and feet and feathers and Zee went down.

Weston swung the gun to the right and pulled the trigger. A shot rang out and blood blossomed on Grace's breast.

"You're not Grace," he said. And pulled the trigger again. The child staggered backward, her eyes huge with shock and pain. An inarticulate cry burst from her throat, outraged and inhuman. Her skin rippled and expanded as her mouth elongated into jaws and her nose into a snout. A long, serpentine neck grew to support the massive horned head, Vivian's pendant dangling incongruously from a chain that had expanded to accommodate the new bulk. Talons sprang out of what had once been hands but were now feet on the ends of legs as thick as tree trunks.

Before Weston could reload, the dragon pinned him to the ground with one foot and held him there.

"Let him go!" Vivian shouted, moving toward the fallen

Dreamshifter, but a warning jet of smoke from the dragon's nostrils stopped her in her tracks. The wound in the creature's breast was a small thing now, not even bleeding. She towered over Vivian, as black as the Gates themselves, sucking up all of the light.

It was all Vivian could do to stay on her feet.

Words formed, soundless, in her mind.

You will take the Key. We will fly to the Gates, and you will open them for me.

"And if I don't?"

All of your companions die.

Weston wasn't moving, and Vivian couldn't tell if he was still breathing. Zee inched forward, flat on his belly. His arm was bleeding again. If he took on a sword battle with this dragon at this time, he would die. He simply wasn't strong enough. She also knew that he was planning to try.

Somewhere there was dragonstone. In Weston's pack, probably, and she felt a flare of anger that he'd chosen the familiar gun over much more effective magic. Still, they might find the dragonstone, get a chance to use it, if she could buy some time. Her mind was still putting together pieces to try to get to the only acceptable outcome. Nobody dying. Getting her hands on the Key. Stopping the disintegration of the dreamspheres and finding her way to the water from the river so she could free all of the trapped undead Dreamshifters.

It took time to solve a puzzle like that, and maybe there was a way to bargain.

"If I open the Gates for you, will you carry us all? And promise our safety after?"

That depends on what you will promise me in return.

"To do my best to open the Gates."

But I have told you—if you do not open the Gates, they will die. And I will continue to cause you pain.

"No matter how much you hurt me, I will not open the Gates for you. And if they all die, you might as well kill me."

Oh, very well. And my safety? Where is the dragonstone?

"I don't know." True enough, although she hoped it wasn't true for long.

Can you control your minions?

The idea of either Weston or Zee as minion almost made her laugh, despite the desperate straits they were in. "I don't seek to control them, and I cannot speak for them. But if you want me to open the Gates of my own voluntary will, then you must carry me there and guarantee their safety."

You strike a hard bargain. I will not seek to hurt them. Or you. Until the Gates are opened.

"And we will also hold our hands until the Gates are opened."

"Vivian—"

She silenced Zee with a look. His eyes smoldered in an unminionlike way, but he nodded, keeping the sword unsheathed while she bent over and picked up the Key that lay by the dragon's great foot. As before, it surprised her with its weight. Only now it felt alive in her hand, as though it were made of pure energy and not just stone.

The energy fed her. She felt her shoulders straighten, felt herself draw a deeper breath. "Another thing," she said, looking way up and into the huge golden eyes. "I want my pendant."

I do not wish to give it to you.

"Doesn't matter. It isn't yours, and if you're planning to leave me alive, as you promised, you won't be needing it and I will."

She knew full well what she was asking. It meant the dragon was giving up control. No more ability to inflict that mind-numbing pain.

The black dragon shot flame out of her nostrils. Vivian waited. At last the great head bent toward her and the pendant was in reach. Surprised at the steadiness of her own hands, Vivian unfastened the clasp of the chain and hung the pendant around her own neck. When the chain automatically shortened to fit, she didn't even feel surprise. Her hand closed around the familiar little penguin.

"All right then," she said. "If you would move your foot so we can retrieve our comrade, we're ready."

I will carry him.

It took a minute for Vivian to realize that the dragon

meant to carry Weston in her talons. She shook her head. "No. He rides with me."

He tried to kill me.

"He tried to kill the sister you were pretending to be. Let me have him."

No.

"Fine." Vivian dropped the Key. "All of us, or none of us. That's the bargain."

A cry of rage, a puff of flame. Great wings clapped together in the air above the dragon's back.

Vivian stood her ground, one arm shielding her face from the dust storm kicked up by the dragon's wings. Zee was on his feet beside her now, steadying her with his warm presence, helping her stand braced against the onslaught.

At last the great wings stilled and the dragon quieted.

You may pick up your comrade.

The monstrous foot lifted, and Zee dragged Weston as far away as the limited space allowed. Vivian ran to join him. The old Dreamshifter's chest barely rose and fell in rapid, shallow breaths. His skin was hot with fever. When Vivian's hand touched his forehead his eyes opened, unfocused at first but clearing.

"Spiked me," he whispered.

Oh no. No, no, no. Tearing away his shirt she found the marks on his shoulder where the talons had pierced his skin.

"What is it, Viv? What's wrong with him?"

"Dragon venom."

"It's all right," Weston said. His lips twisted into a smile. "Looks like I'm gonna burn one way or another. Funny how it all works out."

"Shhh," Vivian murmured, smoothing his forehead. "Don't try to talk."

Weston tossed his head side to side, restless with the fever and the pain. "Damned dragon reached right inside my head and picked up on my memories of Grace. Smart enough to age her to look like me . . ."

"How did you know?" Zee asked. "That it wasn't your sister, I mean?"

"Grace always called me Morgan. She—" His words cut off as his body jerked in a sudden spasm and then went limp.

"Weston, wake up, stay with me!"

But his head lolled on his shoulders and his eyes didn't open.

"Can't you do something?" Zee asked.

Vivian shook her head, fighting back the sobs. She'd dragged Weston here, put him through so much heartbreak. This was so wrong, so unjust, that he should die, in the end, for nothing. And she couldn't even pretend he was going to a better place. Her chest felt so tight she couldn't catch her breath. Tears traced a cold path down her cheeks as she bent and pressed her lips against his hot forehead. "Say hello to my grandfather. And tell him I'm coming."

Enough of this wailing, the Black Dragon said. *Leave him or bring him, I care not. But if you don't wish your Warrior to join him, we go now.*

Without another word, Vivian picked up Poe, Zee dragged Weston up over his shoulder, and they climbed onto the dragon's back for the flight to the Black Gates.

Thirty-nine

✣

Sentient stone just wasn't possible, but Vivian felt the Gates respond to her approach with what felt like watchful consciousness. The Key in her hand began to hum and the Gates responded, producing a chord that ran across her skin in waves of sheer pleasure. Her heart leaped in exultation and the word *home* chimed in her heart.

Behind her, the thudding steps of approaching giants shook the earth in a regular rhythm. Above, the sun was blocked out by dragons flying in formation. Wind created by their wings buffeted her face and hair. So strange, and yet so familiar.

Maybe she had dreamed this moment or maybe it was truly what it seemed—her destiny. Her body moved without volition, drawn toward the singing Gates by an invisible attraction. Metal to magnet. Moth to flame. It didn't matter which.

Poe planted himself in front of her at a complete standstill, and she nearly tripped over him. When she tried to sidestep, he moved with her. Zee called her name, but his voice was no more than a faint tug. Even the thought of Weston, burning up from the inside out, held little meaning.

Vivian moved around the penguin and kept walking. The Gates were almost within reach now. A narrow beam of blue light shone through the keyhole—an octagonal shape that was a perfect match for the carved end of the cylindrical Key. It was that light that made her pause. Weston's face flashed through her mind—night, a campfire, a cup of something bitter.

Dragons fighting over a woman who stood quiet and self-possessed among them, holding a baby in her arms. The wailing of a child. A dragon, black as night with eyes of flame, snuffing out all living things.

Vivian could feel the impatience of the Black Dragon, an irrefutable force, like gravity or light.

Open the Gates.

"Not yet." Resistance was difficult. Her tongue felt heavy and thick, but she was the Chosen and the Key in her hand gave her power. Besides, she had her pendant back, and whatever spell had been cast over her seemed to be broken. No more crushing pain when she thought her own thoughts.

The Black Dragon roared, a spine-chilling sound. *Open the Gates. Keep your promise.*

In that moment, Vivian felt all the parts of her coalesce—sorceress, Dreamshifter, a tiny remaining spark of dragon. And above and beyond all, her own consciousness, Vivian, binding them all into one. She could open the Gates if she chose, or leave them closed, but it would be a decision made freely.

She thought about Jared, twisted and ruined by forces beyond his ability to resist. About Zee, so deeply wounded in body and in spirit, and Weston dying from the dragon poison. She pondered the child the dragon carried—Zee's child—and all of the things that might mean. She thought about the dying dreamspheres in the cave, and the undead Dreamshifters caught in some sort of special hell.

So many things that might happen if she opened this Gate, so many things that might happen if she didn't, two paths, both shrouded in mist and uncertainty. But one thing shifted the balance—the destruction and darkness and nothingness that followed the path of the dragon—and she understood at last what she must do.

She turned toward the Gates and lifted the Key. It was drawn to the keyhole, as though that ray of blue light had magnetic properties, and clicked into the lock with a sensation of completion that ran through Vivian from head to toe.

Home.

An odd euphoria, unlike any emotion she had ever felt before. A crack grew and widened between the two halves, and they swung slowly inward. Tendrils of mist swirled out through the opening, wreathing around her with a living touch, preventing even a glimpse of what lay beyond.

The desire to enter was intense, testing her resolve, and she would never be sure what she might have done if the rest was not decided for her. A gust of wind knocked her flat on her back, in time to see the Black Dragon fly low over her head and through the Gates. Hundreds of dragons followed, their wings creating a gale-force wind that dropped everybody, even the giants, to their knees. Vivian covered her eyes, blinded in part by dust and even more by the intensity of rainbow light refracting off millions of mirror-bright scales.

When the last dragon passed through the Gates, for a moment the plain fell silent. Then the voices of the giants rang out in a shout that shook the earth. They got to their feet and began to march—not toward the Gates, but away, back across the valley.

All except for one.

A female giant separated from the others and approached the Gates. Zee moved to intercept, but she ignored him, bending over Weston's body.

"Leave him in peace!" Vivian said, turning away from the Gates and her deep desire. "Enough harm has been done today."

The giant woman looked up, surprised. "Do you want him to die?"

Vivian could sense the dragons flying away into the Forever, and the lure of following was a driving physical need. It was difficult to pay attention, to find words, but this was Weston's life at stake.

"Of course I don't want him to die. There's nothing to be done."

"I can help him, if you will allow," the giant said.

Vivian's eyes met Zee's. She knew nothing useful about the giants, wasn't at all certain if they were to be trusted.

"Why would you do this?"

"I am a healer, and there is no need for his death. Besides, his sister has lived among us now for years and I owe her a blood debt. Before we marched, she said to me that I should watch for her brother, lest his fate had brought him here at last."

"Please," Vivian said. "If you can. But he is very far gone."

The giant reached into a pocket and brought out a small vial of black fluid. She opened Weston's mouth with one hand and tapped a single drop onto his tongue.

"So Grace isn't angry with him?"

"She is deeply remorseful about something of which she will not speak. She has said nothing of anger."

Weston drew a deep breath and sighed. Already his color was better, his breath regular and even. His forehead cooled beneath Vivian's hand.

She turned from him then and focused all of her will on the Black Gates. They responded to her thoughts, to her need, and began to swing together. There was no sound, no ceremonial clang as they closed, not so much as a whisper, but she felt the moment reverberate through her body with inalterable finality.

"The Gates have closed!" Zee said. "We need to follow that dragon. How do we open them again? Where is the Key?"

"Gone." Vivian's voice echoed inside her head, empty of all of the dragons, all of them gone where she could not follow.

"What do you mean, gone?"

"It was absorbed when I unlocked them. They are sealed tight now."

"The Key was made to be used but once," the giant said. "It would not work again, even should you find it."

"There has to be another way," Zee said, and then he caught sight of her face. "Vivian? You did this on purpose?"

She managed to get to her feet. "She had to be contained, Zee. She wants to destroy everything. This way, at least her damage is limited."

The giant's broad face had gone pale, if such a thing were possible, and she shook her head. "Truly, you do not know about the Forever."

"No, truly I do not. So tell me."

"All things begin and end there. If she destroys all things in the Forever, the Dreamworlds will follow, and then the waking worlds because all must dream or they will die."

Darkness crowded in, buzzing in Vivian's brain. The choice had seemed so right.

"Still, she is, as you say, contained," the giant went on. "It will take time for her to overpower the King in Forever. And there may be another way in. My people would have records."

"Can you take us to your people then?"

The giant shook her head. "My life was forfeit the moment I broke ranks and came to you. If I go back, I die."

"But we have to get in. Without letting her out." Vivian walked over to the Gates and put her hand against the stone. No more vibration or hum, but the stone recognized her touch and responded like a living thing. It wanted her but was bound by the old spells.

"Perhaps it is time to pay a visit to the sorcieri," the giant said.

"Could they open the Gates?"

"They were involved in the making of the Key. Nobody remembers how. If you can persuade them to help—"

"Vivian, no," Zee said. "Think about it. Remember Jehenna. Like she would have been of help?"

"All dragons aren't the same. Or all giants either, it appears. So maybe . . ." She realized what she was saying as the words left her mouth. Right. A kinder, gentler sorceress. Not very likely.

She felt drained and vulnerable and tired, and the

problem was so much bigger than she was. Way back in medical school when things got overwhelming she'd invented a slogan for herself: *Just start somewhere, and take it from there. Do the first thing you can do, and then the next.* Time to follow her own advice.

"First thing, we're taking Weston back to Wakeworld. He's been through enough."

"I have not ever been to Wakeworld, but I will go with him," the giant said. "I owe a life debt to his sister."

"He'll love that," Zee said. "And what will you do, Dreamshifter?" His agate eyes were unshuttered for once, and she saw all that lay behind the single question.

Vivian got to her feet and stood facing him, almost but not quite touching. So much between them, and she didn't know how to bridge the chasm. But her inner dragon was dead, and that was one problem solved, a tenuous bridge on which to build.

Just start somewhere, and take it from there.

"Well, Warrior, I was thinking about this," she said, and rose up on her tiptoes to kiss him. Their lips touched, clung, light as a feather caress. He did not pull away, or respond, but stood perfectly still, neither drawing back nor moving into an embrace.

But beneath her hands on his chest his heart beat fast. She deepened the kiss and felt the tension break as his arms came round her and lifted her off her feet, crushing her against him. His lips claimed hers, soul deep, then wandered to her hair, her eyelids, the curve of her chin.

"This isn't really an answer to anything," he murmured between kisses.

"But it's an excellent question."

The giant broke the moment. "If the two of you are quite done, you might wish to see this."

Warm and sheltered in Zee's arms and feeling like nothing could ever threaten her again, Vivian turned her head.

A solitary dragon had landed. He was small, not much bigger than a draft horse. His left wing drooped a little, as if something in it were broken, and black blood oozed from a tear in his side. He leaned his head against the stone of the closed Gates and gave a mournful cry that twisted Vivian's heart.

All the softness left Zee's body. She felt the change in his heartbeat, could feel the adrenaline burst harden his muscles. As his hand went to the hilt of his sword, she covered it with her own and looked up into his face, recoiling from the hate that shone in his eyes.

"He's just a baby."

"He'll grow."

The little dragon cried again, with a wail of absolute despair at being left behind. In response, Vivian felt a small spark of answering dragon in her belly and knew that her own dragon wasn't quite dead after all.

"He's hurt, Zee. And all alone."

She saw the hatred in his eyes shift to loss and grief as he acknowledged once again all that she was. And then, as she was about to turn from him with a heart so heavy she feared it would break, he smiled. It was a flash of pure joy, utterly unexpected and all the more beautiful for that.

"You," he said, and the love in his voice outweighed the pain in her heart. "If you found a wounded slime toad, you'd want to help it. I kill, you heal. Perhaps there is a balance after all."

Once more she kissed him, then turned to what must be done.

The dragon hissed when she approached, but he was too young yet to flame. Reaching for the spark of dragon that had flickered briefly in response to his cry, she sent into his mind, *You are not alone, little brother. I am here.* She looked over her shoulder at the others and added, *We are all here. And all will yet be well.*

ABOUT THE AUTHOR

Kerry Schafer lives in the town of Colville, Washington, with her family, which includes two cats, a rescue fish, and a preternaturally large black dog. A self-styled perpetual student, she earned an RN from Royal Alexandra Hospital in Edmonton, Alberta; an Honours BA in English from York University in Toronto, Ontario; and an M.Ed. in counseling psychology from Washington State University. Visit her online at kerryschafer.com and facebook.com/KerrySchaferBooks.

*A stunningly seductive debut that blurs
the line between dreams and reality.*

From
Kerry Schafer

BETWEEN

All her life, Vivian Maylor has rejected her mother's insane ramblings about Dreamworlds for concrete science
and fact—until an emergency room patient ranting about
dragons spontaneously combusts before her eyes, forcing
Vivian to consider the idea that her visions of mythical
beasts might be real.

When a chance encounter leads her to a man she
knows only from her dreams, Vivian finds herself falling
into a world that seems strange and familiar all at once…

"A rich wonder of a fantasy."
—Robin D. Owens

"A smart, resilient heroine…A sparkling debut."
—Carol Berg

kerryschafer.com
facebook.com/KerrySchaferBooks
facebook.com/AceRocBooks
penguin.com

M1372T0913

FROM *NEW YORK TIMES* BESTSELLING AUTHOR

Ilona Andrews

MAGIC SLAYS

⇒ A KATE DANIELS NOVEL ⇐

Kate Daniels may have quit the Order of Knights of Merciful Aid, but she's still knee-deep in paranormal problems. Or she would be if she could get someone to hire her. Starting her own business has been more challenging than she thought it would be—now that the Order is disparaging her good name. Plus, many potential clients are afraid of getting on the bad side of the Beast Lord, who just happens to be Kate's mate.

So when Atlanta's premier Master of the Dead calls to ask for help with a vampire on the loose, Kate leaps at the chance of some paying work. But it turns out that this is not an isolated incident, and Kate needs to get to the bottom of it—fast, or the city and everyone dear to her may pay the ultimate price.

AVAILABLE FROM ACE

penguin.com

M828T0111